A
Deeply
Flawed
Quest
Novel

Death by Chicken

Guida M. Jackson

CSU Editions

California

Carson

Dominguez

Hills

With the exception of mention of a great California wine company's suit against Joe Louis Lopez, a one-armed artist in San Antonio, for screen-printing "*Puro Gallo*" on his T-shirts; the description of the founding of *la raza unida* by José Ángel Gutierrez; and the mention of a restaurant owned by Gutiérrez's grandfather where women are not allowed, "Frank's Place" in Hebbronville, all characters and incidents depicted in this novel are fictitious, and any resemblance to actual persons or events just goes to show what a quirky place Texas is.

For Jack Hume

1

Jonathan Tyler received word of his impending death while aboard his corporate jet, halfway between Boston and Roswell. Granted, there may be no good time to get such news, but this was the worst. He was busy: on his way to put out a brush fire before it became a conflagration.

Intimations came first by FAX: a report on the results of his latest lab tests. The experimental drug had not fazed the course of his rare blood disease.

He wasn't too worried, although his demise at any age, much less forty-six, had seldom occurred to him as a possibility. Factoring in his net worth and new medical technology, he could afford longevity whatever the price. He had the finest medical team money could buy. They would figure something out. Yes, shit happens, but not if you get a good education and work hard. And having followed the prescribed cosseted path laid down by his Wharton predecessors, he was entitled to a long life.

Besides which, he was prudent, dammit. He ate five fruits or vegetables daily—got his green leafy one out of the way at breakfast. He drank skim decaf latte and a single glass of red wine with dinner. He could urinate a strong healthy stream with the best of them. Three times a week he worked out with his trainer, and he played racquetball as often as possible. He had all his teeth, all his hair, feathered with enough gray to give him credibility in the boardroom. Even when he was in California he felt thin. At this stage nothing, particularly death, would improve him significantly.

Now, without (much) warning, death stalked him like a hungry she-tiger.

No, wait. A tiger was sleek, beautiful. Death was more of a warthog.

Apropos that the news should reach him in midair: a liminal space, a caesura in his routine, a quantum leap. It was an abrupt transition from one discrete state to another, during which he effectively vanished, to pop back into view, upon landing, in an altered condition: superfluous, moribund. Tapped for early dismissal. Yanked offstage before intermission. Blown off his perch. Sucked down the drain. Extracted. Extruded. Remaindered.

How can you embark in the balmy vestibule of summer and alight in the anteroom of winter? The prospect brought a rush of saliva to his mouth that he had to swallow several times to dispel.

The kick in the head came moments later via a conference call from his wife Sarah and Doctor Allman, who led the army of Sloan-Kettering specialists subjecting him to tests to find whether his chronic listlessness was caused by the drug or further encroachment of the disease. Jonathan dreaded answering, feeling like a truant schoolboy because he'd left the hospital without checking out and high-tailed it back to Boston where he'd alerted his crew to be ready for take-off.

Now, with the doctor listening, he couldn't explain to Sarah that the reason had nothing to do with cowardice. Let her blame his conduct on impatience. Whereas the corporate culture in general preferred the previous government's Shock and Awe approach for global and local problem solving, at Tyler Technologies he preached the subtler creed of Be Smart; Make It Happen. Only this time, with the mess in Roswell threatening to send his company the way of AIG or Enron, it wasn't working.

Neither was his marriage. But that was another story.

Sarah's panic was the catalyst for his alarm. She was schooled to maintain a cool propriety in the face of the most untimely social disasters—even when their teenaged son mooned her poolside guests to show disdain for her celebrity collecting (that day, a Saudi princess, in town for a nose job), Sarah had calmly turned her back, leaving him to hobble off unnoted with his trunks bunched around his ankles. At the time, Jonathan had thought it was her finest hour.

Now her voice shook—surely not with emotion—not Sarah, who considered it chic to be shallow. "Jonathan, how could you leave the hospital without a word? I've been—concerned."

Caught off guard, he nevertheless gave her a clipped dismissal. "Let's not discuss personal matters in front of strangers."

Allman broke in. "Strangers? You're talking about the man who has viewed you through the business end of a proctoscope."

Anyway, the doctors had completed their tests. They should already have dismissed him. Maybe he had left the hospital so abruptly so as to avoid hearing the prognosis, rather than from a need to solve the Roswell crisis personally. He could, after all, have sent an underling.

In the past months, he'd become inured to Allman's bleak predictions, which he suspected were one-fourth medical training and three-fourths salesmanship. Now, resigned to the inevitable lecture, he settled back in his seat, reached for his Evian, and said to Allman, "So, what's the next move, doc? Bone marrow transplant? I'll check with my secretary—"

"No." The doctor's voice crackled flat and impassive across the airwaves. "You force me to discuss what I seldom do by phone. You've already seen the lab results. We've run out of options. Marrow transplants won't fix you, son. Nothing will, I'm afraid, at this stage. We can keep you going on transfusions for a while, but you must get back."

The words fell on him like an anvil. Even the plane's interior lights seemed to dim. He'd always presumed he would have a presentiment of his demise, a protracted, piece-meal gradual initiation, over many years, during which he would wither along with a certain grace. Now sweat sprang from every pore, turning the phone clammy in his grasp. Still he didn't trust his own hearing. He swallowed hard.

"Wait a minute. Are you telling me I'm going to *die?*"

The Right-Hand-of-God intoned, "Everybody does, Jon."

Smart-ass. And this was supposed to make him feel better?

Jonathan found himself trembling so hard that his teeth chattered. He grappled about for his calm, like sweater sleeves turned inside-out. "How—how much... What's the....?"

There was a brief silence before Allman said, "Depends on how soon you can get back for treatment. Without transfusions and monitoring, you're a ticking land mine."

The plane had already crossed over the Mississippi. There was no use in turning back. More than ever, he had to diffuse this mess in New Mexico. Pride wouldn't allow him not to leave his affairs in order. He would probably be dead for a very long while.

He faked a breakup in the connection. After he rang off, he lurched to the head and threw up, then examined himself in the mirror. Surely he hadn't looked so god-awful when he shaved. The ringing in his ears had nothing to do with cabin pressure. Enlarged pupils dwarfing their blue irises signaled terror—and betrayal by the hierarchy of priesthood to whom he'd entrusted his health.

He had believed the prevailing wisdom, had inflated the powers of medicine into a religion: medicinism. He had replaced mace and mitre with scrub suit and scalpel to the same farcical end. Now he discovered that the priests of the new order had violated him, betrayed his trust.

Had he been on the can when life happened? He hadn't begun to do the things he had a right to expect.

If it was true that we spend the second half of life aligning with the grander energies of the cosmos, then lately he'd been thinking that he should quit amassing and start enjoying, before it was time to get serious. The progression was: first you build a career, then have your mid-life crisis, then you settle in to enjoy retirement and finally get around to finding answers to the larger questions.

It was just now time for his mid-life crisis. He'd counted big on it. Contending with Sarah, even Tyler Technologies, had become intolerable. For months now he had yearned for it all to vanish; become a mere palimpsest upon the larger tapestry of his life. He fantasized a future troubled by no more than a shadow image of his present, and on this near tabula rasa he could imprint, say, a melon-breasted lap dancer in a hot-pink thong. But so far he'd had no time to pursue that ambition.

Now he would gladly make a Faustian pact if only he knew where to find Mephistopheles.

Yet maybe he had already met him in the person of Dr. Allman. He had already made the bargain when he submitted to this course of treatment.

He brushed his teeth and went back to his lounge chair and struggled to compose himself by prioritizing a list to get his affairs in order. It was too bad he hadn't shucked Sarah before this news. If she were to meet with an accident—tumble off their yacht, for instance, helped by a gentle nudge. But no, then he would only end up in hell, where she would surely be waiting, looking down that supercilious nose.

There were serious concerns, such as the one that drew him to the New Mexico site, but he couldn't concentrate. Permanent hackles had risen at the base of his skull, rendering it numb. After several attempts to focus, he tossed his planner aside and buzzed for his pilot Arpad, at the same time dismissing the lone steward, who retreated out of earshot to the galley.

The captain, a slender-built quasi-Hindu a decade his junior, soon appeared, his respectful nod almost a bow. This beautiful specimen of manhood, who, except for the lame foot, lacked only Shiva's blue skin, stood waiting for the invitation to sit. Pretty men with penetrating black eyes annoyed Jonathan, but in Arpad's case he was willing to overlook it.

He waved the pilot to a seat, gratified by his deference despite their years together and Jonathan's repeated protestations of friendship. Possibly Arpad sensed a lack of genuineness in this show of equality, but at the moment he was handy, and Jonathan suddenly saw him as his new best buddy. Anyway, he couldn't imagine entrusting information to any of the complicated web of alliances—business associates, racquetball or golfing cronies—who might use the knowledge as a weapon. If leaked, news of his ill health could be felt on Wall Street, sending his stock south.

Maybe Arpad was in fact his only friend. He tried to imagine who would be asked to speak at his funeral. Certainly Sarah would never choose his pilot.

Arpad sat quietly while Jonathan scavenged for words, allowing time for pride to filter out the histrionics. He imagined he detected compassion in the dark expectancy of those incredibly perfect features, something deep in his pagan nature responding as if it already knew.

On second thought, Jonathan realized he didn't dare actually confide in Arpad for fear he might start looking for other employment. So he said, "I could use some unbiased feedback. Here's a hypothetical. Let's say you're in business. A ticklish situation develops. A lot of money is at stake. Let's say you find out you're sick. Bad sick."

Arpad showed no hint of surprise, except that his eyebrows raised a fraction.

Jonathan continued. "Suppose you could prolong your life by staying close to your doctor and —oh, I don't know—getting blood transfusions or something. But an accident occurs at a facility you own. Not an important holding, which is the ironic—"

Arpad held up a warding hand. "Hold on, chief. Even if I knew anything about business, which I don't, I'm not about to give advice to one of the country's savviest—"

Jonathan's voice overrode the pilot's. "The reason it's ironic is that, because of a snafu by the accountants, what happened at this insignificant little holding could jeopardize other larger assets. It'd be very dicey if you don't get the accounting straightened out before word gets out that might affect the price of your stock."

Arpad squirmed in his seat, obviously uncomfortable. "I'm not qualified to have an opinion even on an abstract problem."

Jonathan said, "This is about priorities, not money. Let's up the ante. Let's say the health thing is a matter of life and death. Hypothetically. Let's say you're going to die."

"But I am going to die."

"*What?*"

Arpad leveled his dark gaze at his employer. "Ah. I thought you knew. But then, you're one of the cowboys. Just kidding, chief. I would be glad for the knowledge of when I will die. As far as we know, it's a gift bestowed on no other creature."

"Yeah, right! Some gift. Pops right out of the cake."

"But that may be chauvinistic. Elephants seem to know. And some of the apes.

Knowledge of death gives us motive to fulfill our destiny." Again he smiled. Even without orthodontia, not a glistening tooth was out of line.

Jonathan thought about this. "You're serious. You think we have a destiny to fulfill?"

"I'd say so. Your destiny is a promise you make to yourself when you're very young."

At the moment Jonathan had no patience for remembering childhood promises. Life's a bitch, he thought. A terminal bitch.

He tried again as Arpad waited for the inevitable question. "Anyway, would you go on, work as hard as you could shoring up your assets, or check into the hospital to buy a few more months?"

At length Arpad answered. "I guess it would depend on my philosophy. I might try to better the earth, leave a legacy. Because I'm not married, you see. I don't have a family to consider. If I did, I might ask, would they rather have me a bit longer, or would they need financial security?"

Jonathan suffered a fleeting pang of guilt. The wishes of Sarah and the boys had scarcely entered his mind. He had no illusions about where their priorities lay, and where his concern should be. Regardless of his loss of feeling for Sarah, he couldn't leave her to sort out his affairs.

Anyhow, would he want to die a poor man? He'd been on the cover of *Forbes*, for God's sake.

"I don't know," he said glumly. "You work so hard, and before you can…." He petered off in a miasma of despond.

Arpad took the abrupt change of direction in stride and answered with no hesitation, a hint of amusement lighting the black eyes, for some reason. "There's an ancient teaching that says we must do our work but not be attached to the outcome. It's not a matter of results but of process."

"Process my ass!" On second consideration, life had been nothing but process. Now his affairs had become so complicated that he didn't have time to deal with this new health threat. At this point he ought to be able to kick back—chuck the materialistic squirrel cage, sell the big houses and the rest of the crap, go simple. Buy a spread in Idaho; start over with a string of horses. Or move to Italy and….

But no: the crisis in New Mexico dwarfed all other plans. He didn't even have time to die.

Had he ever wanted any sort of destiny with a passion? Except now: this urgent trip had sent his blood coursing, for once. Even building the company had afforded no real challenge, since his father had bankrolled him. Now, he didn't want to die, but particularly he didn't want to die broke.

Arpad said, "We're about thirty minutes out. If there's nothing else, I should...."

Jonathan gestured a wordless dismissal. But then, Arpad was accustomed to his moods. As the pilot rose and left with only a nod, Jonathan, aware of being alone with only the drone of the engines, stared around at the spacious white interior with its white leather and chrome appointments that suddenly appeared cheerless. He might as well be the only person on the planet. Hurtling through space like a solitary bullet, bereft and friendless.

He picked up his Tylergiz and spent the minutes remaining until landing disciplining himself to see items at a remove, like the credits and debits of a failing corporation he was trying to resuscitate. No more daydreams about pushing Sarah overboard or raising horses in Idaho. He must at least leave an unblemished monument to his business acumen. He could imagine his obit in the *Wall Street Journal.* It would probably run more than a column. But they might overlook some of his accomplishments. Maybe he ought to write his own. If only there were time to do more, leave a fortune that would—well, shock and awe.

The plane bucked a sudden violent down-draft on the approach, catching the sun's blinding glint on a plummeting wing. For an instant he almost wished— but no. The doctor might be wrong.

Yes! That was it! He was wrong! The sonofabitch was probably making one of those regal pronouncements the whole narcissistic profession was wont to make, on the flimsiest evidence. He might as well have said, Take a grain of salt and call me in the morning.

He'd get another opinion at another medical center. Go someplace without an arrogance cluster.

Better yet: go nowhere. The bastards were all on a power jag. Screw 'em. There was a way out of this. Always was. A solution was bound to present itself. He sensed the certainty of it.

Now, he had more pressing matters. The man who propelled him from his hospital bed was somewhere on that drought-wracked landscape below: a man who couldn't even speak English but held the fate of Tyler Technologies in one grimy hand. A man who, under normal circumstances, he wouldn't be caught dead with.

2

Jonathan first learned of the man's existence only a few hours earlier, while he occupied one of those hospital suites in the tower reserved for VIPs. He had selected breakfast from a large leather-bound menu. His meal arrived on bone china emblazoned in twenty-two karat gold with the hospital's crest. But it was cardboard crap, all the same.

Crap or not, he would have eaten it had he known how long it would be before he had another opportunity to eat.

He was set to ring for something decent when his attorney Hal called on his cell with the bad news. There was no mistaking the hysterical edge to Hal's voice. "How soon can you get out of that place?"

"Depends. What's up?"

"I'd rather not say. This is public air space. Look: encrypted e-mail would be safer. Can you log on?"

Jonathan took out his Tylergiz and waited with impatience for Hal's message. The wait wasn't doing his cardboard crap any good, he could tell by the smell. He shoved aside the tray when Hal came online.

At first the news didn't seem so bad. True, a man had been killed in a cave-in at a mine—a property Sarah had recently inherited from a childless great-uncle.

Jonathan couldn't see what all the fuss was about. They had liability insurance; as soon as she received the deed, Hal placed the company under the insurance covering all his holdings.

No need to bother the wife with this, Hal's message said, *but apparently her great-uncle was such an inept businessman that he left holes in his articles of incorporation big enough to drive my Porsche through.*

So the title to the mine was probably in Sarah's name individually, because of the incorporation snafu. No problem. That's why Jon carried a personal liability umbrella policy on Sarah and himself—to cover unlikely circumstances like this.

Here's the catch.

There were several spaces, as if Hal dreaded writing the next sentence. *In the changeover in Accounting, when we eased old Henshaw out before he reached retirement age, apparently the premium on the personal wasn't paid.* Hence no personal coverage at the time of the accident. This was disturbing, but Jonathan was by now far too well protected.

...and possibly no corporate coverage, either.

The lawyer didn't need to draw him a picture. Even if premiums were up to date, if the insurance dogs got wind of faulty incorporation, they could legally dodge liability payment to the worker's heirs. Not only could Sarah lose the mine, but a lawsuit might place their other assets in jeopardy. They could feasibly lose a wad. Enough to jeopardize their credit rating. Certainly enough to send the price of Tyler stock into the toilet.

Henshaw! That inept sonofabitch. Or had he done it deliberately as retribution for being turned out a few months shy of being eligible to draw full retirement?

Was there no one you could rely on anymore?

Your best bet, Hal went on, *is to send an arm-twister down to the site—someone you trust. Make an on-the-spot settlement. Leave the insurance company out of this completely until I quietly file amended articles of incorporation and place this property within your umbrella corporation. More important, get a release signed by the victim's survivor.*

Jonathan shot back, *Why can't you go? Who better to handle this?* Hal was his full-time employee. But of course, he already knew the answer. Hal had another chemo treatment today. So he deleted that and wrote, *How about sending one of those overpaid underlings in your department?*

The answer came immediately. *This information could be worth a bundle in the wrong hands.*

So what did that mean? Was he nurturing Judases on the payroll? Jonathan shifted in his hospital bed, shoving aside a stack of correspondence on matters that he preferred to handle himself. But this was one that could be delegated. Why all the secrecy?

Hal's message explained. *Better for the mine's district manager not to know. Better that nobody knows. The smell of blood and all that. It needs a personal touch. Best to put a sympathetic spin on it for the victim's next-of-kin.*

What were the odds of an accident happening when there was a problem with both insurance policies, with Hal sick and no junior attorney they could trust? Jonathan felt as if the stars were lining up against him.

The insurance "problem" had nothing to do with odds. It had to be a sin of deliberate omission by Henshaw.

As he read, he began bundling correspondence into his valise. Too impatient to wait for more on the small screen, he dialed Hal's number. Hal picked up immediately.

Jonathan chose his words carefully, in case of a leak in the airwaves. "Who're we dealing with here?"

"Next-of-kin's named Miguel Fuentes. The victim was Ramón Fuentes, his nephew. The old man speaks no English, by the way, but in Roswell, finding a translator can't be that tough."

"You sure we can't strike a deal with this old guy by phone?" Jonathan said over the rumble of his empty stomach. The cardboard was looking better by the minute.

"I haven't told you the worst of it," Hal said. "This fellow claims to be ninety-seven years old. He'll have to be sent to live with some other relative, and he's apparently waiting for reps from one of those Hispanic watchdog groups to tell him what to do. If they get to him first—"

Jonathan was already out of bed, pulling his trousers from the closet. Nobody had to draw him a picture. He'd dealt with labor groups before. "Oh lord. Look: Fax me a settlement to the plane. I'll have to disable the old man myself. Oh, and call my wife."

Hal's indignation was obvious. "Why should I face your firing squad? I'm on my way to a chemo treatment. Can't I spend my last few minutes in peace, for God's sake?"

Jonathan grabbed a soggy toast triangle with one hand as he scooped up his belongings with the other. "Then get someone in the office to call. I don't have time to wrangle at the moment. Anyway, I need to get hold of my pilot."

There was no one else he could trust. He figured he could slip out of the hospital, drive up to Boston, have Arpad and his crew standing by at the airport, fly to New Mexico, charm the old Hispanic into a settlement, and be back in Boston before morning. Nothing was as important as securing his assets so that some little *peon* didn't end up with all he had worked to amass. In the no doubt liberal courts of New Mexico, he'd be dog meat. He could see the headlines now: "Technologies Tycoon Buried in Cave-In Judgment. Tyler Stock Plummets."

Now, as the plane touched the tarmac, Jonathan considered the many ways that Sarah could gum up the works but decided to ignore Hal's advice and fill her in. He dialed her cell phone.

When she answered, he said, "Where are you? Are you alone?"

"On the way to get my highlights done. Look, can't whatever this is about wait?"

Apparently his death was somewhere down in the hierarchy of concerns below her hair. It figured. But for all the money she spent on beauty treatments, the results still reminded him that somewhere out there, there must indeed be a God with a sense of humor. "I've just landed in New Mexico. There's been a cave-in at that mine you inherited. A man's been killed."

She evinced no remorse, but then, neither had he. "So what can *you* do about it? Dig him out yourself? You don't know the first thing about mines."

Ire rose up his neck like a warm tide. Before he latched onto the undercapitalized hand-held computer company that was now the centerpiece of Tyler Technologies, he had made his reputation buying failing companies and turning them around. What kind of company was immaterial. It usually boiled down to paring labor costs. Profit and loss, leveraging, it was the same in all of them; production costs could always be managed because labor was a malleable element. He was an expert at labor utilization, one of the best. But she was too wrapped up in herself to appreciate the fact. He waited until he had regained control to answer.

"What I can do is prevent you from losing a costly liability suit and, by the way, possibly a good chunk of our personal assets as well." He stopped, suddenly remembering Hal's caution about using public air space. He had already spoken too freely.

"Keep quiet about this, understand? No confiding to your flitty hairdresser. Unless you want to start shopping at K-Mart and living like—well, the rest of the world."

But when you're bred to believe in your own entitlement, such threats are meaningless. He hung up abruptly and did not answer when she rang back immediately. Besides, Arpad was beckoning; the hatch was open.

The mine's district manager, a sinewy and tanned man whose name was Doss, was waiting by the runway with a dust-covered Jeep Cherokee. Jonathan stepped out into the consuming hot breath of New Mexico at mid-day and scowled around for a limo. Today he needed comfort, not utility. And a tall cold Scotch. With a side of onion rings.

Why hadn't he at least eaten on the plane? Damn Allman, that medical jackass!

Doss removed his cap and whacked its film of dirt against his leg, anticipating his question. "We're a little short on limos out here, Mister Tyler. Anyhow, we'd like to make a good impression on Fuentes. A limo might send the wrong message."

"Gotcha." Jonathan eased himself into the passenger side, astonished at how weak he felt. It was all in his mind, he knew; this morning he had felt perfectly fine. No, now he remembered. It was the damn cardboard crap he didn't have a chance to eat. That explained it.

They rode in silence the hour from Roswell's airport to the dismal mining site east of the city. It was his first visit to the mine. Despite his preoccupation, he registered surprise at how flat the sun-baked land appeared. It didn't look like his idea of mining country. As they drove up to a fenced area designated with a sign, "Llano Gravel," he said, "What the—? This is no mine!"

"Yes sir, it is," Doss said. "Not all mining is underground. Some of it is strip mining. But it's almost as dangerous, maybe more. We have cave-ins just about as deadly."

They skirted the pit and bumped toward a scrapple of mobile homes on the far side, stopping in front of the last, most disreputable. A gnarled old man the color of the barren ground sat in a sagging lawn chair in the shade of a lone cottonwood tree, whittling and addressing a mangy pariah dog too engaged in scratching to listen. A younger Hispanic with a pocked face mangled like a train wreck leaned against the tree, eyeing them with undisguised insolence.

"That's old man Fuentes," Doss said. "I don't know the other one. He's not an employee. Name's Diego—claims to be a friend of the victim—Ramón. Miguel put him up in their trailer. Even Diego can't get anything out of Fuentes about what he plans to do. Maybe you can."

"I intend to." Jonathan jumped from the car as it rolled to a stop. His own life was ebbing away too rapidly to waste it dealing with illiterate Mexicans. "We're going to pay this geezer off and fly him out of here right now. We'll worry about where he's going once we're airborne."

As they approached, the old man squinted up through sharp ferret eyes and shook his head. His brown face was lined and carved as a mesquite stump. Diego, whose partially closed left eye had probably once made contact with a broken beer bottle, took a step away from the tree.

"He says no flying, man," Diego called in a singsong patois. Jonathan got the picture: the pug-ugly Diego must be a member of the watchdog group Hal mentioned. He certainly had the face for it. Jonathan had arrived too late.

But Doss leaned in to explain. "Miguel's got a bunch of fighting cocks, see. We—uh—don't condone cock fighting, but it's pretty bleak out here. A long ways from nowheres. The men have to make their own entertainment."

Doss's attempt at piety was wasted on Jonathan. He didn't care what the men did on their own time—they could play fifty rounds of grab-ass with pack animals for all he cared. He forced an amiable nod toward Fuentes while he said sotto voce to Doss, "Get rid of the birds. And get rid of this Diego. I want to deal with this codger alone."

In a symphony of slow motion, the old man put down his whittling, folded his knife, shifted onto one hip and placed the knife in his back pocket, sealing it with a couple of firm pats. Then with two small horny, distorted hands that looked more like twisted tree roots, he braced himself against the chair's wobbly aluminum arms. Slowly, cautiously, pausing midway as if to allow a seizing pain to pass, he rose laboriously to a height of less than five feet. Never had Jonathan seen such an ancient piece of human flesh. He sighed in exasperation. This shriveled mass of antiquity was no adversary; Doss could have handled him.

And by what right had this *peon* arrived at such an age, while he himself was rapidly passing on at forty-six?

Fuentes stumped toward them at a maddeningly tedious pace, flashing an obstinate grin. As the old man turned aside and spoke in rapid Spanish to Diego, it occurred to Jonathan that Fuentes possessed remarkable hearing—or else he had somehow read their minds.

Diego, stubbled chin jutting in defiance, swaggered up to translate. "He's not going without them cocks. Not taking any money. Not signing any paper till he gets where he's going. Better get a bus. Real big one to carry all them *gallos*. It's a long ways to Crystal City."

Crystal City. At the mention of the name, the old man whipped back around and hurled at him an agate gaze with the force of a lance. It was a command, pure and simple. Jonathan all but reeled back as if he had been hit by a physical blow. The experience rendered him weak, and he felt powerless to look away.

Crystal City. It had the sound of magic.

Had it come down to this, then, that after a sentence of No Hope the thought of magic should enter his head? He almost wished he were going there himself.

3

Maybe it was the heat, magnified by the intensity of Miguel's stare. Jonathan swayed and looked for something to lean against. There was nothing but men, covered in grime and sweat. He braced himself and fought the invisible hold of the man's gaze.

Several workers gathered around talking at once, trying to convince Jonathan of the elder Fuentes' devotion to his fighting cocks. He was a true *gallero,* they explained: a committed cocker. He pampered them like children, they said, carting their cages into the trailer in bad weather, preening them, feeding them special treats, chirping peculiar ancient Toltec noises involving great rolling of the tongue. The idea that Miguel Fuentes would go anywhere without his *gallos* seemed as remote as the notion that he would sign any piece of paper before he got precisely what he wanted: transportation for his precious cargo.

Jonathan heard the men as from a distance. And still he was caught in the hypnotic black stare.

But Miguel broke the spell as soon as Diego translated the men's words. He turned and stumped back to the lawn chair, dropping into it heavily, and folded his arms across his chest. As if no one else were there, he began to rock and hum quietly. The old buzzard was soft in the head.

But being a practical man, Jonathan turned to one of the workers. "Where is Crystal City?"

The miner took off his hard hat and ran a palm across his sweaty forehead, revealing a stripe of pink burned skin beneath the layer of dust. "Only Crystal City I ever heard of is way down yonder close to the South Texas border. Might be five hundred miles or so from here."

Another worker, Hispanic, spoke up, pride evident in his tone. "It's in Zavala County. That's where José Ángel Gutiérrez started *la raza*."

Jonathan, noting that Miguel sat up at the mention of the name, didn't even like the sound. As if the name *raza* meant something to him, Jonathan nodded and waited for an explanation.

"*La Raza Unida*," Doss supplied. "A Chicano political party that caused a big stir in the seventies across the southwest. They took over the whole Zavala County. Folks called it 'Little Cuba.' I figured they'd about died out by now. Could be I was wrong."

Jonathan got the picture: this must be the watchdog group his lawyer Hal had warned him about. Diego must be the advance guard. They were coming to take up Fuentes' cause, create an uproar in the press, supply attorneys to sue the daylights out of Llano for the cave-in. He turned to Doss and said quietly, "Get the old guy a bus. We're moving out today."

Doss frowned. "A whole bus? We might could charter one. Cost us an arm and a leg, though. And today? Not likely."

Jonathan gritted his teeth but kept his temper in check. Motioning for Diego to follow, he approached the old man, addressing him with his most sympathetic somber tone, belatedly remembering the accident that had caused the crisis. Fuentes would have to wait for Diego's translation, but he wouldn't miss Jonathan's look of concern. "Is it because you want to take your nephew's body there for burial? Is Crystal City his home?"

Doss, who had lumbered along behind, interposed. "We've—ah—taken care of memorial arrangements already. The remains haven't been recovered, but we had a very nice service at the pit this morning. The priest happened to be in the area and won't be back for a month, so Miguel wanted to go ahead—"

The Anglo worker said, "By that time we'll probably run acrosst it. If it ain't too rotten, we can go ahead on and bury it somewheres else, or ship it home to Texas, or whatever."

The old man listened to the translation, then spat in contempt, sending a stream of tobacco juice whizzing past Jonathan's Ferragamos. The interpreter repeated his words: "He says hell no. Ramón, he don't care where he's buried. Ramón going to burn in hell anyways for not treating them *gallos* so good. Weren't for Miguel, wouldn't be no cocks. Miguel, he's gonna take them to stay with his aunt, *la curandera*. Got real fine cages there. Used to, anyway, he says."

Jonathan presumed he meant the dead man's aunt, possibly Miguel's wife, or former wife. He watched the old man. Not a flicker of an eyelid revealed pain of grief. Nevertheless, he said with exaggerated gentleness, "We...want to compensate you for your grief. I know you will miss your nephew, sir."

The interpreter translated while Jonathan waited for some reaction. Fuentes shifted and spat out across the back of the mutt and rattled off something the nice version of which translated, "How the hell you know that? Don't know nothin' about it."

Doss drew Jonathan aside and whispered, "We're getting no place. Suppose we go back to town and see what kind of transportation we can find before it gets any later?"

It was out of the question to leave the old man there alone under the influence of a *la raza* man. Before he had signed a release? No way! Jonathan shook his head. "*You* go into town and I'll stay right here with my teeth fastened to his butt. I'm not letting him out of my sight." Jonathan mopped his forehead and peered up at the hazy red sun. It was encircled by a dusty ring. "Maybe I can coax him indoors...."

Doss took a dubious glance at his watch. "Probably be morning before we can get a bus out here."

His employee's insubordination flew all over Jonathan, who was unaccustomed to less than the best, and the best *now*. Besides, he wanted to scream, *I'm dying! Can't you see I'm dying?* He faced the manager nose to nose and growled, "Now hear this: we're moving the old man out *today*. By the time those agitators show up, he'll be long gone. *Buy* a damn bus, if necessary. Do whatever it takes. Just get into town and get back here with a bus this afternoon. Got it?"

Doss's eyelids blinked rapidly a couple of times. His jaw hardened, and he slapped on his cap, wheeled around without another word, stalked to the Jeep and sped off in a shower of gravel.

Jonathan turned to the others and said, "Well? Don't you have work to do?"

As they scattered, he grabbed Diego by the arm and said, "Tell the old guy to pack his things, get those damn birds ready to travel. His bus will be here soon, and he's moving out today."

Belatedly, Jonathan read the contempt in the man's eyes. Diego scuffed back toward Fuentes, appearing suddenly worn down by the heat. Then he stopped and looked over his shoulder, a smirk playing at the corners of his mouth. "Would I *tell* him, or would I *ask* him?"

Jonathan shut his eyes, waiting for the rising explosion to subside. *My God, help*, he thought, then immediately chided himself for the unconscious imprecation. He refused to implore a deity he had denied so vehemently. Now, at the first sign of crisis, he was copping out, returning to the mindless superstitions of childhood.

He had to think, but he was too hungry to think. A thousand miles from home, surfeited with the burden of a death sentence, surrounded by idiots—it wasn't supposed to happen this way. He had even missed lunch, which doubtless accounted for the pain at his temples. Depression seeped into his brain, penetrating as a fog. He needed food, consoling. Forgotten for the moment were any deep-held domestic resentments: he needed to talk to Sarah.

Belatedly he realized he had left his briefcase containing his Tylergiz in Doss's vehicle. He looked at the wretched shack where Fuentes lived and knew without asking there would be no telephone inside. He forced a grin and said to Diego, "Sorry. *Ask* him to pack his things, if you will. I'm going to find a phone."

He hiked back to the foreman's trailer and entered without knocking. A welcome blast of refrigerated air settled around him, bringing sudden moisture to his eyes. He was unused to being so bereft of comfort. He sat on the vinyl couch and wilted, too wrung out to think straight. He felt stripped, drained of stamina, as if he might faint. Finally he forced himself to reach for the phone, punching in the numbers by rote.

Without much encouragement he might allow Sarah to come for him, take him home, hold his head in her lap on the plane. Maybe he would throw in the towel altogether, quit trying to save Llano, quit trying to plan for the future of his family. Forget about the old man and his fighting cocks. Let *la raza* take everything. The gravel mine was a sleazy two-bit operation, anyway. If he'd known how insignificant it appeared, he'd never have bothered trying to save it in the first place, except that this accident had put his estate at peril. But hell, he couldn't take it with him. It would be a great relief just to let go....

The silken voice on the line drove such thoughts from his mind. "Jon, baby, is that you?"

My God, I've dialed Betts out of habit!

He couldn't die yet. He must get back and formally break it off with Betts. Pay her for her occasional company these past seven years. A lump sum in cash, enough to get that brownstone she wanted. With the stipulation that she keep her silence once he was gone. He couldn't risk ruining his reputation.

"Jon? Hello?"

He had to live long enough to intercept his American Express bill, destroy the evidence of their most recent tryst. If Sarah ever found that bill, she would *kill* him.

The irony struck him as hilarious. It was like, during the blackout, the television announcer telling the public to "go to our website to check when the power will be restored in your area."

He dropped the receiver into its cradle without answering and fell back chuckling, wondering how he could have been so careless. Maybe he was losing it already. The illness was affecting his mind.

The old man's magnetic stare—was that his imagination? He'd seen that same knowing gaze in the eyes of a yellow lab he once owned. It was almost as if Miguel were trying to tell him something, or draw him into his sphere for some purpose. As if he sensed Jonathan's condition—my God, did it already show? Did it hang out from some neglected diagnostic zipper?

As if Miguel Fuentes were saying, *You need me more than I need you.*

Crystal City. The name called up visions of The Emerald City from *The Land of Oz.* Too bad there was no real place like Oz, where one could get a heart, or courage, or even a new life.

4

At the Roswell airport, Arpad's co-pilot, Wheeler, patted his midsection and studied the white-hot New Mexico sky. "No sense in frying the follicles in this heat. What say we check out the grub in the coffee shop? No telling how long the chief'll be gone."

Arpad turned back toward the plane, fiddling with the hatch coupling. He was breathing hard, only vaguely aware of why. "Go on in. Order me a coffee. I've got to do something first."

A cloud settled over the features of the younger man, who towered over Arpad almost a head. "What's the deal, Ar? You've been in a funk ever since the chief called you aft. And that phone call just now—was that the chief's wife?" Suspicion darkened the pale eyes. "He's not getting ready to can me, is he?"

"Hell no!" Arpad flared, but quickly regained his composure. "Just go on. Get me a piece of pie, too. Any kind. I'll be along."

He needed a few minutes to sort out the source of his anger. Yes, he resented Wheeler's insinuation that Jonathan could be anything less than loyal to his employees. But that was not where it started, as he knew perfectly well. He was angry because he despised being placed in a position of having to lie to the chief once again.

That in itself was a lie. No one placed him in that position. He simply had to keep the story growing that he'd set in motion when they first met: the elaborate history he had invented about his family and his Indian forbears.

In the beginning, when he had been so intent on doing a good job for the chief, it would have been too humiliating to admit that he had no family and never had—that someone, probably his mother, had placed him in a dumpster, apparently on Christmas eve. He had been tossed away like so much holiday refuse, surviving possibly as many as two bitterly cold nights before his cries were heard on the day after Christmas—cries of hunger and of pain: His body was so frozen that he lost part of his right foot to frostbite. He had explained the disability to Jonathan as being the result of a youthful motorcycle escapade. The truth was that he had never been on a motorcycle in his short, deprived life.

Could Jonathan, could anyone, comprehend the daily degradation of living with the knowledge of having been thrown away, of being reared and schooled by the county, being shunted from one foster home to another, being rejected time and again by prospective parents because of his lameness? Could anyone imagine the surge of unreasoning hope before each adoptive interview that at long last he might have a mother to love him, a father to protect him? Could anyone ever fathom the depths of his despair as he saw each couple turn away, invariably murmuring, "Pity about his foot" or "Such a pretty child, except for the deformity"?

Could Jonathan understand the mortification he felt every time one of a parade of foundlings who came and went called him names like "Gimpy" or "Stumpy"? Could Jonathan, who had grown up with everything, know the years of longing to have a brother, a real friend—and later, a girl friend, a date, even? Arpad had seen that look too often: the first attraction turning to aversion, or disgust, once they noticed his crippled foot. It was the same expression he'd seen all his life on the faces of the couples who came to the Home to adopt a son.

Arpad was destined to be nobody's son, nobody's brother. Nobody's lover.

Perhaps it was partly his fault. Early on he had learned to protect himself, withdrawing to a safe place inside, shutting out both the cruel jibes and the occasional overture toward friendship. And escaping adult rejection before it happened.

Yet it had been one of those whispered comments that set his life in motion. As one prospective father turned to go, he muttered to his wife, "That one will have to depend on brains to get by in this world. I hope he's got plenty of 'em, being lame and Indian both."

He owed a debt to that man for those revelations: most important, that he was Indian! He had a heritage! The man had tossed him a lifeline to his past. The second revelation gave him the key to survival: that he could possibly make his way through life with brains. They had set him on a determined path to educate himself, and to learn all he could about his Indian heritage.

A pang of sorrow twisted his heart as he recalled the true motivation of that child for the hours he pored over great tomes in the back reaches of the public library, thin brown hands turning the pages carefully as he studied with a focused intensity that drew sweat trickling behind his ears, that drove hunger and all sense of time from his eager mind.

That child had hoped, not for a prosperous future twenty years hence, but for another chance to impress the man who placed such importance on brains. Someday he and his wife might come again to the Home in search of a son, and Arpad would so dazzle them with his knowledge that his deformity would be overlooked. The kind woman would rush forward, drop to her knees and draw him against her breast and hold him close, so close he could feel the beat of her heart. The man would ruffle his hair and say, "I would be proud to call you my son."

To his disappointment, as he read more, he realized that to be an Indian in the United States was to be a second class citizen. But at least being Indian was better than being nothing.

Much of the longing for a father had been transferred to Jonathan, even though only a decade in age separated them. Arpad remembered how, after flight school, he had tried without success to find work, until the chance meeting with Jonathan outside the office of the private airport where Arpad had gone to apply for employment. This was prior to the time that Jonathan hired a full-time crew of his own.

Even from that first glance, Arpad had felt the aura of fate. Jonathan, red-faced with exasperation, was in heated conversation with his pilot, a man in his fifties.

When Arpad realized they were discussing a no-show pilot, he edged close enough to listen.

Jonathan was saying, "What about Casper? Hell, he's better than nothing."

The older man said, "Casper's already logged the maximum flight hours. There's nothing to do but wait until morning—or else go commercial."

"I need to leave *now*! There's an important deal hanging." Jonathan spun around, almost colliding with Arpad, who drew himself erect and tried to look competent enough to fly a plane.

Even his first words had been a bluff. "I hear you're looking for a pilot. My flight has been cancelled. Maybe I can help you out."

The older man intervened, eyeing him with suspicion, doubtless because he'd never seen him around before. "*I'm* the pilot. Our co-pilot's a no-show." He pointed outside toward Jonathan's jet. "Are you checked out in that baby?"

"My favorite machine," Arpad said, and meant it. If this man would put him on for even one flight, that plane would be his favorite from now on.

The inevitable happened, the moment he always dreaded. Jonathan frowned down at Arpad's foot. "I need an able-bodied man."

Arpad flushed but held his gaze steady. This was too desperately vital to risk any waver. "I can do anything any other man can do, and furthermore, I know how to use my head. My *brains* aren't handicapped. Which would you rather have in a tight spot, a quick thinker, or a man who can run fast from a burning wreckage?"

Jonathan laughed and clapped him around the shoulder. "What's your name, kid?"

The touch was the nearest thing to an embrace he'd had in years—perhaps ever. It sent a warmth coursing clear to his gut. He didn't even resent being called "kid."

"Arpad Patel. I'm older than I appear." The need to invent an acceptable history dammed the threatened rush of relieved tears. "My family came here from Bombay when I was an infant. All my education has been in American schools." He did not add that he had paid his own way by the most menial of dishwashing and janitorial jobs, often going for days without a decent meal.

He paused before continuing, desperate to make his point. "I'm a very, very good pilot."

The next few years had been spent proving that he was worthy of Jonathan's trust and acceptance, so that when Jonathan put on a permanent crew, he was part of that crew. He was so beholden to Jonathan for offering him a chance that he gave more than was expected, arriving early, staying late, personally overseeing mechanical maintenance and even the plane's interior custodial care. In six months he had made himself indispensable, not for job security, but simply out of profound gratitude.

Yes, he should have confessed his deception long ago, as their relationship deepened into friendship. He always intended to confide the truth about his deprived past, but pride prevented it. Jonathan seemed in awe of his Indian background, as if it automatically conferred upon Arpad a degree of oriental wisdom. So as not to disappoint him, Arpad returned to the library during off-hours and steeped himself in Hindu mythology, which he spouted forth when the occasion arose.

When Jonathan bought a larger plane, Arpad went back to school to learn its intricacies, as if his assignment to it was a given. And when the older pilot retired and Arpad moved up into the captain's seat, he all but forgot his mean beginnings for long stretches of time. He could almost believe that he belonged here, in this luxurious life that had been his for over a decade.

Now, if what Sarah Tyler had just told him over the phone was true, Jonathan was seriously ill—maybe fatally ill, and there was nothing Arpad could do. She wanted him to bring Jonathan home immediately, but he couldn't even do that; could never go against the chief's wishes, and obviously the chief wished to be here, in New Mexico. Sarah had sworn him to secrecy, asked him not to mention her call to Jonathan. One more secret he'd have to keep from the chief. He couldn't even tell Jonathan a plain truth about himself, not now, certainly. But worse—

If Jonathan were to die, Arpad would be left with no family whatsoever. For the chief didn't realize that he had become father, brother, all Arpad had in the world.

The thought angered him, or he willed it to. He longed to remember every single time he and Jonathan had clashed, every incidence of Jonathan's arrogance and high-handedness. It would be an easy matter then to withdraw, return to being the remote, careful, defensive youth he had been when Jonathan took him in. Except that he was no longer young.

A sudden whirlwind kicked up dust that stung his face, and he became aware that his right palm, still gripping the hatch handle, was almost blistered from the metallic heat. Shaking free of the morose introspection, he turned and headed for the airport coffee shop to join Wheeler and the steward, glancing at his watch on the way.

The sight of the expensive timepiece, a gift, one of many from Jonathan, brought a jolting insight and stinging eyelids. If something ever really happened to Jonathan, Arpad wouldn't want to live, either.

The thought struck him as heroic. If Jonathan were terminally ill with something slow and debilitating, he could at least give the chief one lasting gift.

If anything ever did happen, if the end seemed near and painful, he could lure Jonathan into the old two-seater that he had bought as a collector's item, take him up for one last flight, make a plunging nosedive into the Atlantic at full throttle.

The fantasy sent a surge of adrenalin through him. It would be the sort of heroic act he'd dreamed of performing ever since he first began reading the great Hindu epics, the *Ramayana* and the *Mahabharata*. It would be a selfless sacrifice that would be worthy of King Rama or the Bharatas.

It would be the kindest thing he could do for them both.

5

The miscue with Betts had disabused Jonathan of the idea of phoning Sarah, who would probably somehow sense his guilt. She was, after all, only a couple of thousand miles away, well within wifely antenna range. Instead, since chances of Doss returning before late afternoon seemed more remote by the minute, he rang Arpad and instructed him to book rooms for himself and the others in a Roswell hotel. He didn't want them waiting around in a bar, partaking of light refreshments like tequila with the natives, arriving back at the plane bleary-eyed and under the impression that they could perhaps avoid the troublesome tailwind off the Rockies by taxiing much of the way across the Panhandle of Texas.

Arpad betrayed his concern, despite obvious attempts at nonchalance. "Okay chief. We'll catch a catnap and be set to fly you back tonight, no matter how late it is."

In uncharacteristic carelessness, having left his briefcase in Doss's Jeep, Jonathan had neither the corporate checkbook nor the settlement agreement and release Hal had faxed him. Although he couldn't pay off Fuentes until Doss returned, he could at least negotiate the amount. He determined to do it immediately, before Diego put any delusions of grandeur into the old man's head. Hal had advised him to low-ball it: "Don't give the rest of them ideas."

He had been too upset to eat lunch, but flying west, they had gained two hours. Many of the workers had apparently been gathered in the sparse shade of the tool shed to eat lunch when his arrival interrupted them. Now they had returned to finish. There was an air of festivity in their banter, as if the memorial service had offered a welcome respite from routine. As he hiked past, the pungency of bologna assailed his nostrils, causing his mouth to water and almost bringing to mind—what?

Something from his childhood…

If he had delusions of negotiating without Diego, he was disappointed. He found them both behind Miguel's trailer amid an astoundingly large array of home-made cages. Forgetting the old man spoke no English, he said, "Hey! You're taking all these?"

Miguel continued directing Diego in securing the coops with wire, chirping to the birds with obvious affection, ignoring Jonathan as if he were another scrap of the unending clutter of the place. Jonathan counted the cages: there were fourteen in all. No wonder Fuentes wanted a bus. Because of their size, each cage would require a seat of its own.

As he watched, Jonathan had another idea. He addressed the old man as if he could understand. "How about this? It's going to get woofy in the bus. What's Spanish for chicken shit times fourteen? What if we send the birds on the bus, and I fly you to your relative's? You could be there ahead of the cocks." *To prepare her for the shock of being descended on by a menagerie.*

After the briefest consultation between the two, Diego rose to his full question-mark posture. "You just don't get it, man. Miguel, he's *gallero*. He's not going to leave his *gallos*. Anyways, where would an airplane land? The old woman lives out in the mesquite."

Jonathan hadn't thought of that. He returned to his original purpose. Again he addressed Miguel, still bent over the coops, apparently oblivious to his presence. Summoning a country-parson solemnity, as if Llano Sand and Gravel were the aggrieved party, Jonathan intoned, "Although the company is not required to make restitution for an accident of this kind, it regards its employees with great affection. We're tremendously saddened by this act of God, and I'm prepared to give you a generous sum to compensate for your loss—"

Diego interrupted. "How much?"

"Thir—" He blanched and gulped hard under the younger man's murderous glare. Good lord, this man was capable of planting a shiv between his ribs without blinking twice. "Forty—" Still the Hispanic glowered. "—and ten thousand for moving expenses. That's fifty thousand, altogether."

Diego spat; his retort was a savage bellow. "Rot in hell, *gringo*! Miguel ain't going to settle for twice that much!"

Jonathan had been prepared to go much higher, but he balked at being railroaded by this young scar-faced hood. Sooner or later he'd get Miguel alone and find a different interpreter.

He shook his head sadly. "Too bad. That's my best offer." He wheeled abruptly and headed back toward the foreman's trailer, buoyed by the transient illusion that he had excelled at hardball. *Slash and burn—wasn't that what he'd learned at Wharton?*

But again the heady odor of bologna wafted past like a silent breeze and brought with it a stab of memory: Jonathan and his boyhood friend Lidge sharing lunch in their tree house, their futures spread before them like a gigantic patchwork quilt. Everything had been implicit back then, like the plant in its seed, their successes assured by their idyllic entitled childhood.

Instead, he had been catapulted in a flash to an inglorious premature dotage that was even now gurgling down the sewer with the other detritus, like Streisand ticket stubs and Trump fan club membership cards. He felt wounded by his own raw self-pity.

Afternoon dragged interminably, heat-beaten to submission. It was almost sundown—shot with orange spears and pink plumes of light that should've stunned him if he weren't so miserable—when Doss returned, followed by a dilapidated recycled school bus, now painted white, with *Spring Acres Missionary Baptist Iglesia* stenciled across each side. The bus was driven by a dour and swarthy Hispanic with a troublesome near-sighted squint. Doss introduced him as Reverend Ramos, the assistant pastor. He looked more like an extra in a Godfather movie, except that he wasn't Italian.

"It was the only thing I could get on short notice," Doss told Jonathan while Ramos went off to inspect the chicken cages. "Had to do some fast talking at that, once I mentioned the chickens. To safeguard the church's property, this preacher Ramos insisted on driving the bus himself—for an extra fee of course."

It mattered little to Jonathan how the old man traveled, just so he was out of there immediately. He said, "I only hope that contraption will make it over the county line. Round up all the help you can get to load up." He started toward Miguel's trailer to pin down the old man and get his signature on the release. The hours of inaction had left him edgy, anxious to get back to his own agenda. One of the first things he planned to do, after a large pepperoni pizza with extra cheese, was dump this mine. Or maybe just close it the hell down.

Dusk quickly crept in like a fast-closing eyelid, bringing its inevitable melancholy, made worse by hunger. All around the settlement he could see lights coming on in the workers' kitchens. Smells of pinto beans and ham hocks mingled with those of beef stew and the unmistakable odor of Mexican chili. Jonathan almost regretted now that he had declined the foreman's invitation to supper, especially when he stepped into the old man's trailer and found Diego and Miguel, whose chin barely cleared the table, sopping their chili bowls with rolled-up tortillas. Jonathan swallowed his starvation, amending the large pizza to prime rib medium rare and baked potato with sour cream when he got back to the Roswell hotel. He didn't plan to spend the night, but he felt too exhausted to fly back to Boston without food. Dripping in fat.

Jonathan directed the ever-present Diego what to say to the old man, who continued eating implacably even as two of the workers arrived and began carrying his belongings out of the trailer. "Tell him we've kept our end of the bargain," Jonathan said, pulling out the settlement release he had retrieved from Doss's Jeep. "Get him to sign these and I'll hand him a check. *Mucho dinero.*"

Diego spoke to Miguel at length, but it was obvious that the old man had no intention of signing. Speaking around a mouthful of tortilla, chili glistening from the corner of his mouth, he let out not much more than a half-dozen sounds: "*Todavía no estoy en casa.*"

Diego turned with an indifferent shrug. "He says he ain't home yet."

"What does that mean?" Jonathan sputtered in exasperation.

The old man swallowed and rattled off a string of rapid Spanish, peppering the table with chili droplets. Diego translated. "He says the bus might break down. His chickens could die. Then he would have no livelihood."

"He's going to receive a great deal of money. Have you told him that? Enough to buy—hell, cages full of fighting emus."

Diego nodded. "It's not the same. He loves them *gallos.* Somebody might steal them."

"Tell him…tell him we'll send someone along. Doss can follow in the Jeep. He could phone for help—"

Miguel interrupted with another objection.

Diego said, "Even if he gets there, his aunt might be dead. He would have no place to go."

"His *aunt? His* aunt? How old is this woman, for Christ's sake?"

Diego obtained the answer. "He's not sure. One-hundred-eleven. Maybe more."

"Es *una curandera*," Miguel said with obvious pride.

"She's a healer," Diego explained.

"*Muy famosa*," Miguel said. Jonathan got it. But as the old man continued to speak, Diego's eyes—even the mutilated one—grew large. Jonathan waited impatiently for the translation.

"I know of this woman," Diego said with obvious awe. "But I did not know she was kin to Miguel. She is the most famous *curandera* in the country. She has performed many miracles."

One of the movers, overhearing, stopped and said, "Josefina Carlota Rulfo! She saved my cousin's arm when it got mangled in a threshing machine. She made it where you can't tell nothing ever happened to it."

Miguel added something more. Diego, all arrogance vanished, said solemnly, "She has brought many people back from the dead."

The three men fell silent, nodding reverently in agreement.

Jonathan couldn't resist the sarcasm. "If she can do all that, then why is Miguel worrying that she might be dead? If she's that good, she can just resurrect herself."

Diego and the mover stared at him in shocked disapproval. Miguel, black eyes darting from one to the other, seemed to sense Jonathan's meaning. He drew himself up so tall that his chest was visible above the table top. He spoke in a quiet voice laden with hauteur.

Diego said, "She has brought herself back from death many times, but now that most of her family is on the other side, she may want to go of her own accord."

Jonathan felt outnumbered. The air was pendulous with the men's awe. He shook off the sudden sense of defeat and addressed Miguel directly, as if he could understand. "So what you're saying is that you won't sign this settlement until you get to Crystal City?"

Diego translated and Miguel nodded, then got up and followed the movers out, barking instructions, moving with sudden surprising agility. Diego shrugged again and stumped out behind them. Jonathan eyed the leftover meal whose pungent odors lingered. He wished to high heaven he had something decent to eat. He could hardly think of anything else.

Doss stuck his head in the doorway and announced, "They're ready to roll. The bus is jam-packed, allowing breathing space for the birds. We'll have to ship the rest of his stuff—"

Jonathan cut in. "He didn't sign the settlement and release. Says he won't until he gets to Crystal City. Looks like you'll have to follow them there in the Jeep."

Doss started as if he had been struck, and Jonathan glimpsed the steely core which fitted him for his job. "Look, sir: I've sacrificed a lot for this outfit, but at this hour I'm late for a rehearsal. My daughter's wedding is tomorrow night. There's no way in hell I'm going to miss it!"

"Oh. Of course not." Jonathan mentally inventoried the motley crew of workers and their foreman. He did not trust even the foreman to follow through on this assignment; it was too important. And Hal was right: best not to draw in too many people. He slumped in pretended resignation. "Guess I'll have to go myself."

Actually he felt a buzz of anticipation. Or maybe he was light-headed from hunger.

"You can take my Jeep," Doss said. "I'll get someone to drive me back to town."

It must be more than lack of food that made Jonathan feel giddy and weak, he decided. He knew he hadn't the stamina to drive all night. "No. I'll ride in the bus with the other two. I could fly down, except that there's no place to land, I'm told." He couldn't risk letting Miguel out of his sight, but he saw no reason to mention that to Doss.

He would have to phone Arpad, but what could he say? How to explain that Jonathan Whitley Tyler IV was set to board a school bus of doubtful vintage, with a near-sighted Hispanic preacher at the wheel, to accompany another Hispanic old enough to have fought in World War I and crates of illegal fighting cocks across miles of desert to the home of an even more ancient witch doctor? It would sound like the ravings of a lunatic madder than an outhouse rat...someone in a hypoglycemic fog, or suffering from starvation dementia. And yet he *felt* lucid.

What was it Arpad had once said, about the forces of nature being in charge? Jonathan experienced an unbidden surge of elation, an irrational hope, as if Fate intended for him to meet this famous healer. Well, what would it hurt? No one in Boston or New York need ever know. He must warn Arpad not to tell Sarah.

Allman and his gang of over-paid medical assassins had already passed his death sentence anyway. Even now the blade was poised atop his assigned guillotine back at Sloan-Kettering. Maybe this old woman, with her ancient Mayan wisdom, possessed some arcane herbal concoction, some magic bullet-dodger.

Yes, he must definitely keep this bus trip from Sarah. If she thought he was doing something foolhardy, she might feel compelled to do what he had forbidden her to do: blurt out his diagnosis to Arpad—or even to him, for that matter. From the beginning he had informed his doctors that he wanted no exact label attached to his malady. He had an intuitive sense that to give his illness a name might impede his recovery; a so-called fatal condition would be a self-fulfilling prophesy. Surprisingly, Allman had not considered that an unreasonable attitude.

But the doctor had argued, "Medical ethics require that I inform someone. Your wife, at least, has a right to know."

With reluctance Jonathan had agreed, but he warned Sarah, "If you repeat it to anyone—me, the boys, your parents, my dad, your hair dresser, that nose-picking yardman, *anyone*—Tyler Technologies and I will both do a vanishing act. I'll hit Atlantic City and with one monumental roll of the dice turn you into a pauper. You'll have to bury me in Potter's Field in a Dell box."

Not that she believed him, of course. Jonathan was far too rich to lose it all that easily.

Now, as Doss retreated, temptation overpowered Jonathan, outweighing his usual cautious nature about botulism and salmonella and just plain filth. Ignoring the chili speckles on the table, he waved off several swarming flies, reached over and grabbed a cold tortilla, and dunked it into the remains of Miguel's bowl. He'd never tasted anything so good.

6

For the few hours of their stay in Roswell, the steward, being gay, had felt more comfortable taking a room to himself. Arpad and Wheeler shared a two-bedroom suite with a commodious sitting room in which Jonathan could relax and perhaps have a meal before they returned to Boston. It was in this room that Arpad left his cell phone while he went to the bathroom. While he was gone, he heard it ring, heard Wheeler answer.

The co-pilot had just finished talking when Arpad returned. "That was the chief. Change of plans. We've got hours to kill. Guess we might's well go eat and scope out the poon situation."

Arpad staunched his heightened concern. He was accustomed to sudden alterations in Jonathan's agenda, and this time should be no different. He reached for the hotel phone. "I'd better call the airport and notify them of a revised flight plan. What's our ETD now?"

Wheeler was examining his stubble in the wall mirror. "Unknown. The chief's off on a little bus trip....Think I ought to shave if we're going out on the town?"

"*What?*" Arpad pressed the disconnect button. "Did you say bus trip?"

"My guess is he won't get back before morning. He didn't say anything about our reserving him a room for tonight."

Arpad punched in the numbers of Jonathan's cell phone and heard the recorded voice saying the party he was calling was not online. "Turn on your phone, dammit!" he muttered. Without leaving a voice mail, he turned to Wheeler, his anxiety mounting. "Where is he going? And why?"

The younger man studied him quizzically in the mirror. "How should I know? Since when has it been in my job description to keep tabs on the boss? I does me duty and asks no questions."

He faced around, leveling a pale accusing gaze at Arpad. "What's with you, anyhow? You're not his freakin' mother hen, for God's sake."

"It's just that—he was anxious to get back…home." Arpad stopped, not wanting to betray a confidence. Sarah Tyler had phoned shortly after their arrival and confided how important it was that Jonathan return to the hospital quickly. She had warned him not to tell a soul of the seriousness of Jonathan's condition. If the chief ever found out how much Arpad knew, it might be impossible to induce him to take a "mercy ride" in the Piper Cherokee. He would never allow Arpad to take the plunge with him.

He tried not to panic. "He didn't sound sick or anything, did he?" Maybe Jonathan had suddenly taken ill and had to be rushed to the nearest clinic.

"Relax. He said something about—uh—delivering an old man somewhere, I think. Said he'd call us before he started back, give us an idea on our departure time. Lighten up, Ar. We got a freebie here. Let's go check out Roswell. Nothing's going to happen to your meal ticket."

Lighten up? he wanted to scream. *But you're not the one who's about to die.*

He wondered if he had the valor to make such an offering, the kind his Hindu ancestors had taken for granted. Did he have the courage that even many present-day women had in remote villages of India—to commit suttee? To climb atop their husbands' funeral pyre and sit with dignity through unbearable torment while they went up in flames?

Perhaps the whole suttee tradition had been a patriarchal idea, a way of ridding the tribe of the troublesome problem of caring for widows. Even so, back-country women embraced it to this day: an outward declaration of their connubial devotion: "If you can't live this life, I won't, either." An overt manifestation of their avowed belief in other lives to come. And hadn't he thrilled to accounts in the *Mahabharata* of filial sacrifice of one warrior for his fallen comrade? Was this not also the standard of Mohandas Gandhi, the Mahatma, the Great Soul?

When Sarah Tyler divulged her husband's diagnosis, Arpad's secret vow to sacrifice himself had seemed high-minded, even romantic. Now that he thought about it, lately there were clear signs that Jonathan was sinking, and the concrete action, so noble in the abstract, caused his palms to sweat. If he dwelt on it too deeply, he might not be able to go through with it. So he would allow himself to think about it no more. He would put one foot in front of the other and walk through it with grace. He could do no less for Jonathan Tyler, who had given him the very life that he had, the only security, the only happiness he had ever known.

7

His name had been Guayo Cutzal from the time of his naming ceremony for the whole of his life, until he got to the States. Then he quickly learned what a handicap it was to have a Mayan name among Chicanos, to say nothing about Anglos. So when he purchased his ID card from the vendor in El Paso, he had chosen the name Hector Mendoza.

That was the name he gave to the fortune teller in Hobbs when he went in to find out about his family. But maybe by misleading her, he directed her attention to the wrong family, because of what she said about them. At least that was what he thought at first.

The woman ran a combination gas station, grocery, and curio shop on Hobbs' outskirts, but behind the beaded curtain at the back of the shop, she read palms. Although she spoke Spanish of a sort, she was *gringa*, with stringy yellow hair and a chipped front tooth and elbows like grasshopper knees. But she was the only fortune teller he knew of, and she charged just two dollars.

His fears were allayed about having possibly misled her when she looked him square in the eye and asked in her own brand of Tex-Mex, "Where 'bouts in Central America are you from, hon?"

Still he lied and said, "I am from El Paso. I am American."

"Yeah, yeah." The woman flashed a snaggled sneer. "And I'm Martha Stewart." Her eyes narrowed in recognition. "I've seen you around. You work at that garage up the road, right?"

He nodded. "I am lube man."

"My Robbie used to be their lube man," she muttered. "They couldn't hold his job for him for six lousy weeks until he served his sentence. Now what do you want to know, boy?"

They were seated on nail kegs across from each other over a metal TV tray with rusting legs. Hector scooted forward. His voice grew husky with earnestness he could not hide. "I have not heard from my family since I left home. I am weak with worry. What can you tell me about them?"

She pulled his broad stubby hand to her and studied his palm with exaggerated concentration. "I see that your baby's sick."

"I have no baby," he said, sure now that his false name had thrown her off track.

She looked up sharply. "How long you been gone?"

"Three years."

"Your baby was born a few months after you left. Your wife—you *do* have a wife, don'tcha?"

Hector nodded as the image of his squat little Chacach rose in his mind. Chacach would never lie with another man; his mother would not permit it to happen.

"Your wife was pregnant when you left, but she didn't know it yet. He's now...uh...over two years old."

Hector felt a rush of pride, and his spirits soared. "I have a son?"

The woman nodded and pushed his hand back. "Yup. So you better high-tail it back to Honduras, or wherever, and quit taking jobs away from good American boys like my Robbie."

"Belize," Hector said. "I am from Belize."

He did not tell her that, to seek his fortune, he had traversed the western mountains of his homeland and the swamps of northern Belize, had walked the length of Mexico, had swum the Rio Grande at Villa Acuña, then trudged west to El Paso looking for a cousin he never found. By the time he got there, he had lost half his body weight, and his moccasins had worn through to the skin. But it would be worth any hardship to pull his family out of the poverty that had driven them far into the highlands near the Guatemalan border. He had promised Chacach that he would become a rich man and then he would send money to the whole family.

"I am from Belize," he repeated proudly. "But now that I have a son, I need to stay here even longer. Got to earn money to send to my mother, to take care of my family."

The woman grabbed his hand again and peered intently at the lines of his palm, tracing one with a long jagged nail. A deep frown gathered across the leathery skin of her brow. "Oh no. Here's something I didn't see before. Someone in Belize is very sick, all right. But it isn't your son."

"My wife?"

She shook her head over and over, the brittle ends of the yellow hair sticking to the sweat on her cheeks. "No, no, no. It's your mother." She looked up and let out a long, tragic sigh. "I'm afraid she is dying. She is asking for you."

Hector gasped. His mother was the backbone of the family. She could not die. He said, "Can you do anything?"

"Me?"

"Do you have magic?"

"No. The only hope for your mother is for you to get back home to take care of her. The burden you left her with is too much."

Hector stood, weighted by this new responsibility. Yes, he must go home, he could see that now, even though to return without the promised fortune would be a disgrace. But could he face that torturous trek southward with the worst of the summer still ahead? He had almost died on the way up here. But he couldn't spare the time to wait for winter. Maybe he should head home through El Paso, even though it was out of the way. Try again to locate his cousin, who was supposed to have connections. Word in the family was that his cousin knew someone with a fruit truck. If only he could ride part of the way....

Yes, he would get to El Paso by the fastest route.

That in itself would be a challenge. If only he had a gun.

8

There were no amenities on the ancient bus: no toilet, no air conditioning to dispel the reek of chickens and the emanations of a chili-bloated nonagenarian, no cigarette lighter into which to plug the cell phone, and—Jonathan was sure after the first half-mile—no shocks. He wadded the spare shorts he always carried in his briefcase to use as a pillow, to absorb some of the jolts as he rested his head against the window glass. He sat on the bench behind the driver, not because it had the fewest sprung springs, but because it was the only one with leg room.

Every window that could be, was opened to ventilate the rolling aviary—some, like his, were permanently stuck shut. The roar of wind and road noise made talk impossible, which suited Jonathan. He was exhausted and hungry and had nothing to say to the Reverend Ramos, whose constant small adjustments of the wheel, made necessary by his near-sightedness, kept the bus and its contents in a constant shimmy. With each swerve, Jonathan had to grab for the upright post to keep from being thrown into the aisle.

Miguel, inheritor of short Aztec genes, and further shriveled by age, curled up two rows back, across from his favorite fighting cock, to whom he continued to croon or tongue-click the incessant soothing message. The chickens ceased their squawking as soon as the sky turned black which, Ramos patiently explained as if Jonathan were an imbecile, was their nature to do.

Sometime near ten Jonathan started from a fitful doze as the preacher pulled into a seedy-looking truck stop lit by several thousand watts of buzzing zapping lights. He turned to Jonathan and said, "I got to stop, Mister Tyler. I'm falling asleep sittin' here, and anyways, I don't feel so good."

"Where are we?" Jonathan said. Across the highway from the truck stop a large cantaloupe moon hung over a completely empty landscape, illuminating nothing else for as far as he could see.

"Oria, Texas. The last chance to stop for a long ways."

Jonathan sighed in relief, envisioning at long last a shower, a full dinner, a comfortable bed. "Is there a decent hotel nearby?"

Ramos gestured toward the truck stop, to which a second floor of grey stucco had been appended by, it appeared, an unsteady hand. "This is it. There's rooms upstairs."

Jonathan strained to see beyond the glaring lights of the truck stop, toward a range of distant hills scalloping the horizon to the west. "Where's the town?"

"This is pretty much it right here."

"What's the next town of any size?"

"Pecos is the next place. But it's too far to drive. I'd never make it." He shifted and called out to Miguel in Spanish.

Miguel had risen and was sitting stiffly erect. He said something that sounded to Jonathan like an objection. Ramos shrugged and told Jonathan, "He won't leave his birds out here alone. He's going to sleep in the bus."

Jonathan pointed a finger at Miguel. "*Don't move* till I get back," he growled, hoping his tone alone would convey his meaning. He got off behind Ramos and said, "Go on to bed, then. If I can't convince the old man to come in, I'll sleep in the bus with him."

Ramos's chortle bore elements of an outright scoff. "Where's he going to go? Who's going to get him?"

Jonathan didn't explain about the ominous *la raza* civil rights group that he was protecting the old man from. He headed for the pay phone on the outside wall and called Sarah.

She sounded almost hysterical. "Where have you been? You didn't have your phone turned on. I've been frantic."

"Slight problem there. Low battery, and no cigarette lighter on the bus. It's—a very unique vehicle. I should get you one for your birthday."

"Can't you buy a new battery for the phone?"

He peered through the sooty truck stop window and saw the lone attendant-cum-chef hand Ramos a room key. "Not likely. Anyway, I'll be home tomorrow."

"Why not tonight? We need you tonight, Jonathan. Something else has come up."

His mind immediately flashed to their younger son. "What's Chip done this time?"

"Don't be sarcastic. An officer called. A *policeman*. Chip and his friends were stopped for speeding—"

Jonathan's fury spewed over the top. No one in that crowd was old enough to drive. "What ninny gave them a car?"

"—and they found marijuana. They're holding him in juvenile detention, Jonathan. Until morning!"

He looked at his watch. In Boston, it was after midnight, too late to call his attorney. Since Hal's chemo treatments began, he had adopted a policy of turning off his phone at bedtime.

Sarah pleaded, "I don't know what to do. Can't you just fly back now?"

"On what? There's not even a taxi in this place, much less a plane."

"Where's the jet?"

"Back in Roswell, hours from here. Look—I don't know anything to do except leave Chip there overnight. Maybe the experience will do him good."

Sarah's control shattered. Her atypical hysteria, with its incumbent shrillness, set his teeth on edge. "Jonathan, he isn't experiencing *anything*! The officer says he's too spaced out even to care!" Her voice broke with a sob. "He thinks it's funny!"

The news left Jonathan shaken. Besides, he couldn't abide Sarah's new emotionality, any more than he could abide her usually meticulous self-control. Their union was a paradox, a conflict that couldn't be resolved. Holding paradox is wrestling with angels, he figured, feeling righteous.

"That's not even the worst of it," she went on. "When he left home this evening, he was wearing eye shadow and mascara, and do you know why?"

Jonathan sure as hell didn't want to know. Why couldn't Chip have put this off a few more months, until Jonathan was reduced to some fine siftings in a bronze urn?

"It's because he wants to appear less upper class, can you believe it? He hopes, if he looks kinky enough, he'll be more *interesting*."

In other words, he's ashamed of us, Jonathan thought. "The stupid little twit!" Good thing the kid wasn't old enough to be thrown in the drunk tank. Someone would be bound to find him interesting there.

He promised to check in with her in the morning and hung up. Weakness overtook him, reminding him of how long he had gone without a decent meal. He went into the truck stop, sat at the counter, and ordered bacon and eggs from the grizzly fry cook. At least he need no longer worry about cholesterol; that was something. Even a death sentence has its up side.

Where had he gone wrong with Chip, mascaraed pot-smoker? And with Whit, whose idea of meaningful activity was throwing himself against a Velcro wall? Now that every moment of his life had turned into an inventory, he would like to be remembered as a good father.

Secretly, he hadn't wanted children, not really, not yet. Maybe not ever. He hadn't been ready to assume the role his own negligently attentive father had filled with such apparent ease—and his grandfathers. Even his peers seemed to welcome fatherhood more than he, or were they all merely acting a part as he was?

Still, despite that, he had been a conscientious parent, calling up from some deep well the knowledge and perspectives of his ancestors, albeit less frequently as his business duties mounted. He thought he was as good a dad as his own had been, as good as his friends....

But then. Friends. He didn't want to go down that path at the moment.

Who would bear his coffin to its grave? Or his urn to its mausoleum? He ought to make a list. Make some donations, endow something. Throw a party.

Good lord, he couldn't die until he made some friends!

He shoveled in the eggs without savoring them as he had meant to, and hurried back to the bus. Belatedly he wondered if he should have brought Fuentes something to eat. The old man had resumed his makeshift bed on the worn vinyl seat. Jonathan took a gulp of untainted air from an open window, removed his shoes and tried to make himself comfortable in the cramped little space. Damn school kids! Why did they have to be so freaking short?

Despite his great discomfort, he soon dozed off. His sleep was peopled with knife-wielding doctors in bloody coats who were trying to harvest his organs. Several times he woke with a start, cramped and aching from his awkward position, but once he felt to be sure he still had his liver, exhaustion soon reclaimed him.

Toward morning he became aware of a banging on the bus window. A raw red sun was already beaming in.

The chickens had begun their maddening chatter; he had fitted their talk into his dreams. Now their cries became raucous, as if they sensed danger. Before Jonathan could rouse himself, Miguel hurried up the narrow aisle and opened the door. The station attendant, now with a new growth of chin stubble, leaned in, wild-eyed and panting.

"Better come quick, mister. Your buddy's having some kind of friggin' fit!"

In his stocking feet, Jonathan bolted past Miguel and they both followed the attendant into the truck stop, where a circle of truckers stood around the prostrate body of Ramos. He had stopped writhing and lay as if comatose, a stream of spittle oozing from the corner of his mouth. Suspicious stains darkened his khaki trousers. Gradually his eyes flickered open and his squinty near-sighted gaze wandered until it found Jonathan.

"I forgot my medicine," he said, weakly apologetic.

The truckers helped the preacher stand and led him to a booth, then quickly dispersed in embarrassed silence. Jonathan and Miguel dropped down opposite him.

Jonathan said, "You're an epileptic? And you never told me?"

Ramos shrugged. "I'm fine long as I take my medicine. But I left it at home, and the attack sneaked up on me." He grinned timidly. "Guess we'll have to turn around and go back. Maybe you'd better drive."

"Not on your life! *You'll* go back; *we're* going on." He reared up and called to the ring of coffee drinkers perched on stools around the counter. "Anybody going to Roswell who'll give this man a ride?"

No one looked up. Jonathan rephrased it. "For a hundred bucks?"

Two men got off their stools and came over. Jonathan surveyed them. "Which one of you will take this man on to Spring Hills?"

One of the truckers stepped forward. "That's on my route."

Ramos said, "Wait a minute! I'm not going to leave our church bus with you. No way, man!"

"How much is it worth?" Jonathan said.

When Ramos appeared dumbfounded, Jonathan added, "Let's put it another way: how much for a new bus? Cash donation."

Instantly restored to health, Ramos curled smacking lips and turned to the trucker with a questioning look. The trucker sized up Jonathan and said, "I'd say seventy grand. Maybe a hundred."

Jonathan edged past Miguel and went out to get his corporate checkbook and his shoes. On his way back inside, he thought of Sarah and stopped by the pay phone to give her a call.

As she answered he glanced toward the slightly listing old crate. Inspiration struck. "Know how you refer to RVs as 'tacky little peasant-mobiles'? Well, love, prepare to eat your words. I'm about to buy you your own private recreational vehicle. You'll travel like a rock star."

It occurred to him that he would indeed present the bus to Sarah. It would never make the trip under its own power, but he could have it shipped by rail and delivered to the front door of their fashionable Beacon Hill address. He would have a video cameraman on hand to record her expression. Maybe he would have the video played at his funeral.

He cackled out loud as he replaced the receiver, cutting off the dumbfounded Sarah in mid-sputter. Figuring he sounded like a native, he called out to a passing trucker, "Hey man! Which way to Pecos?"

Belatedly he remembered that he hadn't even asked about Chip, which should have been the purpose of his call. But guilt's bi-product is insensitivity, he decided. He was actually beginning to find the whole thing ironically amusing. Anyway, Sarah would have to get used to handling crises without him. And that little shit would think twice about wearing eye makeup in a jail cell again.

Still, how could he forget so easily? Chip's welfare aside, what kind of father would he be remembered as—*that* was the important thing. He should be there now, chastising, admonishing, cutting off his allowance, grounding him, or whatever fathers are supposed to do. Making an *impression* on the boy. Building an *image*. Ward Cleaverizing himself. Giving both Chip and Whit and even Sarah something positive to remember, after....

He must find time to revise his list, reprioritize. Yet already he seemed to be slipping farther and farther away.

9

While Miguel, with a watchful eye on the bus, decimated a breakfast of *migas* and refried beans, Jonathan paid off both the trucker and Ramos, writing the second check to Spring Hills Missionary Baptist *Iglesia* and marking it as a charitable donation. The amount obviously impressed the truckers watching from around the counter, men who never read *Forbes* or *Barron's,* and Jonathan was reminded that a man's success is more likely to be measured by what he gives away.

Ramos pocketed the check and promised to mail him the title. Meanwhile, he cautioned Jonathan not to push the bus too hard: "She heats up real quick. Remember that water jug behind the driver's seat? I was you, I'd stop about midway of Pecos and Fort Stockton and add a little water to the radiator. Same thing between Fort Stockton and Sanderson. Then when you get to the next town, be sure to fill up the jug again."

"I can't just stop at a service station?"

The preacher shook his head. "It's fifty-two miles between stations on one stretch and sixty-five at another place, without even a stream along the way. That's a mighty long walk."

Jonathan made a mental note to check the glove box for a map before he left. He ordered pancakes and eggs and settled in Miguel's place as the old man got up, tossing a comment over his shoulder as he went.

"He's going out to feed and water the birds," Ramos explained. "He says take your time at breakfast. This is going to take a while." He chortled and added, "Guess it's getting woofy in the bus by now. And when that mid-day sun gets in there—"

Jonathan didn't want to think about it. As one of the newly superannuated, he didn't feel like hurrying, anyway. He had slept poorly and very little. He would eat a leisurely breakfast and call Arpad, then talk to Sarah once more before starting out. He looked at his watch. It was only a little past seven-thirty—nine-thirty in Boston. At home he would be having his juice— freshly-squeezed by the faithful cook-in-residence Florence—and, depending on the weather, heading for his exercise room or his pool. Even if he didn't leave Oria until eight-thirty, he ought to be in Crystal City by mid-afternoon.

"How much farther to Crystal City?" he asked Ramos.

The preacher did some calculating on a paper napkin. "From the mine to here, we've come about a hundred-fifty miles..."

"Is that all?"

"That's pretty good time for that old bus. Pert-near fifty miles an hour. That's because it was night time and cooler. You won't do near so good today. Especially counting for stopping to fill the radiator. Also, you got to wait a good long while till she cools off before you get the cap off, or you'll burn the pee-waddlin' out of your hand."

He went back to his figures on the napkin. "Let's see...here to Pecos, that's about thirty-eight miles." He looked up. "I always figure an hour from here to Pecos. Them truckers can make it in half that. You can't drive fast, anyways, on account of the chickens. The cages, they buck around a lot, I guess you noticed. Them chickens get sick and die, old Miguel's liable to die right along with them."

Jonathan moved his arrival time forward to late afternoon.

Ramos said, "It's about three-hundred-eighty-five miles to Crystal City from here, figuring five or six to get to *la curandera*'s. Stopping to eat a couple of times, stopping to water the bus and fill up the jug—I calculate you'll roll in there by bedtime. You might even get there in time for c*ine telemundo*."

By way of explication, he added, "If you stay in the motel, you can watch Letterman. If you stay with *la curandera*, you'll see *cine telemundo*."

After Ramos left with the trucker and most of the other truckers headed out, Jonathan sank into a slough of despondency. For all he knew, he was spending one of the last few precious days on this earth in the company of an ancient Mexican and fourteen gag-inducing cocks, driving a rolling bucket of loose bolts and springs, leaking hoses, and broken shocks across the backroads of the most desolate land he had ever traversed. How had he come to this? It occurred to him that in times of strong emotion and difficult decisions, he had generally displayed to his "public" great forthrightness and presence of mind, then proceeded to act rashly and rather stupidly. It was probably as Freud claimed: the display of something was a sign of its lack.

Still, given his upbringing, his careful adherence to plan in the matter of school, career, associates, and marriage, he could not ever have imagined ending up in this milieu. It was almost as if he was condemned to live out what he could not conceive, as if Fate must be trying to exact all its lessons quickly before his time ran out.

He braced for another call to Sarah, guilt having moved her ahead of Arpad on his list.

That she was a long time in answering was a clue to her disposition: she would be decidedly cross and out of sorts.

"What was that other silly call about?" she said. "Are you *on* something?"

"Sorry." He intended to be sober this time. "Tell me about Chip. Have you called Hal yet?"

"Hal won't be in until much later. I would feel awful bothering him with such a mortifying situation, anyway. I talked to his secretary. She's going to send a little clerk or something down to help get him out. But she warned me that, at his age, he'll only be released to a parent or guardian. Of *course I* can't traipse down to the juvenile detention center *myself*, so Peters will have to go." Peters, the trusted houseman, had many years ago been given legal authority to act as guardian to the boys in their parents' frequent absences.

"You know I'd planned to leave for Fox Hill on the early flight this morning, to check on Mums—and fly back in time to be here when you get in. When *will* you get here, by the way?"

Jonathan dreaded telling her. "It appears that I still have a day's drive ahead of me. After I finish arranging this settlement, there'll still be the problem of making connections with Arpad. So it could be past midnight—later than that, considering the two-hour time difference. Don't wait up. In fact, stay out on Long Island overnight. Have a nice visit with your mum." It would be a relief not to face her tonight. Their flagging relationship had staggered on for years, long after its heart had stopped beating. It was a corpse, actually.

"Then you'll be coming here? Instead of going back to the hospital? Oh Jonathan—"

For one pleasant moment he had forgotten about the hospital and the doctor's death sentence. A dark curtain settled over his spirit, and his sick feeling swept over him like black tide. "No, you're right. I should check myself back in."

When he hung up, he tried to reach Arpad in Roswell, but he was apparently out to breakfast without his phone. He called Doss and told him to have the pilot locate the nearest landing field to Crystal City, and to meet him there about six o'clock.

"I'll check with him later about the location," he said. Surely he could pick up another cell phone battery in Pecos.

As he headed out toward the bus, parked by the side of the truck stop, he saw the old man get off carrying the water jug, now empty. "Damn chickens drink more than we do!" he grumbled to himself. He met the old man at the water hose and offered to carry the full jug back for him. But Miguel waved him off and hefted the heavy container onto his shoulder, a remarkable feat for a man of his years. Jonathan was not even sure he could do it comfortably himself.

He followed Miguel onto the bus and closed the door, then checked the glove box of his new possession, locating the insurance papers but no map. Well, he could make it to Pecos without one. Pecos, so it was said, was a much larger town.

The driver's seat proved impossible to adjust, so he settled in as best he could. It was a stretch to reach the pedals; he wondered how Ramos, who was shorter than he, had managed. A fresh irony presented itself: after a lifetime of smooth sailing, now he was the one doing all the adjusting and accommodating. Maybe it was a myth that it had ever been otherwise.

He glanced at his watch and discovered that it was almost nine o'clock. Breakfast, phone calls, and chicken feeding had eaten up more time than he had realized. He ground the engine to life and tried the gear shift. It was loose as a goose.

"Well, so long as it runs," he muttered, recalling his outrage when the beemer felt a little rough after Peters took it for a check-up. But that had been a quantum leap ago.

The bus groaned off the caliche lot and onto the highway. Jonathan grappled with the gears until he got the old tub into high, then floorboarded it and watched the speedometer climb all the way to 49 MPH.

Belatedly he remembered to adjust the rear view mirror. In its reflection he saw, much closer than usual, the face of his passenger, which appeared several shades darker.

And about seven or eight decades younger.

Jonathan was looking into the face of another man, and what he felt against his right ear was a cold point of steel.

10

Graduation ceremonies were over by nine, after which Elise Harwood and her mother had a quiet celebratory dinner at a restaurant near the hotel. Salome wore a disguise, even though her face was not so easily recognizable anymore. But word around Boulder was that a graduating senior's mother was an old movie star. That, and Salome's flamboyant appearance: black jumpsuit, black wig, dark glasses even indoors, would make her suspect. Elise had to admit that Salome still looked the part, even though she hadn't had a leading role, outside of cable TV, for years.

Elise was used to the stares and whispers; she'd had it all her life, although, as a rule, in public, Salome walked—no, swept—several paces ahead so that no one would suspect that the two were related. These days it wasn't so much that it wouldn't do Salome's career any good if it were known that she had a twenty-year-old daughter—no. It was that it wouldn't do Salome's love-life any good: her men were sometimes nearer Elise's age.

Elise had not a smidgeon of her mother's glamour. On visits home from boarding school, she had invariably dismayed Salome, whom she would never have dreamed of calling "Mother." Elise's hair was mousey blond, shades removed from the flaming red that had inspired Salome's first stage name of Flame. Elise's was perpetually frizzy and unkempt, which went along with the rest of her appearance. She went directly from awkward first form-er, whose plaid school uniforms hiked up in back, dipped on one side, and sagged in front; whose skinny calves could never hold up her school knee socks, and whose regulation black patents were always scuffed and run-down at the heels; to gawky teenager, whose jeans bagged too much to be stylish and whose tees always had something dribbled down the front.

In a more elemental way, the young Elise had sensed Salome's disappointment that her daughter had always been far more excited about seeing Nana Vanderpool, her old nanny, than her own parent. Salome was accustomed to being in the spotlight, being fawned over. It was humiliating to be upstaged by the hired help.

Nana was long gone, being summarily canned after being caught in mid-boink with a yacht captain Salome had considered her private property. No matter how hard were the times, Salome always managed the upscale life, the grand gesture, the retinue of drooling attendants. Only occasionally, one of them strayed, a behavior Salome could not fathom.

It would have been nice, Elise thought, to have someone here on this day who cared. Nana would have been genuinely proud.

On the occasion of Elise's graduation from the University of Colorado, Salome arrived sans entourage, driving all the way from Las Vegas in a snappy little cream Mercedes 320 SL convertible with a blue rag top. Tragically, because of Colorado's high spring winds, the top had to remain up, thus denying the public the sight of all that luxuriant flaming hair as Salome tooled around the streets of Boulder. Except that of course she was wearing the black wig and keeping the low profile, if you what you call low is wearing a jumpsuit unzipped almost to the crotch. Couldn't the woman wear underwear just this once?

That she had openly attended her daughter's graduation pleased and delighted Elise, but she should have known that her own accomplishment would be overlooked. Since when had she not taken a back seat to her mother? Not that it mattered. It was a fact of life, the only certainty she had known since the cradle.

Another fact that Elise had been forced to face with increasing urgency in the past few years was that, once she was out of college, Salome's obligation toward her was over. Elise would be on her own. No showing up for unexpected visits to crash on Salome's white leather couch, even for a weekend.

After a lengthy meal during which her mother had consumed a fifth of Dom Perignon unaided, Elise called for the check, figured the tip, and passed if over for Salome to sign. Then, voicing a weariness she didn't have to feign, she convinced Salome it was time to hang it up and firmly guided her out of the place while the old girl could still manage under her own steam.

At the car, Elise held out her hand. "I think you'd better give me the keys, considering—well, I know my way around town."

Salome, who was tilting several degrees off vertical plumb, shrugged and handed over her whole handbag. "Sure, lamb. Find 'em yourself in that rat's nest."

As they drove back to the hotel, Elise wondered how her mother managed to afford this obviously new car that still smelled of top-grain leather and just plain money. "Nice wheels," she said.

"You like it? Present from Buddy. He's such a dear. He's completely besotted by me." She sighed over such a burden.

"And Buddy would be...."

"Haven't I told you about Buddy? We met in Vegas in February. Buddy loves to gamble. He's some sort of salesman. Crude oil, I think he said."

"Business must be good," Elise murmured. She doubted that Salome's new boy friend was aware of Elise's existence.

It was plain that her mother couldn't make it up to her room without help. Elise wheeled into the hotel parking garage over Salome's protests.

"Darling! I always get out at the front door! Let one of the little dark men park the car."

This was one time when no one was going to stagger through the lobby snockered to the eyeballs. From the garage they could take the elevator directly to the fifth floor room. Elise stepped on the gas and said, "Oops, too late now. Anyway, it's safer to park and lock. Keep the keys to this baby yourself."

"Mmm. And the title too, I suppose."

"The *title?*"

"It's in the glove compartment. Buddy just gave it to me especially for this trip. Of course I didn't tell him where I was *really* going. He'd never have believed me if I tried to convince him I have a teenage daughter."

No need to point out that she hadn't been a teenager for almost three years. So. She was right: Salome had no plans for her ever to meet Buddy, which meant she had no plans for Elise to come home—wherever that was at the moment.

Elise retrieved the document from the glove box. "You'd better take it with you." But Salome's head was lolling to one side, so she tucked it into her mother's handbag.

Despite Salome's sudden desire to render a retrospective medley of John Denver tunes beginning with "Rocky Mountain High," they made it up to Salome's room without mishap. But at the door, as Elise steeled herself for the inevitable lame goodbyes, Salome balked.

"Oh, but you *must* come in. I—didn't have time to buy you a graduation present, so instead, we must have a drink."

"I think not. Save it for another time...."

"Then I'll give you an ever better present. I'll do something verrry special in honor of the occasion."

"Uh, I don't think I need..."

"Oh but you *must* come in. Don't you want to know what my surprise is? I'm going to tell you about your father."

It was the one thing she hadn't expected that could have lured her into her mother's suite. That and the fact that the alternative was hoofing it back to the apartment she shared with her perpetually stoned roommate, who had missed graduating by several grade points and who was by this late hour higher than a Parton hair-do.

Salome had always been close-mouthed about Elise's dad, except to say that he had drowned off the coast near Carmel before Elise was born. Maybe there had been snapshots, stowed away in a long-forgotten album. Maybe that was what Salome was going to give her.

They settled in the small sitting room, Elise on the loveseat and Salome in a club chair beside the portable bar. Salome poured them both a neat Scotch and handed one over, ignoring Elise's protests.

"Just a little nightcap, lamb. Anyway, you may need it."

That was all the warning she had. Hair bristled on the back of her neck. She'd never become accustomed to her mother's surprise revelations. What was she going to tell her this time? That his death was no accident—that something more sinister happened to him? She took the glass and gripped it with both hands.

"He—wasn't murdered, was he?" she asked in a dry voice.

Salome collapsed in a spasm of laughter, sloshing Scotch onto the arm of the chair. "Not by me! Although once or twice Jerry was tempted. But all that's behind us now. If I ever see him again, I'll probably hug his neck."

Surely she meant Jerry, the agent who had groomed her for stardom, bankrolling her acting lessons from his own pocket, but eventually dumping her when her box office appeal began to wane.

"You're talking about hugging Jerry's neck," Elise said warily.

"No. I'll never forgive that chicken snake! I was talking about your father."

Elise let this statement sink in with no outward reaction. She took a hefty gulp of the Scotch and waited for it to burn its way to her stomach before asking in an even voice, "So you're saying he's not really dead, then."

Salome shrugged. "He could be. But I doubt it. That whole clan is long-lived."

The whole clan. "Then he wasn't an orphan?"

"Hardly. But of course none of them know about you. Your father doesn't know." Salome, lost for a moment in the past, glanced at her daughter and tried a fake, too-bright smile. "Oh don't look peevish, lamb; it doesn't become you. You must learn to be more Zen, go with the flow. If you keep screwing your face up like that, you'll have permanent forehead wrinkles before you're thirty."

Before she lost control and slapped the daylights out of her mother, Elise got up, stalked into the bathroom and slammed the door. She leaned against it trembling, waiting for her outrage to subside. It was even worse than she'd imagined. She had been an embarrassment since before she was born. There had never been doting grandparents, a loving father; Salome had seen to that. The woman outside that door was a monster who had deprived her of her birthright to keep from jeopardizing her precious career.

It occurred to Elise that if she stayed there feeling sorry for herself for too long, Salome would pass out and she would learn no more about her father. Because after tonight, she sure as hell would never be in the same room with the witch again. She splashed water on her face, took a deep breath, and opened the door, prepared to be civil for a little while longer.

She was too late. Salome was sprawled face-down across the bed, the black wig clutched in one hand, her red mop bound closely to her head in a white wig-cap.

Elise landed on top of her, flipped her over, and smacked her hard across the cheek. "Wake up, dammit! You're not going to pass out until you've told me everything there is to tell!"

She forced Salome to sit up, pulled her arm around her own shoulder, and heaved her to her feet. "We're going to walk and you're going to talk."

Salome's head drooped forward. She was essentially dead weight. But adrenalin provided the strength Elise needed to lug her mother across the floor. "No! You're not going to drift away like you've done all your life. You're going to stay on your feet until you tell me every detail about my father, my whole family, you hear me? You had no right to keep this from me."

Somehow she kept Salome conscious and, after a couple of barf recesses in the bathroom, extracted enough information that the enormity of the older woman's neglect appeared to be dawning on her. Still Elise forced her to walk, dragging her along, making countless circles of the apartment, until Salome was reduced to blubbering tears.

She tore away from Elise and lurched for her purse on the night stand, extracting a pen and paper. With shaking hands, she managed to scribble something, sobbing noisily. Elise was reminded that years ago Jerry had advised Salome, "Don't ever cry on camera, darling. Your nose looks like a lighthouse beacon."

Salome had been making dramatic gestures for so many years that Elise had ceased to view them as phony. It was just the way she did things. Long ago one of Salome's boyfriends had termed it the three H's: high Hollywood histrionics. With a grand sweep, Salome fished out the car keys from her bag and, head thrown back, chin held high, thrust them and the paper at her daughter.

"Here's your graduation present. Take it. See? I've signed the title over to you. That ought to make up for a lot."

Elise stared at her mother, whose mascara streaked down her cheeks and blended into the corners of her mouth, and thought, What do I need with a hundred-thousand-dollar car when I have no place to go home to?

But she took the keys, kissed her mother on her sweaty, Esteé-caked forehead, and allowed her to fall limp onto the bed at long last. Salome was a zero before Elise reached the door.

She let herself out of the suite, rode down to the garage, and said hello to her new car. She got in, patted the leather seat fondly, and drove to the nearest service station to look for a roadmap.

11

Doss's call served as Arpad's only notice that this might be the last day of his life, that this opportunity to dive to his death with Jonathan was too tailor-made to pass up.

Arpad had slept poorly, having failed to get any solid information as to Jonathan's whereabouts. He lay awake most of the night, aware of a dark hovering cloud of apprehension that nothing would dispel, wondering what was behind Jonathan's veiled questions on the plane, questions about the meaning of life. Did Jonathan have a premonition that the end was near, or had the doctor told him so?

It occurred to Arpad that his life was not one of action, but of reaction—to Jonathan's. It was an inevitable consequence, he supposed, of being beholden to Jonathan for his life. Now it was impossible to plan his next move until he knew Jonathan's.

Toward morning he drifted off and slept until Wheeler woke him at eight-thirty. Arpad told the co-pilot to go on to the coffee shop while he showered. They should be prepared to leave as soon as they heard from Jonathan. Thus he was again in the bathroom when his cell phone rang.

His caller I.D. indicated a number from a pay phone at a place called Manny's Truck Stop. But repeated rings to the number went unanswered, and he didn't even know where Manny's was.

On the off chance that Jonathan would locate the right hotel and try to reach him on the room phone, Arpad ordered breakfast sent up. When the call finally came an hour later, it was not from Jonathan, but from the Llano manager, Doss.

"The boss wants you to fly to the closest big airport to Crystal City—that would be San Antonio—and he'll contact you there," Doss said.

"Crystal City?"

"It's a place down in Texas about a hundred miles or so southwest of San Antonio. There's a little airport in Uvalde, which is nearby. You can probably rent a small plane in San Antonio to ferry the boss back to the jet."

Why not? Arpad thought. His own Piper Cherokee was classic. It would be a shame to destroy such a beauty. A rental would work just as well, better in fact—in case the time had already come.

He got his things together and rode down to the lobby to pay the bill while Wheeler went outside to hire transportation to the airport. The co-pilot was exuberant, glad to be on the move again after a night of inactivity. But Arpad's mood was nearer to chest-tightening dread.

So. This could be it. He looked around at the lobby with its gleaming Spanish tile floor, splashing fountain, rich tapestries, subtly piped-in guitar music. He hadn't noticed its loveliness before. A pang shot to his core. At once life never seemed so sweet. Nothing is so precious as that which is lost.

12

Once during the heat of argument, Betts had flung out her usual charge at Jonathan of his being left-brained, giving it a pejorative spin by attaching it to a region considerably south of the cerebrum. "A wholly left-brained anal person can fake anything because he doesn't have feelings to give him away," she had accused.

Although at the time he had successfully argued, "Then explain why the left frontal lobe is the location of the sense of humor," now he hoped to God she had been right, that the knife-wielder in his rear-view mirror couldn't smell his fright. Dear Jesus, this brown-skinned man meant to *kill* him. Perspiration stung his eyes, distorting his vision as his gaze darted from the road to the mirror in an effort to assess this new threat. And where, I'd like to know, is the humor in this? he asked the universe in general.

The youth looked Central American: short and squat; he was barely as tall as Jonathan in his sitting position behind the wheel. The knife blade he held at Jonathan's neck was a good seven inches long; still, he might have been at a disadvantage against Jonathan had he not caught him from behind—except that his muscular upper torso hinted at a compact power that Jonathan would be reluctant to tackle.

"*¡Váya a Juarez!*" The young man's throaty snarl erupted next to Jonathan's ear. The knife was so close that even a swerve in the road might jugulate him.

From somewhere behind them Jonathan heard Miguel say, "*El gringo no habla español.*" Jonathan breathed easier: at least the stranger hadn't slaughtered the old man.

In response the intruder pressed the blade harder against Jonathan's neck and yelled, "Juarez! Juarez!"

"Okay, okay!—uh—*sí!*" Jonathan moved an inch away from the knife just as the bus hit a bump in the highway. Good lord, was he going to be decapitated before he had a chance to die?

As the bus jounced over the pot hole, the man grabbed the support pole to keep his footing. The chicken cages rattled, sending the cocks into a squawking tizzy. Jonathan did not slow down to accommodate the rough pavement; in fact, he pushed the bus even harder, intent on covering the distance to Pecos as speedily as possible. Somehow he would signal for help there. In the meantime, he couldn't even communicate with this wild man. He cursed the day he chose to take French, first at Choate and later at Harvard, Spanish not being considered *degage*. It occurred to him that none of his education had been useful except to open doors. In this situation, they all the wrong doors.

The man sat on the bench seat behind Jonathan and turned to bark orders at Miguel who, in a voice gone suddenly nasal, kept whining over and over, "*No tengo. No tengo nada.*"

Because of the poor condition of the pavement, Jonathan could not keep the speedometer sitting on 49. After a while he gave up trying, fearing that he would tax the old engine beyond its capacity and he would be stuck in the middle of the desert with no way to phone for help. In that case, he thought wryly, they could drink the jug of water and barbecue the fighting cocks—if they had so much as one match between them.

He settled back and concentrated on breathing normally and covering the distance to Pecos without riling the wild man.

They had traveled approximately twenty miles when they left the protection of a bluff to the east. The landscape flattened out, and suddenly the morning sun burst like a flash across the plains, beating into the dozen side windows of the bus, raising the temperature inside the old crate in an instant. Surely the heat would lessen when the sun moved higher overhead, Jonathan told himself, so that its rays weren't shining directly into the windows. But common sense informed him that he was living the last hours of his life in a rolling pressure cooker that was only going to build up steam as the day wore on.

Eventually the buildings of Pecos hove into view against the southern horizon, its squat church spires already swaying in the rippling heat. Jonathan unclamped each clenched hand from the wheel in turn and worked it, trying to restore circulation. Everything would be all right. He would signal the attendant as he paid for gas; he could talk without moving his lips. The Central American would be none the wiser.

But as they entered the city limits and Jonathan slowed down, the man leapt to his feet in an irruption of screamed threats, brandishing the knife in wild reckless arcs. Miguel rushed up the aisle and shouted at Jonathan, *"¡No álto! No stop! ¡El dice no álto! ¡Váya a Juarez!"*

This time the man again pressed the knife against Jonathan's neck until it drew blood. At first he did not feel the cut and only became aware that the skin had been pierced when a sticky trickle warmed his flesh. Then the cut began to sting, and Jonathan began to sweat worse than ever. Salty perspiration only caused the cut to burn all the more.

"¡Cuidado!" Miguel called to the young man, who answered by barking more instructions to Jonathan, punctuating them by pointing the knife with darting jabs toward the road ahead. There was no need for translation; Jonathan increased his speed and the bus rattled through Pecos without stopping.

The intruder failed to notice the bank of highway markers at the interchange, pointing to Juarez off to the right. Jonathan headed due south, in the direction of Fort Stockton and Sanderson, two towns he remembered Preacher Ramos mentioning as being on the route to Crystal City. According to the sign, Fort Stockton was 52 miles away; Sanderson was 117. He had no notion of where to go after that, but it hardly mattered now. If he couldn't escape the hi-jacker, he was probably going to end up in Mexico. *Muerto. Muerto en Mexico.* It sounded like a song title.

Surely before he reached Fort Stockton he could think of a way to signal someone as to their danger.

As they left the Pecos city limits, the youth, who had been standing by Jonathan's side, showed obvious signs of relief. He swiped the knife blade across his jeans to clean it before retracting it into the handle with a quick snap of the spring trigger. But he didn't return the weapon to his pocket; it remained within his grasp, his thumb at ready on the switch.

There had to be some way out of their dilemma. If he could get the youth in front of the door, he might be able to open it quickly, kick him out, then burn rubber taking off. But the plan was so ludicrous that, even in his dire frame of mind, he had to smirk. To begin with, the door wouldn't creak open—or close—without Herculean effort, and second, the bus couldn't gun away. It was doing well to sputter ahead, chugging and coughing for several minutes until all the pistons decided to fire.

If only he could communicate with Miguel, the two of them might devise a plan, unless...

A niggling finger of doubt insinuated itself into his thoughts: maybe Manuel and this man were in cahoots. Maybe they planned the whole thing. Maybe Miguel had always intended to go to Mexico. Jonathan felt his deep betrayal, his naiveté. He'd been had.

But his spirits leaped when up ahead, coming toward them, he recognized the light rack atop a patrol car. Frantically he searched for his headlight switch, which finally presented itself as an insignificant unwieldy button beneath the speedometer. He leaned forward casually so as not to alert the two men, and flipped the switch on and off several times. The cop car responded by flashing its headlights twice in greeting as it sped past.

On this deserted stretch of highway obstacles became visible miles ahead. A dot on the horizon stirred his hope: from its size, he figured it must be a car, parked by the roadside. If he could somehow alert the driver, maybe he would phone for help.

As they drew nearer, that hope vanished, for the car—an old Volkswagen—had its rear hood raised, and the driver stood beside it frantically signaling to them. Obviously, if the driver could phone for help, he wouldn't attempt to flag down passersby. Anyway, he didn't appear to be muscular enough to overpower anyone, even if Jonathan could stop and somehow get the idea across to him.

Within a quarter of a mile Jonathan realized that the driver was, in fact, female—a girl, really. The high forehead, pale face and large eyes with, seemingly at first, no mouth—like the common conception of an alien from outer space—reminded him of the *wondjina* cave paintings of Australia. Except that a *wondjina* figure's feet are shown as footprints, and its head is surrounded by a halo or horseshoe shape with lines radiating outward from it. This *wondjina* wore a billed cap and sneakers.

Automatically he downshifted, but his unwanted passenger was instantly on his feet, and Jonathan heard the dreaded snap of the switch-blade. *"¡No álto! ¡No álto!"* he commanded.

"But she's only a girl, a *chica*," Jonathan protested, nevertheless picking up speed, not wanting any more pricks to the neck. He gave the girl a helpless shrug as they rolled past. It was returned by the traditional Italian salute and, from the now plainly evident mouth, a stream of high-pitched invectives that were quickly lost on the wind. He glanced longingly out the side mirror: she was still hurling imprecations like stones.

As the youth put away his knife, Jonathan let down his guard and returned to casting about for a plan. He was so lost in thought that it was several minutes before he recognized the guzzling sound and realized that the man was drinking from the water jug. Without thinking, Jonathan jammed on the brakes, throwing the man off balance and sending the plastic jug flying against the windshield. Jonathan lunged to catch it, to right it before their precious water supply spilled out and ran down the dashboard, but he was too late. The jug came to rest upside down against the gear shift, and he watched in dismay as the last of its contents disappeared around the rubber gasket on the floor, sizzling as it went.

In the same moment Miguel was on his feet, and before Jonathan knew what was happening, in a surprising show of strength, the old man had lifted one of the cages over his head and brought it crashing down against the intruder's skull. The blow, which momentarily stunned the man, broke the bottom from the cage, and Miguel tenderly removed the dazed but outraged cock and cuddled it like a baby, crooning to it. With a surge of elation to know he hadn't been the ploy of a plot between the two Latinos, Jonathan regained presence of mind to step on the man's wrist and relieve him of his knife. Then he attempted to pull the lumpen body toward the bus door, where he planned to dump it unceremoniously on the road's shoulder.

But behind him the old man began to yell instructions. "¡No!" was all that Jonathan could understand, but the meaning was clear: Miguel did not want to abandon the young alien to the ravages of the desert. As the youth slowly regained his faculties, Miguel stood over him and barked orders. The youth, gingerly feeling the bump on his head, picked himself up with obvious reluctance and dragged onto a seat, where he hunched, quiet and subdued, not looking up.

Satisfied, the old man turned to Jonathan and pointed ahead. "*Ándale.*"

Jonathan murmured, "That shoots the conspiracy theory," and grinned his thanks in the mirror, but Miguel didn't notice.

The bus, being so rudely brought to a sudden stop, had quite naturally died. Jonathan ground on the starter, but the engine would not catch hold. Then Miguel, still cradling the chicken under one arm, came forward again and pointed through the windshield.

"*Mire.* Look," he commanded. "*Hace mucho calor.*"

Steam rose from under the hood and wafted off into the boiling day, forming a shimmering mirage between them and the road—a road upon which they were not likely to travel. Jonathan checked the temperature gauge. The old bus was ready to explode.

13

He could be the Culture of Entitlement poster boy, so what? He'd never considered it a hindrance. As the only son in a Philadelphia mainline family, it had been acceptable for Jonathan to display his temper if his expectations were unmet. The practice was not discouraged by his father, who, out of earshot of his mother, would say, "That's it, kid. Demand the best and never settle." Jonathan didn't consider himself unique; most of his peers reacted with the same outrage toward disappointment. Some things in his life had not changed much, if at all, since he was an infant.

Now, in the aftershock, with their water supply gone and the Central American safely unarmed, Jonathan turned upon the man, venting all the pent-up rage that had been building ever since Dr. Allman pronounced his death sentence. He stood over the alien flailing blows at his head, screaming, "You idiot! You frigging slimeball idiot! Do you see what you've done, you disgusting little bastard?" It was the best he could do, and it left him breathless, with throbbing knuckles.

The Indian, seated on a front bench that faced outward toward the aisle, covered his head with both arms and drew his knees up to his elbows, shouting over and over, *"¡Lo siento! ¡Lo siento!"* until Miguel, in a manful effort for one so elderly, dropped the rooster and clamped Jonathan in a bear hug, pinning his arms against his body. The disgruntled cock flew to the overhead rack and perched, shaking his feathers into place in an attempt to restore his dignity.

The bus's sudden stop had dislodged many of the cages, tilting them off the seats at odd angles. When Miguel appeared satisfied that Jonathan had calmed down, he released him and went back to right the cages, first pointing a menacing finger at the perching cock and issuing a string of maledictions. The cock apparently understood them better than Jonathan did.

Once his initial anger was spent, Jonathan dropped onto the bench opposite the Indian and allowed the irony to sink in. He, who was going to die anyway, was the only one who seemed upset about their plight. What did it matter if he died of dehydration or from a bus explosion? In hindsight, the absurdity of his reaction struck him as highly amusing, and he began to chortle inwardly until, from overhead, something landed with a splat on his forehead. As he swiped it off with his bare hand and realized that it was a chicken dropping, he burst into convulsive howls of laughter. It must be so: into each life a little rain must fall.

Gradually the Central American uncovered his head, at first eyeing Jonathan with perplexity, finally smiling in broad relief, then guffawing when he noticed the defiled forehead. Miguel soon joined in the hilarity, with which the cocks competed, setting up such a ruckus as would have roused the most intrepid highway patrolman, had there been one anywhere within miles.

When the lunacy abated, Jonathan cranked open the bus door and stepped outside to survey the forsaken landscape. Miguel retrieved his chicken and followed, pointing off into the distance at a small stand of what appeared to be cottonwood trees, and jabbering in Spanish. He turned and barked orders at the Indian, who leaped off the bus, jug in hand, and lurched off in the direction of the trees at the pace of a potted palm.

Jonathan yelled out, "Wait a damn minute! Come back with that jug!" Then, forgetting that neither of them could understand, he stormed at the older man, "Oh great! Now we don't even have anything to collect water in, even if we found it."

Miguel, obviously understanding the cause of Jonathan's concern, waved him off, saying something with great confidence as he returned to the bus, pointing to the man's knife abandoned on the narrow dashboard. Presently Jonathan could hear him hammering, probably trying to repair the broken cage. He considered chasing after the illegal, but the intense heat had sapped his already ebbing strength. He sat on the bus step and watched the retreating figure grow wavy as light shimmered off the barren ground between them. Maybe Miguel was right: the Indian probably needed the knife and would be back to get it.

Surely a car or truck would pass soon and he could flag it down. Fortunately, discounting the chicken crap, he was still fairly decently-groomed: he didn't look like a hijacker. Surely he could get *somebody* to stop, if he weren't rear-ended first. The bus had stalled squarely in the middle of the lane, and pushing it onto the shoulder was out of the question.

He climbed aboard the bus to locate the hazard lights, or better still, the sort of flashing caution lights that were standard equipment on school buses. He examined the dash panel but found nothing of the sort: the bus, probably sixty years old, predated all modern warning devices.

Outside, as if by a prearranged signal, the buzzing song of thousands of cicadae rose on the hot air. It was an eerie sound, made more mysterious by a lack of any visual sign of them. He wondered where on earth they could be. They must be hidden in the random mesquite that dotted the sparse terrain, their gnarled stunted trunks a testament to the arid surroundings. Idly he wondered if the creatures were edible. He seemed to remember reading about some African tribe that fed on locusts—or was that biblical? On Odysseus' trip back to Ithaca, hadn't he come upon the Land of the Locust-Eaters? No wait. That was Lotus, not Locust. Eating the fruit had made his men forget their homes and their pasts, and they lost all desire to go home.

Lost all desire to go home.

From the back of the bus Miguel called out something. Jonathan, hoping he was heralding the return of the Central American with the water jug—unlikely as that seemed—scanned the horizon in the direction of the cottonwoods, but saw nothing. Still, intermittently the old man repeated: *"Allí viene la muchacha."*

Gradually, from some lame portion of his memory of junior high Spanish, the significance of *"muchacha"* kicked in: "girl." He looked out the back window and saw on that flat approach the unmistakable figure of the stranded motorist they had passed earlier. She was still a good quarter-mile away. By his reckoning, her stranded VW must have been at least five miles behind them. In the hour and a half since they passed her, she had covered more than four of those miles. He marveled at her stamina in this punishing heat.

He watched her steady progress until she was within a hundred yards or so, then got off the bus and walked to meet her, raising his hand in the sign of peace and calling out, "Hey."

Her eyes were shaded by the billed cap, but there was no mistaking the hostility in her voice. "So why didn't you stop, buzzard-bait?"

"Didn't you see the guy holding a knife on me? Some weasly little illegal alien hijacked our bus."

"Oh sure! That crate? Why not just hijack a skateboard? So where is this wild man now?"

"He left with our water jug. It's a long story."

Now that he had reached her, he fell in beside her and studied her obliquely. She was probably in her early twenties, flushed red now and freckled, her short bunchy pony tail of frizzy blondish hair running rivulets of perspiration from under the cap. Remnants of white iridescent lipstick had made her appear mouthless from a distance. She wore a hot-pink sleeveless tank top and faded jeans, and slung over her shoulder was an olive-drab backpack. His gaze was drawn to her belt, where a canteen was clipped. As he eyed it, her hand moved protectively to cover it.

"I suppose you're thirsty," she said.

"I can make it okay," he said, lying, "but there's a ninety-seven-year-old man on the bus—and his fourteen fighting cocks."

She spat out a short snorty laugh. "There's got to be a story behind this, too." She considered him with frank interest as they neared the bus, and in the billed shadows Jonathan caught a glimpse of pale blue eyes intense with need.

"You don't *look* like a fighting-cock sort of guy." She read the lettering on the side of the bus and added, "Or a Baptist preacher. Where's your matching white patent belt and shoes?"

As she climbed aboard the bus ahead of him, Jonathan thanked whatever powers that be that at least his last hours wouldn't be spent completely devoid of beauty: hers was the most perfect little rear he could remember being privileged to observe from this close range.

She said, "Come to think of it, you don't even sound like an American."

"I resent that! Don't you recognize a Harvard accent when you hear it?"

"Oh crap. Not one of those. So then you're gifted with almost infinite talents. Tell me: What did you sound like before you got tainted?" She whirled in the aisle to face him. "I'm not going a step more until I get all the sordid details."

Suddenly Jonathan wanted desperately to share his terrible secret. The need to confide it seemed to well up out of nowhere. "Well, for starters, I'm dying."

She paused, not batting an eye. "And your point would be?"

"You don't understand. I really am going to die."

"As opposed to…?"

Exasperated, he shrugged and held out his hand. "It can wait. I'm Jonathan Tyler."

"Elise Harwood." Her hand was impossibly slender and cool in his grasp. She was, he realized, quite pretty in a wholesome sort of way.

She turned to examine the cages and exclaimed, "Murphy Reds!" Miguel beamed and nodded. To Jonathan's surprise, she approached Miguel, offered her hand, and spoke to him in fluent Spanish. The old man's face broke out in a broad flash of teeth as he answered her.

"Glory be," Jonathan said. "A translator."

The two talked for a few moments, Miguel gesturing animatedly and Elise nodding, then she offered him a drink from her canteen. He took only a sip, bowed politely, and returned it. She came back and handed the canteen to Jonathan.

"Go on," she said. "Even dying blue noses must get thirsty."

As he took the canteen, she settled on the front bench and said quietly, "Your statement was excessive. There are many levels of yourself that know nothing about extinction."

He held the canteen poised before his lips, frozen. Still stinging from the memory of Betts' indictment of his left-brained-ness, he would like to think he maintained a noncommittal cool while he waited.

"Your atoms, for example, were actually billions of years old when you were born, and they've still got billions of years left. Even then they won't die but will only get transformed into some other form of energy."

He took a grudging swig from the canteen and handed it back, studying her with curiosity. "You called those chickens Murphy Reds, but you don't belong out here either, do you? What's the story?"

"It's a long one. Got an hour?"

Jonathan, recalling the jaunty, paint-drying clip of the Central American, said, "Take two."

14

Elise Harwood's Story

I learned about fighting cocks from one of my mom's boy friends. But he was just a footnote. My mom used to be Cherilita Huff from Utopia, Texas. If the name doesn't ring a bell, stick around, because her screen name is recognized by the remotest K!ung of the Kalahari.

My dad was Chuck Harwood from Uvalde, better known in high school as Chucka-Block, a fullback for the Uvalde Screaming Javelinas. You know the type, major stud; he'd laid half the cheerleaders in Uvalde and Zavala Counties. He stayed in rut so much, his teammates referred to him as Up-Chuck.

Okay, crude. I made that up.

It's still a wonder that he and my mom ever met, since her folks were strict Jehovah's Witnesses who wouldn't let her be a cheerleader or anything else except a *Watchtower*-toting yutz.

Despite that, her fame grew, because besides being unattainable, she was drop-dead ravishing. Word spread about this strawberry blonde with big perky bazooms and long dancer's legs that her parents tried to hide under enormous floppy clothes.

And a pot developed...you know: where everyone puts in twenty bucks and the one who makes it with Cherilita wins the pot. Some jocks in Utopia started it, but at football games word spread, and so Chuck was in the pot before he ever laid eyes on her. By that time it stood at seven hundred dollars.

You had to work at getting a look at her, because her parents kept her on a very short rein. But during the fall of Chuck's senior year, they let school out for the county fair, and Cherilita showed up with her jalapeño jelly. And that's where Chuck saw her: standing in the booth behind her jelly.

The sight of her was a tweak to his hinter parts. Gone was any thought of seven hundred dollars, or Saturday's game, or of graduating or college—or that he was going steady with a Briscoe, one of several ranching families that you didn't jerk around. But at that point Chuck'd forgotten his girl friend's name—his pals irreverently referred to her as the Chuck-Hole. He only knew that he had to have Cherilita.

She claims she was smitten, too, when she looked into Chuck's freckled face. He must've reeked raw, sticky masculinity, or maybe he came along at just the right time, when her own long-simmering juices were set to boil over. They began seeing a *lot* of each other, although it took monumental acts of subterfuge.

Chuck gave her the first taste of ambition. Her parents had hidden the fact that she was beautiful, so the news came as a surprise to her. Chuck thought she was pretty enough to be a movie star. He used to tell her over and over, "No lie, babe, you could go far" and she'd say, "Which way?"

As the semester wound down, Chuck began to talk about A&M in the fall. Cherilita, who was just a junior in high school, knew it was now or never. She heard about a western being filmed at Brackettville, so she got Chuck to take her over to try out as an extra.

According to her, she was an instant hit. The director took one look and literally *created* a speaking part for her in the movie. When the rushes hit Hollywood, an agent named Jerry Wegner flew down to Texas and put her under contract.

Chuck, being guided by his gonads, took Cherilita off to Ciudad Acuña and married her, so her parents couldn't refuse to let her go to California. Chuck didn't tell his folks about the wedding, just announced he'd decided to go to UCLA instead of A&M—a kick in the nuts to his dad, who'd been in the Corps, and to his mom, who'd counted on an "I'm an Aggie's mom" bumper sticker for her Lincoln.

Chuck stayed in Uvalde until graduation, then followed Cherilita. They were apart about four months, during which he began to regret he ever put the movie idea in Cherilita's head. With the seven-hundred-dollar pot, his pals threw him a huge send-off, which they called—you guessed it—a Chuck Roast.

After that show of sentiment, he truly hated to leave, and he started scheming how he could extricate Cherilita from her contract and get her back home and into the sack more often.

Meantime, Hollywood's version of reality was settling around Cherilita. Jerry Wegner set her up in a fancy apartment, explaining he had to create a mystique.

He decided to present her as a smoldering sex bomb, which she picked up on quickly. It was her idea to color her hair, to match her red-hot image.

Obviously, the name had to go. Jerry decided on Salome. Just one name. On her, it worked. The accent *of course* had to go. Jerry paid for speech lessons, singing, dancing, even walking lessons. Finally she was ready to make the studio rounds.

Big problem: Only a handful of producers and casting directors didn't expect sexual favors in exchange for a break. When she learned this, she blew up and told Jerry, "I'm not about to sleep around! What would Chuck think?"

More to the point, what would Chuck *do*? Jerry could see his investment heading east on Amtrak while he moldered in intensive care in a body cast. But he knew that gorgeous women were thick as gnats in a dumpster and without an occasional hump, Salome wouldn't get a chance. Unless....

Unless she created sufficient furor that the public would *demand* to see more.

But how to create a craze short of having her streak at the Rose Bowl—and even there she might not be noticed, California being what it is.

Enter Jerry's main poke, who happened to be a well-known costume designer who has since switched straight and married a chewing gum heiress. When Jerry lamented his plight to the designer, how he was sitting on a virtual gold mine if only he had a gimmick, that great talent said, "How about if I create The Dress?" referring to an idea they once discussed about the ultimate costume for the Academy Awards, which is the epitome of gross tackiness every year, with every female in California trying to out-raunch all the rest.

Jerry knew he'd never get Salome to wear it if he described it. So he told her, "If you *don't* wear it, you might as well kiss a career goodbye, because your acting isn't all that great."

As if that mattered.

But she didn't know, so she agreed, having just a vague notion about what The Dress looked like.

He had two obstacles: how to get her into the ceremony, and how to keep Chuck away. The first was easy. He had a client, an old letch who'd paid his dues to the Academy since forever but hadn't had a decent role in years. Jerry convinced him that taking Salome to the Awards was the shot in the kazoo his career needed: he'd get camera coverage and a ton of ink about his relationship with the woman who dared to wear The Dress.

Then there was Chuck, who expected to be consulted on everything, and he was so wild-eyed jealous that he was an even worse impediment than the Jehovah's Witnesses. Jerry feared that Chuck might deck him with a flying tackle. Or castrate him with a cocktail fork.

First Jerry took the direct approach. He told Chuck, "Kiddo, Salome needs to be cut some slack. If she's going to amount to anything, she's got to make some personal appearances without you sniffing around like a hound after tail."

Wrong tack. Chuck's temper shot off like a rocket and Jerry's vision was blocked by large bristly-haired knuckles.

He told Jerry, "I am just by-God fed up to the eyeballs with this phony shit! I'm going to cart that girl on back home where we don't have any flittly little pervs trying to leech a living off of decent regular horny people."

Jerry could see that finesse was not to be Chuck's *raison d'etat.* So he got a gay cop who owed him a favor to pick Chuck up on Awards day and hold him overnight in the drunk tank. By the time Chuck got out, Salome's picture—appropriately censored—had made the checkout counter tabloids nationwide. The Dress was immediately dubbed the Shock Frock and Salome, the Shock Chick.

In case you've never seen the Shock Frock, it was a white sequin sheath with three strategically placed cutouts in front—two circles and a triangle—the likes of which not even Cher had ever worn outside a porn flick.

Before the evening was out, Jerry had received a dozen bids for her services. He finally settled for a starring role in a film not yet written to be called, naturally, "Shock." The movie grossed seventeen million the first week, an unheard-of amount back then. Not that Salome got much of it.

But the film almost wasn't finished, because a little embryo—that's me—came along before the shooting was over. The studio kept Salome's pregnancy a secret by closing the set and substituting someone else's body for long shots. As soon as the picture was in the can, they spirited her away to a tacky little house in the Palisades. She gave birth under her real name at a local clinic.

You'll notice no mention of my dad. That's because when he saw the pictures of the Shock Frock, he told Salome, "Screw you and the horse you rode in on," left for Uvalde in a blind rage and secretly filed for divorce.

He transferred to A&M, then went home to learn cattle ranching from his dad. So his folks never knew about the marriage, and Chuck never knew about me, because Jerry forbade Salome to contact him.

I was reared in seclusion, which was easy after Salome married Baron di' Trevitino, the original Continental Drift. Besides the estate in Brentwood and the villa in Tuscany, there were homes all over, but no other kids. For a while I thought the baron's Pomeranian was just an ugly sibling. The only constant in my life was my governess, Nana Vanderpool. I loved Nana, and how I missed her when she was sacked for making jig-jig with a Eurasian chef that Salome had her eye on.

I saw very little of my mom after I was about twelve, when the Baron's grown son tried to force himself on me while we were aboard the yacht anchored in the Aegean. I ran to tell Salome—she never allowed me to call her Mom—and she was so furious, she tried to push him overboard. I'll never be sure but what her fury was because he hadn't made a pass at her instead.

I was sent to a snotty Swiss school that I didn't escape from until Salome and the Baron divorced. By that time, fame being fickle, the Shock Chick was no longer a chick. She had money, thanks to the divorce settlement, but even Jerry Wegner wasn't terribly interested in finding her a job. She'd dropped out of films during her jet-set days, hadn't made Jerry a dime. Besides, she wasn't a fresh face anymore, and her other parts weren't so fresh, either.

She was plenty pissed when he offered her a couple of matronly supporting roles. She threw a jar of wrinkle cream at him and yelled, "We can't all be Marilyn Monroe" and he said, "Dear heart, we can't *any* of us be Marilyn Monroe. We can't even be *Vaughan* Monroe!"

He returned her contract—in a Baggie, after it had been passed through the shredder.

She became frantic to recapture her youth. The cosmetic surgery industry rallied manfully, but frankly, she could have worn a dress with the whole butt cut out, and no one would have done more than gag. Everyone can spot reconstructed floozy flesh.

But she struggled on to stave off the inevitable. She dated men in their twenties—pool cleaners, meter readers, cock fighters, whoever crossed her path, just so they were studs. She even married a few, then paid beaucoup to flush them.

She couldn't afford Europe for me anymore, so she dumped me in a boarding school in Utah where I finished high school at age sixteen. Then I went to the University of Colorado at Boulder.

It wasn't easy. I got razzed about my phony accent— I'd picked up some weird speech patterns, and maybe I had something of an attitude. I tried to figure out how to get along—went through several roommates. Finally decided to settle for one friend, if I could manage that, instead of trying to dazzle the whole student body.

See, to figure out who you are, you need to be attached to this whole chain of people—family. You hear the family stories and your soul develops. So you might say I'm retarded.

College took forever because I started out in psychology but ended up in physics. Turned out I have a low tolerance for bliss-ninnies. I probably only chose shrink studies to solve my own problems, which never happens with those twits. You just grind along on the same treadmill of woundology into eternity.

Then a really wow professor introduced me to Sartre and I discovered action. Action cures anything, right? We can, like, guide our own evolution. So I evolved into a physics major for which employers are lined up to offer me vast sums of money—*not.*

There's been one semi-serious relationship. It ended two weeks ago. He was the wow professor. But dating students is verboten, so we had to keep our deal under wraps. He said once I graduated, we'd, like, come out. He'd leave his wife, and we'd move in together. He never suggested marriage, but that was cool.

But when it became apparent that I'd passed my finals, the turkey found a hole in the fence. I couldn't get him on the phone, my e-mail was ignored, the secretary said he couldn't work me into his agenda. Into his drawers, yes, but not—oh well....

All this time I thought my father died before I was born. Two days ago Salome showed up for my graduation, and afterwards we got drunk in her hotel room. I didn't mention being dumb-assed by the professor, but she told me the story I'm telling you now. She said all the surgeries, the alimonies, keeping up appearances had left her broke. Then she gave me the keys to my graduation present and passed out. All that nurturing flat wore her out.

It'd dawned on me that I didn't have any place to go after that. My mom kissed me off; so did that sonofabitchin' professor. I've got no job prospects, and my roomy recently discovered the hard stuff. She sees copulating macaroni in our fridge, and she tries to douse all that ardor by spraying it with the fire extinguisher. It's hard on the leftover pizza, I can tell ya'.

So I left my mom zonked in the hotel, and the next day I went to a used car lot, traded my graduation Benz for a beat up Beetle and a wad of cash, and headed south. But the VW passed away five miles back. Already buzzards are circling the carcass.

All the same, whether he wants to see me or not, I'm going to meet my dad...if I can hitch a ride the rest of the way to Uvalde with you guys.

15

As if she could read Jonathan's mind, Elise stopped her narrative abruptly and reached into her backpack, extracting a roadmap which she attempted to flatten out on her knees. A sudden gust of wind rattled the crisp paper viciously, threatening to rip it from her grasp.

The three sat side by side in the meager shade of the disabled bus, Elise between Jonathan and Miguel, who got up every few minutes to peer into the windows at the cages.

Elise pointed to a spot on the rustling paper. "Miguel says you're headed for Crystal City. See? You can go this route, by Uvalde, and it's hardly out of your way at all."

Jonathan was so elated to see a map, to get his bearings at long last, that he readily agreed to the detour, if they ever got the old wreck running again. But he remained dubious of the whole undertaking, which had assumed the surrealism of its heat-baked surroundings. He asked, "Does your father know you're coming?"

She shook her head and grinned like an impish ragamuffin. "I decided to get the drop on him...see what he looks like first. Might not like what I see. He may be a real barfer."

Her bravado didn't deceive him. "You're afraid he might bail if he had warning, right?"

She began wrestling with folds of the map, the flush on her freckled face deepening. "What're you trying to be, Sigmund-freaking-Freud? An amateur shrink is not a pretty sight, so spare me the analysis, Mr. Baroque-brain."

But he had an glimpse of her abrading despair and quickly changed the subject. "So if this doesn't work out, have you thought about grad school?"

"Living on what?" Angrily she wadded the recalcitrant map and stuffed it into her pack. "That's the trouble with you Ivy-league types. You don't have a *clue* that things cost money!" With deliberation she turned her back on him and began translating her tale for Miguel.

Jonathan got up to stretch and to scan the horizon. When Elise first began relating the story of her life, the broad side of the bus had offered enough shade so that they could settle well onto the shoulder, giving him a clear view of the highway in both directions, in case a car should come along. But the sun's advance and the receding shade had gradually forced their retreat closer against the bus's side, so that now oncoming traffic, if there was any, would no longer be visible.

As he rounded the front of the bus, he heard the whine of the heavy treads on hot asphalt and soon saw an eighteen wheeler barreling toward them from the south. He shouted to the others, "Here comes a truck! Get out here and help me flag him down."

The two scrambled to join him by the roadside, waving and jumping up and down as the vehicle neared. Jonathan breathed in relief when he heard the truck downshift. As it neared, it pulled off onto the shoulder opposite them, and Jonathan could read the logo of a beverage distributor out of San Antonio. Talk about luck!

A stubble-cheeked driver of about thirty leaned out the window and asked, "Got problems, pal?"

Jonathan sprinted across the road, making a mental note to soft-pedal the Harvard accent. "I hope all we need is water for the radiator. Think you could spare some?"

The driver studied the awkward writing on the side of the bus, then his gaze traveled over Miguel and Elise before returning to take in Jonathan's obviously expensive clothes. He said, "I never knowed a Baptist to come off without a little dunking water, in case he was to make a convert."

"It's a chartered bus," Jonathan said, realizing the description more than bordered on hyperbole. "I'm transporting that old man over there...he has chickens, you see..." As the driver looked dubious, Jonathan hurried on. "I'll pay generously for your trouble."

The driver, having apparently decided that this was no hijacking trap, cut his motor, got out and walked across the road to peer into the bus for himself.

"I-gannies, that's a passel of cocks, all right! Reckon we can't let 'em all croak, can we?" His gaze lingered on Elise, and Jonathan, with his newly awakened sensitivity, recognized what he felt as unreasoning ire. Why, he could not imagine. The two of them were not in competition for the girl—and that's all she was. She was much too young for him. It was just that she had not spoken at all, and yet the driver was clearly addressing her instead of him. Jonathan was unaccustomed to being ignored.

The driver trotted back to his rig and slid open the side door. "Let's see what we got here..." He pulled out two cases of bottled water. "Sorry it can't be more. As it is, I'll be short on my deliveries. And I *will* have to charge you for these."

They filled the radiator with designer water, watered the outraged chickens, and drank their fill. The driver, who introduced himself only as Borger, waited until Jonathan started the bus and it was established that the old crate would actually run. The driver accepted payment and cautioned them to stop in Fort Stockton, some 27 miles ahead, for some liquid radiator patch. Then after one last leer at Elise, he trotted across the road, and drove away.

Jonathan waited behind the wheel of the bus, whose idling motor caused the whole chassis to rock. But Miguel, having tended to his birds, had climbed down and was squatting again in the shade. Elise had followed and was engaged in earnest conversation with him. Then she appeared in the doorway and said, "You might as well turn off the engine. Miguel's not leaving."

"Not—Why, in God's name?"

"He's waiting for Hector—That's what the Indian's called. He says we can't abandon him."

Jonathan swore loudly and, without waiting for Miguel to get out of the way, pulled the bus onto the shoulder and cut the ignition. Maybe he would run over the old coot and end this whole fiasco. In his second rant of the day, he bolted from his seat and stomped down the steps yelling, as if he might make the old man understand by the sheer volume of his argument. "Are you nuts? The man's a bloody criminal! A high-jacker! He's not coming back to bring us any water, you idiot! He's halfway to the border by now."

Miguel said something which Elise translated. "Miguel says Hector will be back. He's positive of it."

"What possible reason could he have to think that?"

"Hector's mom is very sick in Belize. Apparently Miguel promised Hector that *la curandera* would help him get back home." Her eyes darkened with a peculiar sense of earnestness. "He said she would *transport* him there, whatever that means."

The old man spoke again, looking Jonathan squarely in the eyes, fastening on him that same black stare that had caught him in thrall back at the gravel pit. Jonathan ran his clammy hands down the sides of his chinos and tried to look away, but he could not.

Elise said quietly, "Besides, Hector would die if we left him here."

Miguel pointed to a spot beside him, a silent invitation to sit that was actually more of a command. The spell broken, in exasperation Jonathan flung up his hands. "We'll wait one hour, no more." He glanced at the sky. "By that time the sun will be overhead and there'll be no shade to sit in. We'll all bloody die of sunstroke." As if it mattered to him, he suddenly realized.

Elise settled between them and said, "That ought to give you time to explain why you're so all-fired set on dying."

He felt like smacking her for her irreverence. His second impulse was to refuse to dignify her impertinence with an answer, not wishing to trivialize his plight again.

But then he thought better of it. Maybe he *could* make someone understand, even if it was only a frivolous coed and an ignorant old Hispanic. If not, he needed to clarify it for himself, at least.

He leaned back against the hot surface of the bus and acknowledged to himself that it was time—it was past time—for a recapitulation of his life. Ideally, he would have gone off alone, to a favorite spot in the Maine woods, perhaps, and tried to make some sense of his short life. Now it appeared there would be no time for that, just as there was no time to fulfill his secret aspirations, or even to figure out what they were. He would have to settle for this: sitting on the roadside in a place as arid and desolate as his soul, if he had a soul. He wasn't sure about that.

Perhaps, in the telling, some secret to the meaning of his life would reveal itself. Perhaps something deeply profound and mysterious, like a wild creature crouching at the very heart of his life, was just waiting for the light.

Too, perhaps his voice would drown out the drip, drip, drip of the radiator's precious contents and their sizzle on the hot pavement, a metaphor for the juices of his life.

16

Miguel lagged behind as they reassembled to hear Jon's story, but the old man's absence was not the reason for Jonathan's hesitation to begin. He was stalling, censoring, culling out those portions, namely, his relationship with Betts, that he would share with no one.

But how to leave Betts out of it? She had been a seasonal fixture since childhood. He could scarcely recall a time when he hadn't known her. And from the beginning she had been associated in his mind with naughtiness.

She lived with her several siblings in a modest South Orange estate on Ridgewood Road, down the hill from where his grandparents lived on Tillou Road. Despite the stringent discipline exacted by his Teutonic paterfamilias, Jon looked forward to his visits to the big house at the top of the hill as times of great freedom, when he could roam the nearby woods without a care, munching on some delicacy purloined from the larder of Florence, maid-of-all-work who lived on the third floor.

One brilliant Labor Day when he was seven or so, he and his cousin Clifton headed toward the woods with nothing more pressing on their agenda than looking for mischief, when two gangly little girls whom he had often seen before stepped from the cover of the trees. Prodded by the taller of the two, the shorter one challenged them.

"Where do you think you're going? You're not allowed to pass without—" She looked to her companion for encouragement. "—showing us your hootuses."

Jonathan felt his ears go hot with mortification even as Clifton, who was a sophisticated eight-year-old, shot back, "Not unless you do something we tell you to do."

"Like what?" the stingy-haired wonder sneered.

"Swing by your knees from a tree limb."

The taller girl snorted. "Is *that* all? Deal!"

"—Without no pants on!" Clifton finished triumphantly, while Jon stared at his audacious cousin in reverent awe.

In a great mixture of bravado and misgivings, the four proceeded to a secluded spot under the trees and carried out their forbidden voyeurism, the aftermath of which brought that same adrenalin rush that any feat of daring accomplishes. And although they never repeated that particular escapade, there were other experiments during subsequent visits to South Orange.

As years passed, Jonathan often encountered the younger of the two girls, whose name was Betsy. They met in the village deli, on the shores of the small municipal lake, even, in later years, up on South Mountain.

He had last gone there to escape the cacophony of mourners who gathered in the front rooms on Tillou Road following his grandfather's funeral. As he stopped on the familiar path to view the distant towers of New York City, Betts, now a comely adolescent, stepped out of the woods, much as she had appeared before him so many years before.

"Bummer about your grandfather," she said.

He turned away to hide the first tears he had shed, although his eyes had ached with grief for days.

She covered his awkwardness by clearing her throat and saying, "So! I guess they'll be selling his house."

The implication that he would no longer be coming to South Orange fell leaden between them. He could not now remember the sequence of events that followed, that culminated in a frenzied bout of lovemaking among the leaves on South Mountain, a stint which she immediately dubbed "the farewell frig." He had recalled that she no longer wore braces, which made portions of the process decidedly less painful.

They had exchanged letters briefly, but Jonathan never considered her romantically, even when they met at Harvard several years later. True, they came together occasionally for casual sex—once furtively wedged upright beside a soft drink machine—then went their separate ways as in the past.

He had lost track of her after college, had run into her years later at the Four Seasons when he, an old married man of forty, was in New York on business. She was dining with friends and didn't see him at first. He had recognized her immediately, despite that the once straggly brown hair was now a stylish tawny blonde, and the angular schoolgirl body had rounded and softened, lending contours to the unadorned silk shift she wore so elegantly.

He waited until she rose to leave before intercepting her. He left his own party of business associates and hurried across the restaurant, calling out her name. She wheeled and gave a squeal of obvious pleasure, then introduced him to her friends. He was gratified that neither of the men was her husband.

When the formalities were behind them, he blurted, "Do you know where we could find a tree limb?"

Deep dimples that he had forgotten marked her smile. "I've learned a few tricks since then," she said.

She made excuses to her friends while Jonathan detached from his dinner companions. He took her back to his hotel room where they engaged in a mutual all-night ravishment. He never felt a moment's remorse; he had, after all, known Betts much longer than he had known the cool, bloodless mother of his children. He and Betts had a long history, and it had always been sexual, always clandestine.

She was an acquisitions editor for Oxford. Recently divorced, she had moved back into the family home on Ridgewood Road in South Orange, where she lived with her widowed mother, commuting daily into the city. The arrangement wasn't entirely successful. "I'm in the soup the minute I hit the door," she said with a sigh. "I wade into the hallway ankle-deep in gazpacho."

During the intervening six years, down to the present, his outlook on life had brightened considerably. When he could no longer face another round of Sarah's interminable charity balls and dinners, he would phone Betts and steal away to New York.

After the first hot flush had subsided, she had told him about her marriage at the age of thirty-two to a marine lawyer whose given name, Proctor, was shortened to Proc. After two years of marriage, she shortened it to Pric. They battled incessantly for six more years about everything from where they would eat dinner to which side of Zubin Mehta's head his part was on.

"Anyway," she said stubbornly, "Pric never knew the first thing about how to—" She suddenly grew coy. "—you know...."

He did know. He knew so much about her, despite that they seldom had a serious discussion. He seemed to have been born knowing about her. In some ways, Elise reminded him of Betts, which is why he was willing to open up to her. Betts, too, had the tongue of an anteater. But as he thought about it, one Betts was more than ample for any man. One, in fact, was a luxury; two, a gross excess.

Betts was the sort of woman he should have married, he realized in an overdue flash of insight. In one sense, they had always been married.

If he made it back to Boston, maybe he ought to change his will to reflect his obligation to Betts, not that she needed his money any more than Sarah did. It would be his way of expressing the love he had never once voiced in words in all these years.

But now he faced a more daunting task: figuring out where else he had gone wrong and confessing it to a disinterested audience of two, accompanied by a Greek chorus of fourteen foul-smelling cocks.

17

Once more Elise sat between them on the baking highway shoulder, this time translating to Miguel as Jonathan went along:

"I should begin with my parents. My father, also named Jon, grew up in South Orange. Gran'dad was a Wall Street broker who took the train to Hoboken every morning, then caught the tube to Manhattan, where he had his own firm. Grandmother regularly took the children to the city, except from Hoboken they went by the ferry that dropped them off not far from Fifth Avenue. They went there to shop, visit museums, or attend the symphony, ballet, shows.

"Before leaving the city on Friday, cook's day off, Gran'dad would stop at the greengrocer and the fish monger and bring home something special which he himself prepared. He took great pride in his culinary concoctions. The point is, the ingredients had to come from New York. You'd think New Jersey had no grocers. Life revolved around Manhattan; it was the central presence that informed and colored their whole existence. They shunned Newark like a poor relative, except that even as a young boy Dad was sent there by train once a week for violin lessons. The only hopeful sign, from his point of view, since he was obliged to sing in the choir, was that South Orange's two Episcopal congregations, Saint Andrews and Holy Communion, had to consolidate because of poor attendance.

"My mother was a Philadelphian, imbued with a sense of entitlement, who met Dad at Trinity College, Hartford. After he finished Columbia Law School, they married and moved to Brooklyn Heights. But again, the world revolved around Manhattan.

"Mom never got over her revulsion of its crassness. To her, Philadelphia was founding fathers, gentility, ruling class, the ambition of mankind. Manhattan was squamous cell carcinoma. When she became pregnant with my older sister, having found no viable niche for herself in New York, she engineered their removal to Philadelphia, where Dad joined a law firm in which he eventually became the senior partner."

Jonathan glanced at his watch, wondering why he'd found it necessary to begin so far back. And then of course he knew.

"My parents were very much alike. The only emotion it was proper to display was disdain. Possibly occasionally mild outrage. Mom used to say, 'It's so tawdry to display one's feelings, so Mediterranean.'

"They both sprang from a long line of evaluators. Dad evaluated Mom's activities in the light of how they would affect his career. She evaluated his and ours as to what impact they would have on our social standing. On her deathbed, I recall her asking Dad, 'Am I doing the right thing?'"

"No bull!" Elise said, and Jonathan marveled that he had never found this excessive before.

"We were functionaries," he mused, "without free will, none of us, not even Dad—maybe particularly not Dad...."

"I was born in 1955 in Devon, Pennsylvania, and lived my boyhood with my parents and sister in the same house on the main line, the railroad that runs out to about Paoli station, bringing businessmen in from their country estates. So I had what you might call an idyllic childhood."

Elise pretended to gag. "You know what Jung said about impediments."

"Afraid I don't."

"Being too rich, too good-looking, holds you back. You're better equipped to face the world if you have something to overcome." As he frowned at her, she said, "Sorry. That's my cast-aside shrink babble nosing in. I'll keep quiet."

Jonathan couldn't allow her comment to pass unchallenged. "It's very well to extol the virtues of hardship, but statistics don't bear you out. The leaders in every field come from the so-called privileged class. For every person who's made it after struggling against an impoverished childhood, I can name a hundred whose futures were planned and secured from birth."

She held up both hands, warding him off. "Mea culpa. Truce. I didn't mean to jump over the moat." She gave the royal wave. "Carry on."

But the interruption had evoked a surprising recollection, which he found himself blurting out. "I could have blown it. I thought seriously about doing just that during my first year at Choate: chucking it all and embarking—but never mind."

"Hold it. Embarking on what?"

He snorted, shaking his head at his folly. Odd how even the remembrance brought an unexpected pang, almost a sense of grief. "Like all boys, I was subjected to a variety of lessons aimed at civilizing me and giving me an appreciation for the finer things. I learned to play polo, soccer, cricket, tennis. I studied piano and violin, neither of which I showed the least aptitude for.

"To further broaden my education, I was carted off regularly to the city for performances of every ilk. Once I saw Gregory Hines onstage and bingo! I knew dance was the epitome of what my soul was born for. The man was doing more than just telling a story with his body, like a ballet dancer. He was making music—with his feet! The idea captured my imagination. He needed no instrument to accomplish this; he *was* the instrument. Thereafter I managed to see Sammy Davis, Gene Kelly, Savion Glover—every dancer I could."

"So you wanted to be a hoofer," Elise said.

He studied her hard to be sure she wasn't smirking. "I was never that bold. It just seemed such a fine thing, to dance like a cork on the surf, swirling in the breakers. Or beat a rhythm that lured others into moving, themselves. It wasn't so much the desire to dance as to escape constriction, structure. What can be more liberating than spontaneously moving to music?"

Receiving no answer, he went on. "The Beatles came along when I was ten or so. I became the Ringo of our band that held traveling practices in various rumpus rooms. But making rhythm with drums isn't nearly so empowering. You have to haul around a load of equipment, and you're no good without it. You can't improvise at a party on a moment's notice. It isn't the same."

"Did you never take dancing lessons, then?"

"I did, once. Mother enrolled me in a pre-cotillion ballroom dance group that we all had to endure. To my surprise, I was monumentally heavy-hoofed. The teacher, at her niners, thought I might benefit from boxing lessons, where I'd be forced to bob and weave and lose my woodenness. But Mom wouldn't hear of it because of the gym's location and the caliber of people I'd be exposed to. She suggested fencing, but I was too self-conscious to wear a leotard. At that age, one's private parts are so damned unpredictable.

"It was Dad who thought a few tap lessons might help me get the hang of rhythm. But rhythm was not my problem. My problem was what happened to my gonads when I got that close to girls.

"I managed to convince two friends that tap would be a good workout and provide us an unexplored avenue for meeting chicks, but the miserable truth was that all the beginning tap students were either six-year-old moppets or sixty-year-old matrons. We couldn't take it. After the first lesson, we never went back.

"But one good thing resulted: I had tap shoes that made noise. I have them still, but they pinch now."

"You could buy others. I'm sure it wouldn't bankrupt you."

He shook his head. "The dancing episode was just a metaphor for breaking out of the mold. I got it out of my system."

Recalling Arpad's words, he was positive the dancing phase was not his missed destiny, the promise he made to himself as a boy. So what was? Arpad intimated that letting nature take its course was the only way to reach it, echoing Zen: that even to be attached to the idea of enlightenment was to go astray. But his impatience would not allow for inactivity. He was dying! Already his body was in the process of floating to the top of the tank.

At once he wondered how he'd wandered so far afield, as if he had no control over what emerged. "So much for rebellion. I went to Choate and had my first love affair during a summer outing that Choate sponsored in Belgium." First, he thought, not counting Betts. "We trekked through the low country, visiting castles and flaking grottos, presumably learning about Burgundy, the various dukes of Hainaut and Brabant, the numerous Baudouins. We stayed in inns and ate regional cuisine, drank in the culture, and at night did our best to sample the local feminine charms.

"We did more boasting than making out, but in Brussels, my luck changed. Dad had given me the name of a business associate there, and he notified the family I was coming. They were distantly related to the family of King Leopold II and Baudouin—very well connected. I was invited out to their chateau for the weekend, but I believe I stayed a bit longer.

"There was a girl, not part of the house party. She was the daughter of the chatelon's secretary, a learned man. Her name was Margaret—I couldn't resist tagging her Black Meg after the thirteenth century countess of Brabant who ruled Belgium for a while. Her position was awkward. Being neither fish nor fowl, she didn't dine with either the family, or the servants. She and her father lived on the third floor, one level below the servants' quarters, in an opposite wing from the nursery and the governess' rooms—and worse luck—a long way from mine on the floor below."

He recalled the first time he saw her, astride a tall Arabian, galloping across the verdance, her brown hair caught in the wind. She leaned forward, back slightly arched, her body so much a part of the animal's fluid movement they seemed to be one.

"I met her while riding," he said. "The others could see that I was smitten, so they left me to ride on after her when they went in for mid-morning beignets. I chased her for about a mile before she took pity and let me catch up."

He paused to allow Elise to translate, while he plunged into the memories he would never share: how Margaret had turned to him, dark eyes dancing with mischief, and said, "We go to the shed, *oui?*" indicating a small open-ended structure nearby.

Even as he dismounted and followed her slavishly, he had to ask. "Why?"

She caught his hand and ran toward the shed's interior shadows. "You tell me." She had already unbuttoned her blouse when she pulled him onto the hay.

Elise, finishing her translation to Miguel, turned an expectant look toward Jonathan. But he was thirty years away, grappling with buttons and fastenings in a white heat that still caused his head to throb and his breath to quicken.

Again he lied. "I—ah—lost my virginity in Belgium. Thought I was in love. And Meg cared for me, too. We began to plan our future together. We both cried when I had to rejoin my Choate group in Brussels. I phoned her every night. Then one day, soon after we returned to the States, I was told by her father that Margaret was no longer living at the chateau. He was brazenly curt and warned me never to contact her again."

"Sounds like he found out about your nik-nik in the nook."

"As it turned out, that's what happened."

He made no mention of the long months of paralyzing bereavement that only a lovesick boy can suffer. Yet when Meg's letter arrived informing him that she was in a convent awaiting the arrival of his child, he had felt a sudden revulsion that she should defile her body, should allow it to become distended and misshapen. When he saw a film in health class about childbirth, he had fled the room, nauseated.

He never answered her letter, and now it struck him what a cad he had been. It also occurred to him that he doubtless had an offspring who might have carried his name more honorably than his two insufferable sons. He wondered if it was a boy or a girl, and whether Meg had put it up for adoption. If there were more time, he could trace it; he had connections. But then, he'd had thirty years to do something, and he'd done nothing.

Now he wondered why the memory of Meg was so imminently alive.

Elise broke into his thoughts. "So you never saw her again?"

"No. I considered that fling my one great act of rebellion, outdoing even my secret dreams of quitting school to become a dancer. I went on to Harvard, then got an MBA at Wharton, married the girl my mother picked out, and began building my fortune."

"Fortune!" Her sarcasm cut, deeply. His fortune was the only part of his life he had gotten right. "That sounds impressive. Or are you just bragging because we'll never know the difference, and to one-up me because my step-dad was a baron?"

With contempt for her ignorance of his importance, he said, "For one thing, I buy failing tech companies, make them solvent, and sell them for a profit. It has paid very well. Forbes did a profile on me."

Elise picked up a stick and scratched out a large dollar sign in the dirt. "So when does the dying part come in?"

He heaved with the sheer dread of telling. "I went in for a routine physical and the doc said there was something suspicious about my bloodwork."

Elise repeated this to Miguel, who spoke up for the first time. She said, "Miguel says there was your big mistake, seeing the doctor. Doctors are trained to think in terms of pathology."

"I *doubt* that Miguel said 'pathology'."

"Actually, he used the word *susto*, an Indian term for a sickness that comes on like a curse–that someone wills on you. Miguel says in Spanish it means fear. The fear is the curse."

He considered this. Maybe Sarah willed him to fall ill. Maybe she'd had intimations of his liaison with Betts. Sarah didn't need him. She had her charities, her circle of bluebloods whom he could scarcely keep straight. His presence was doubtless a bother to her. Certainly he had contributed nothing to her love life in—how many years? He rather fancied that she got her jollies at the spa, where she partook with great regularity of the services of a variety of masseurs and masseuses. It pleased and relieved him to believe this was so.

His sons could well wish his malady on him. Ever since they reached puberty, they had all butted heads. He could barely stand to be in the same room with them. He was certain the feeling was mutual. What sane person could stand two cocksure adolescents?

Or maybe—the thought shocked like a thunderbolt—he willed it on himself. It had been years since he had felt any degree of self-satisfaction, years since he had done anything for the sheer pleasure it brought him. Or why didn't things bring him pleasure?

Elise said, "I gather the doc gave you bad news."

"More than once," he said. "We've—*I've* been fighting this thing for over a year now—no, two! God! Two precious years when I could have...." He had been so intense, so submerged in licking his illness, while refusing to allow anyone to name it. How could he have lost two whole years? For sure he hadn't been living.

When he didn't go on, she said, "Could have what? What do you want to do?"

"I don't know." With an awful numbing certainty he knew it was the truth. He couldn't say the only words that came to mind: I just want to live, whatever that means.

At that moment Miguel interrupted Elise's translation by scrambling stiffly to his feet. He pointed off toward the row of cottonwoods and yelled, *"¡Aquí viene Hector!"*

18

Hector's progress seemed painfully slow. To Jonathan's relief, the way the young Indian dragged the jug, it appeared to be heavy, full of water, he hoped. So why did he feel like Napoleon, waiting at the snow-shrouded gates of Moscow for the arrival from the rear of several thousand woolen blankets, being met instead with a corporal bearing a single chenille throw? Because the radiator continued its steady drip. By the time Hector reached them, it would probably need refilling, and they would still be miles from the next pit-stop. Jonathan stood, cupped his mouth, and yelled, "Hurry up! ¡Ándale!" But it was doubtful that Hector heard from such a distance. Or maybe he didn't want to hear.

Elise had been conversing with Miguel in Spanish. As Jonathan rejoined them, Miguel, with an uncharacteristic easy grin, shrugged and said, "¿Cómo no?"

She said to Jonathan, "Miguel has consented to tell us a little of *his* story while we wait. So sit down and quit pacing. It won't make Hector get here any sooner. Conserve your energy."

Jonathan hadn't the slightest interest in learning any more about the old Hispanic than was absolutely necessary. The two had nothing in common, no possible meeting ground. One doesn't lift the head of the albatross tied around one's neck and say, "I say, old sport, what's your name and where're you from?" Still, the seconds were beginning to throb against his temples. If this kept up, in another twenty minutes he would need to be trussed in a strait-jacket. He sighed in resignation. After all, he had sat through several nights of Wagner's Ring Cycle in a box seat with a broken spring; he could certainly endure this.

Miguel pointed upward and gestured toward the bus. Elise said, "Good idea. Miguel says it'll be cooler inside, now that the sun's directly overhead."

The three boarded the vehicle, where the stench from the cages steeped in the hot air. The cocks dozed in a stupor of heat. Elise and Miguel settled on the front seat facing the aisle, so Jonathan sat across from them, noting that at least what breeze there was carried the smell in the other direction. He turned his attention to the deeply-lined countenance, whose pockets and trenches testified to long and deep inhabitation, although the old man's thinning hair was not totally grey. He was truly a remarkable specimen. Some matrons might even consider him mildly attractive.

Timidly the *viejo* began to speak in a voice grown husky with age, forced through passages corroded by tobacco, peyote, marijuana, tequila, Dos Equis—no telling what else. There was no justice, Jonathan thought bitterly, remembering his grim sessions with his fitness trainer who was supposed to keep him in the pink of condition.

Elise translated rapidly:

"Ninety-seven years ago I was born in Nana, near Piedras Negras in Coahuila State, Mexico, in a one-room house with a dirt floor. The cooking was done outdoors, and often many of us slept outside, for we were a large family. Later I learned that my older sister gave birth to me, but she was never my mother. Our mother, really my grandmother, died while I was still a boy. Soon after that I crossed the river and lived on the streets of Eagle Pass.

"When I was old enough, I hired on as a ranch hand. Got to be pretty good at roping and branding and breaking, so I could usually find work, if someone would lend me a horse.

"I had relatives around. You know about my aunt Josefina Carlota Rulfo, in Crystal City. When I would be out of work, I would stay with her sometimes, if she had room. She wouldn't let me stay unless I went to Mass. So she kept me close to the Church, yes. She saw that I married my women, too. Over my lifetime, I've had nine wives. So far. Don't ask me how many children. I lost count.

"Three of my wives died, and the others mostly ran off. Maybe I was no good for some of them, I don't know. *Tía* Carlota said I should treat them better. Sometimes she made me go to confession about hitting or cutting them. Some of them were cheaters or just plain lazy. Anyways, even with all them wives, it seems like I been without a woman most of my life.

"One of my wives knifed me and killed me dead. But lucky for me, *Tía* Carlota had come into her powers by then, and she brought me around from water stage. But oh, the wonders I saw before she brought me back solid again!

"I think it was from *Tía* Carlota that I inherited my talent, but I didn't never notice it until after I got brought back from the dead. Maybe it was a present to me or something by my aunt at that time—for coming back, you know.

"Pretty soon after I last married, my great-nephew showed up, the youngest son of my older brother's daughter. She had died and he had no place else to go. Just a *niño* he was, hardly big around as my arm, crossed the river on the shoulders of a stranger, he told me. So we took him in, and later when my wife left and took our kids, she left Ramón. So I raised him, I guess you'd say." Miguel laughed. "Maybe we raised each other."

Jonathan interrupted. "Ramón. That's the one who died in the cave-in?"

Miguel's face clouded in remembrance. "*Sí.*" He sighed and lapsed into silence. Jonathan was sorry he had reminded Miguel about his nephew's death.

They waited in the reeking, steamy gloom until Miguel was ready to continue. Finally he seemed to brace himself to go on.

"Ramón, he always had big dreams. He used to strut around and brag, 'Me, I'm gonna be rich!' and I would say, 'How you gonna be rich without you rob a bank?' And one day he figured it out. 'Cocks!' he said. 'Fighting cocks.'

"He started betting and winning until he got enough to buy him a cock of his own. Named him Pancho Villa."

He pointed to the rear of the bus. "That's the tough old bird back there in the back cage. Pancho don't fight no more but he pays his way in stud. Half these other birds here—maybe more—are stud payment, pick of the brood, you know.

"So Ramón was doing real good with his cocks and then he up and got him a wife...*Tía* Carlota had him by the ears, too, even though Ramón had a place of his own. And man, that Inez was the meanest woman outside of Guadalajara! She moved into that house and first thing that had to go was them cocks. I don't mean she made him sell 'em, but she made him get 'em out of the house. See, up until then, they'd had the run of the place, just like they was part of the family. So Ramón built them a real nice pen in the yard, you know, moved the porcelain-topped table where we played dominoes and put the pen right where it used to sit, under the shade of the china berry tree. Only good shade in the yard. Ruined our game. After that we could only play when the sun went down and cooled things off some.

"Next thing, Inez started objecting to Ramón taking off to McAllen or Del Río for a fight, and they had some real lively arguments. But he went, anyway. Then one night Ramón came home and Inez had fixed him a real fine dinner of chicken fajitas. The meat was stringy, he remembered afterwards. And the next morning when he went out to feed his birds, one of them was missing. Well, it like to have killed him to think he ate his own bird. But Inez, she didn't back down one bit. She told him, 'Every time you go off, you gonna come home to chicken dinner.'"

Miguel looked at Jonathan intently, as if to convey something Elise was not likely to understand. "You get the idea that Inez wasn't no ordinary woman or he would of kicked her out right then. I told him that's what I would do, but he only shook his head and said, 'You wouldn't if you knew how she is when the lights go out.' Still, he knew it had to be done, but he couldn't bring himself to do it himself. 'It'd be like cuttin' your throat to keep from drinkin',' he told me.

"So Ramón went to *Tía* Carlota, who always fixes things, and said, '*Tía*, that *mujer* is driving me to the pauper's grave. You got to help me get rid of her before you have to bury me.' And *Tía* said, 'I am no *bruja*. I only use my powers for good.' And Ramón said, 'Don't you think it'd be *good* for Inez to visit her relatives in Matamoros—for *good?*' And *Tía* Carlota said, 'Well, I guess I could do that much. Since you put it that way.'

"So she mixed up a potion for Ramón to drink and burned her incense and said a little incantation. And when Ramón got back home, Inez was gone.

"But pretty soon the next door neighbor got suspicious and told the sheriff she thought Ramón had killed Inez and buried her somewheres. Ramón figured that *Anglo* sheriff would never believe what really happened, and anyways, he wanted to protect *Tía* and also his fighting cocks. Didn't want no nosy *Anglo* sheriff poking around out in the back, even though he'd purposely never had them birds fixed."

Jonathan interrupted. "What does he mean by that?"

Elise explained. "Owners of fighting cocks have their vocal chords cut so they won't make any noise in the ring and bring the law running. I wondered about that when I first got aboard this bus, but Miguel told me the cocks had always been fought in remote areas so he and Ramón wouldn't have to cut their chords."

She turned and patted the old man's knee. "He's an old softy. A real teddy bear."

Miguel had waited for her explanation before continuing: "So he loaded up the birds and the two of us took off, heading north. We never stopped until we got to New Mexico, where Ramón signed on with the gravel company. That was ten years ago. We traveled from place to place in the area, but always with Llano Gravel. And that's where we was when the Border Patrol got to nosing around, looking for him. I betcha old Inez was the one put them onto him, wherever she is. So Ramón got so worried and distracted, he got careless and got killed, without ever fulfilling his dream.

"After we went up there and had to start hiding from the Border Patrol, something seemed to happen to Ramón's spirit. He quit trying to fight his cocks so much, quit even caring for them. Got to spending his paycheck on tequila. Wasn't for me, them cocks'd of died and of forgot how to fight. I was the one rounded up the matches and took the bets.

"One time along about then Ramón told me, '*Abuelo*'—that's what he called me, even though I wasn't his grandfather—'seem like I been running and hiding all my life. Sometime I wish I could see *Mamacita*.'

"He missed the *Día de Los Muertos* celebration we had in Crystal City, because at least he could visit with his dead mama once a year. *Tía* Carlota makes a nice shrine for the dead and everybody comes, you know. But up in New Mexico, with no woman to decorate, why, we let the day go by. Anyways, I don't think the dead travel that far from home. So I begun to worry that Ramón was thinking about joining his mama. Guess I don't need to worry no more.

"Anyways, me, I got a duty to carry on: to go back to *Tía* Carlota's and try to strike it rich for Ramón. That ways, I can make a real nice display for him for *Día de Los Muertos*—once they find him and dig him out."

He lapsed into thought but they could tell that he was not finished. Finally he bucked up as if he had just come to a new conclusion, "A man got to start over once in a while. He got to have many lives, like a woman. When a man can't be a *vaquero* no more, he got to invent a new life, like fight cocks. When he can't fight no more, he got to think of something else. Too many men, they keep doing the same thing their whole life and after a long time they get sour, you know."

Miguel barked the briefest chuckle. It was more of a cough. "See? Even in an old man, them fires still burn hot." To cover his obvious embarrassment, he rose and peered over Jonathan's shoulder out the window, then yelled, *"¡Hector! ¡De prisa!"*

Jonathan, who had been mulling over one aspect of Miguel's story, didn't turn around to gauge Hector's progress. He said to Elise, "Brought him back to life, did he say? From water stage?"

She shrugged. "That's what he said. Don't ask me what that means. And he got some kind of present at that time, from his magical aunt."

"Rot!" Jonathan stood, dismissing the subject, or trying to. Then he checked himself. He must quit using descriptive language that might be applied to the status of his own body. He took out his handkerchief and mopped his face. His life was seeping out of his pores in the form of perspiration.

"Yeah, sure," she said. "So then, what do you suppose did happen to Inez?"

19

A sudden displacement, like plate tectonics, threw Jonathan off guard. So swiftly did it come upon him that he had no chance to cry out. Or maybe he attempted to speak; he wasn't positive. He braced against the bench with both hands and tried to draw his feet under him so that he might pull himself upright without asking for help. But his body betrayed him and slithered off the seat onto the floor. He felt all his systems shift, the way the earth's plates scrape along a fault line, altering previous reality irrevocably. No alarm went off when this happened; in fact, he seemed to be observing his own decrepitude from a safe distance. So, no, he probably hadn't called out.

Even before his collapse—or before his awareness of it—his gasps brought Elise to his side and he heard her say, "Oh Jesus, he's freaking cashing in!"

Miguel's much calmer voice drifted down from somewhere over his head. "Could be only dehydration. I have seen it before. When Hector gets here with the jug—"

"Oh sure! Give him ptomaine from drinking river water."

"Typhoid."

"Whatever." She had Jonathan by the arm, attempting to drag him aright. "Help me get him back up onto the seat. Do you really think it might be dehydration? God, I'd give anything for....We might drain the radiator...."

Jonathan commanded his hand to raise in protest, but it ignored him.

Miguel said, with some reluctance, it seemed to Jonathan, "There's the chicken water."

She hesitated a split second. "Get it."

Jonathan observed the two as they lifted his head and forced the smelly liquid between his lips. It wasn't going to do any good, he wanted to tell them. But perhaps he was wrong. It dawned on him that the fluid in his body was an extension of the ancient sea. He carried the primordial ocean inside him, the concentrations of sodium, potassium, and chloride in his blood, and the cobalt, magnesium, and zinc in his tissues being replications of that sea. The struggles in that ocean had been going on for three billion years, but its tides were not so much palpable, as patterns, just as his life was merely a pattern: a movement, or a million interstices of "incidents," or "events," a syncopation, dancing in counterpoint to the rhythms of contingency. His world was a network of processes, creating order through fluctuation. Nothing more.

He saw this plainly, as he hovered a few feet above their heads.

Gradually he ceased his inner struggle, flinging open his portals, suffering the ethereal tides of the universe to roll through him, becoming that which he was taking in. The act almost immediately brought his rhythms into balance, at the same time forging within him a small degree of strength as he returned from his remote place of observation. Apparently the effect was noticeable to Elise, for she said, "*Mas mejor.*"

Miguel answered, "*Sí. Basta.*"

A tremendous lethargy swept over Jonathan and, as he slipped into a welcomed doze, it occurred to him that for a few minutes while he was semi-comatose, he had understood Miguel's Spanish. Or maybe the old man had spoken in English, or some universal language. Or had the entire incident been a hallucination?

He heard Elise shouting out the bus door to Hector. "Hurry! *¡Ándale!* Get the freaking lead out!" She fumbled with something in the driver's seat, and he heard the horn's feeble but insistent beep. "Jesus H. Christ, the man is a friggin' zombie! Can't he go any faster than that? A sand cactus could *grow* here quicker."

Later the cacophony of several jabbering voices overlapped with the sputters of the motor and the raw complaints of the birds when the jouncing began. Jonathan was aware of rough hands holding him onto the seat and of rumbling movement beneath him, as if he lay within the crater of a threatening volcano. It was not an unpleasant sensation; he pictured himself being shot up and suspended on a geyser of lava, the life-blood of Mother Earth herself.

He no longer worried, being secure in the certainty that he would never fall, never reach bottom, for there was none. The warmth of sunlight on his face soothed him with the knowledge of its perpetual brightness. He rested in confidence, watching an infinite round of one thing succeeding another out of nothing. It appeared to be a generative procession in which effects might just as often precede cause as come after them. It occurred to him that Nothing was not what he had supposed it was: Nothing was, in fact, Something. And he was a part of a participatory universe. But he needed to know about this Something—except that maybe knowing, or trying to find out, might bring about instant destruction.

He had slipped easily into what he recognized as a new state of consciousness, knew it to be a fifth state, beyond waking, sleeping, dreaming, meditating. It was a less noisy, more coherent state, in which he could perceive physical reality more directly. It seemed to be an amusing condition, as he'd always hoped. Yes, he chuckled, I am amused. Definitely amused.

But the motion abruptly stopped and the shrill cries of someone vaguely familiar—certainly not his mother or any mother he knew—interrupted his observation. They sucked him quickly back to partial wakefulness, calling from the foot of his bed for help. "Hey you guys, call nine-one-one. Get an ambulance here quick!"

His conscience prodded him to help the woman. He imagined rising and going to her aid, lifting her in his arms and carrying her to safety, out of reach of the lava flow. Eventually he would manage to look into her face and learn her identity, although for now she turned her head away from him. Then he drifted off and surprised himself by his new capacity for remote viewing: he observed his wife Sarah pacing in her room, eyeing the telephone, willing it to ring. He saw Arpad touching down on a bleak airstrip in San Antonio, not knowing that he was hours ahead of time. He saw his older son careening recklessly along the expressway, sure in the knowledge of his invincibility and immortality.

Later his reverie was interrupted again. He had the sense that he was being manhandled by upperclassmen, like back in prep school. "He's coming around now. Seems to be stabilized. Bring in the stretcher. I think it's safe to move him." The voice sounded like Hoss Cartwright from an old "Bonanza" rerun. But the actor—what was his name?—wasn't he dead? *Am I dead, too, Hoss?*

Jonathan felt a pressure against his cheekbones, then realized that a mask covered his nose and mouth, sending freeing mountain air into his lungs. When he attempted to examine it with his hand, a weight tightened against his arm, holding it immobile.

"Easy, fella, don't detach that IV," Hoss said.

"I don't think we can do this in those tight quarters," came a voice from somewhere below them.

"You're right. We'd never negotiate the turn without making a pretzel out of the patient. Here, lady. If you'll hold the IV pouch and the oxygen canister, Joe'll take the knees and I'll get this end—"

He felt himself being hoisted aloft and tried to think how he could help. Guilt swamped him. Surely he ought to take charge.

Eventually they settled him in a new place. As his head cleared, he opened his eyes to find a lovely girl bending over him, eyes dark with concern. From the ether a name settled upon her shoulders like a mantle: Elise. Perhaps they had met somewhere before. Above her head he saw the white metal ceiling of an emergency vehicle. She squeezed his arm and said, "You'll be okay now. Don't worry about Miguel and the chickens. I'll take them the rest of the way. Oh—here's your stuff."

She held up his briefcase, then tucked it beside him. He tried to take it but found that his arms were strapped to his sides. Yes, he must know her from somewhere. Before he could ask or protest her leaving, she was gone. The back doors of the vehicle slapped shut, and the ambulance shot off, sirens blaring.

Through the mask, Jonathan screamed with every ounce of his breath, at the same time writhing against the straps, frantic to free himself. He must not lose— who? Again a name materialized: Miguel. Must not lose Miguel before—he couldn't remember why—

Like sunshine bursting through the clouds another name shot across his mind: *la curandera*. Yes, now he remembered. Must not miss this chance to see *la curandera*. Now he knew what to ask her.

Her culture was very old, dipping back into times when people thought deeply about the wonder and nature of things. Maybe she carried this wisdom into the present. Maybe she could help him regenerate, at least buy enough time to begin to live as he should have all along. He must not have wasted his days on this planet. If he died now, he would have missed the whole point of living, without ever knowing what it was. And if he lost Miguel, he would never be able to find *la curandera* to ask her.

Ironic, a perverse trick of fate, that at the moment of this clear revelation of what he must do, he was strapped onto a gurney, unable to help himself. It was as if a cunning trickster hovered out there in space, pointing and laughing, guarding the portals of meaning, batting away any attempt to look inside. Jonathan didn't know whether to join in the laughter—his usual response to irony—or to sob. The straps seemed to bind him even closer, and he made his decision. He thrashed and bellowed until he thought the vessels on his temples might burst. His heart pounded like a jungle tom tom, threatening war.

An attendant on the jump seat beside the litter put a heavy palm against Jonathan's forehead, forcing his head back onto the stretcher. "Easy, guy...Hey Stu! This nut's going ballistic. I'm going to have to knock him out before he hurts himself."

From a long way away, even as he fought, Jonathan thought he heard: "Don't do it! The guy's vitals are too unstable. You might—"

Jonathan forced his eyes open to see the brute leaning over him. He tried to cry out, but no sound escaped as the man's iron fingers tightened on his neck.

20

Hold it! I still have goals to—
Of course. Goals are all that's left after dreams die.
Okay, forget that. Problems! I've still got problems that—
It is necessary to be at peace with unsolved problems.
There must be something left for me to do.
Yes, talents carry three-layered burdens.

The bright light penetrating his lids was no inducement to open his eyes; in fact, he frowned, squeezing them tight against it. He wanted to remain dormant, to listen, reclaim his essential rhythm of activity and rest, wake and sleep, inhale and exhale—and that suspended void in between, like the unmeasured hiatus when the trapeze aerialist hangs mid-air between handholds.

But another sound intruded. He recognized the voice of the attendant who had rendered him unconscious with unremitting pressure against his carotids.

"Here he comes. See? Just like I said."

"No thanks to you," Hoss said. "How many times I got to remind you, Shit-for-brains Hawkins, that you ain't no friggin' grunt and this ain't no by-God Chu Lai?

One of these here days you're going to press just a little too hard and kill somebody."

As Hoss removed the oxygen mask from Jonathan's mouth and nose, Jonathan recognized the strong antiseptic smell of a hospital. But there was an even more pungent odor like somewhere else—someplace he had been long ago, when he was a child. He couldn't quite identify it, unless it was flea-dip....

Hoss called out, "Hey doc! Your patient's coming around. Want to have another look?"

Oh God no. Not more doctors. Now I'll never get out of here.

Jonathan took a deep breath and willed himself to look healthy as the light stopped beating against his eyelids. Someone must be standing in its path. He opened his eyes and looked up into the face of a somewhat seedy-looking clay-haired young man wearing a white coat with muddy paw prints on the front.

The man shone a penlight in Jonathan's pupils and said loudly, as if he were deaf, "How're you feeling, old fella?"

God! Jonathan thought. Do I look that bad?

He cleared his throat before answering, hoping his voice would come out strong. "I feel fine. But 'old fella'? I couldn't be that much older than you."

The doctor grinned, showing coffee stains on his none-too-straight teeth. He was sickly pale as if he'd never been outside of this glaring, fluorescent-lit room. "Sorry. I call most of my patients 'old fella'—unless it's a mare, and I call her 'old girl.' I'm a vet, see. There's no people doctor available right now, and after we found out how sick you are...some kind of auto-immune disorder, huh?"

Jonathan tried to cover his ears but found his arms still strapped down. "Don't tell me! I don't want to know!"

As if he hadn't heard, the vet clucked his tongue, shaking his head. "Lotta that going around these days. We even see it in animals, you know, who aren't so very different. That's because there's a little bit of everything in all, right? Mostly it's city animals: they become at war with themselves."

"War!"

The doctor loosed the restraints on Jonathan's wrists, an act of faith, Jonathan figured. Again he flashed the penlight into Jonathan's pupils. "Well, that's what allergy is, isn't it? You're allergic to your environment, or, in this case, allergic to yourself."

Jonathan steeled himself to blunt his hostility but he was not too successful. "I didn't ask for a medical opinion. Anyway, how did you deduce that diagnosis on such a brief examination of my retina?"

The doctor looked up sharply, grinning at the note of sarcasm, but Jonathan kept his expression bland. The doctor said, "Well, good as I am at on-the-spot eyeball diagnosis, I have to admit that your wife told me. Although those retina are awful brown, indicating a possible shitty outlook on—"

"My wife! How'd *she* find me?"

"She didn't. We found her. Sorry, we had to look in your briefcase, found your TylerGiz cell phone—your battery's dead, by the way."

"I know, but…" Jonathan glanced around. The ambulance driver and his assistant had left the room. He could see them in the adjoining office, opening the outside door.

"It was no trouble to substitute my battery, so I could check your rapid dial. Number One turned out to be your office, but Number Two—well, you know all this. After I talked to her and found out about your plane, I located your pilot on the rapid dial. Long story short: he's on his way from San Antonio in a little rented Cessna to pick you up. He didn't think our runway would accommodate your plane. Must be some kind of buggy."

Jonathan tried to sit up but the doctor restrained him. Forcibly Jonathan took the doctor's hands from his shoulders and leaned up onto his elbows, reminding himself that he must remain calm and rational if he were to avoid having a net thrown over him. In this place, he might very well wind up in a cage with an outside dog-run.

He flashed an amiable smile. It took all his strength. "Doctor—what's your name?"

"London. Sim London."

"Doctor London, don't let those EMS men get away. I need to ask them something."

The vet, moving with the speed of a slug on a tomato plant, turned and shuffled into his office and called out the door. "Stu! You and Bud got a minute?"

Jonathan sighed in relief as the two men returned. Again he attempted to appear amiable, even toward the one who had so recently rendered him unconscious. His neck still hurt where the burly attendant had applied pressure. That must be against medical ethics, and the thug ought to be reported. Still, Jonathan grinned from one to the other, trying to look like one of the boys. He wished to God he had a chaw of tobacco to offer.

"I want to thank you for coming to my rescue." His Boston accent grated on his own ears. He attempted to tone it down. "The girl and the old man and the bus— where did you leave them?"

The driver with the Hoss Cartwright voice, the one they called Stu, answered. "We picked you up at the truck stop on the edge of town."

"Town. Which is...?"

"Fort Stockton. That's where you're almost at. And the last time I seen that bus, it was heading down Two-Eighty-Five going south, toward Sanderson."

Jonathan sucked in his breath, sat erect, and swung his legs off the side of the examining table. The effort made him dizzy. "You mean she didn't do anything about the radiator?"

The two men exchanged blank looks. Bud said, "All's we know is, the girl said they needed to haul ass if they was going to make it to Crystal City before dark."

Stu broke in. "Oh yeah. She said to tell you that you could get somebody to pick up that old bus at Harwood's ranch in Uvalde...if anybody wanted it. Howsomever, seems to me like them New Mexico Baptists'd do well to commence praying for them a new set of wheels. It'd take an awful big miracle for that bus to make it back to where it come from."

Bud examined Jonathan with narrowed eyes. "You some kind of Baptist missionary? From England or somewheres?"

Jonathan ignored him, focusing on Stu. "How long ago was that?"

Stu looked at his watch. "About forty-five minutes. If you want me to check the log—"

"No!" Jonathan turned to Dr. London. "Doc, could you call the airport tower and ask air traffic control to contact my pilot? Tell him, before he lands, to follow the highway heading south and get a fix on an old white bus."

The vet went into his office to look up the number. While they waited, Bud nudged Stu and snickered. "'Air traffic control.' Never heard old Arliss called *that* before."

Stu snorted. "We gettin' by-God uptown, all right."

Jonathan lay back down, hoping he didn't look as grey as he suddenly felt. That small exertion had left him wrung out. But the last place he wanted to go was back to Sloan Kettering. The only way he'd ever get out of that place again was feet first. With a tag tied to his toe.

Presently the vet returned and settled on a stool beside him. "Caught him just in time. Depending on how fast the bus is going—"

"Thirty-five miles an hour is its top speed," Jonathan said, and the others hooted.

"Then he ought to find it, come back and land in about fifteen minutes. Maybe less." Dr. London hesitated. "You're probably not going to like this next part. We decided you're too weak and debilitated to sit up for the trip back, and the only helicopter around is on the fritz. He's hired the hearse to cart you back in rather than try to stuff you in the Cessna. But don't worry. It doubles as an ambulance. They got two flashing lights they stick up on top."

The telephone rang in the next room and the doctor jumped up to answer it. Apparently he was his own receptionist. He came back and handed a portable phone to Jonathan.

"They got your pilot on the line. He wanted to be patched through."

Jonathan grabbed the phone. "Arpad?"

"Yes, chief. I spotted the bus. It's stopped on the roadside about thirty miles out. The hood appears to be up."

Jonathan groaned. "Waiting for it too cool off enough to put in that muddy river water Hector brought back. I knew she'd forgotten." On second thought, maybe it was for the best. He added, "Let's just hope nobody comes to their rescue."

"Sir?"

"Never mind. Just hurry."

"Won't be long. I'm practically on my approach now."

Bud whistled and said, "The hearse from Baldwin and Sons Funeral Directors! Now that's what I call going in style!"

Or going out, Jonathan thought grimly, sinking back to wait, willing himself to last a while longer. He handed the phone to London, who returned it to his office.

Stu and Bud followed, arguing about where they were going to eat, and speculating if the hearse driver would be sober this early in the day.

Before the vet could return, the phone rang again. Jonathan could hear him suck in his breath. "Gunshot!"

Bud and Stu stopped in the doorway, eyes bright, like coyotes onto a sheep kill.

Vultures! Jonathan thought. They're all alike: everybody connected with the medical profession. Profession! Racket's more like it.

The doctor sounded reluctant. "That's a little out of my line, but, sure, bring him on in. I'm getting used to doing charity work on two-legged critters....How long will it take to get here? I've already got a patient occupying the examining table."

When he came back, he cast a worried glance around the room, then, apparently seized by inspiration, returned to his office and with one sweeping motion, cleared the top of his desk. Papers, cans, coffee cups clattered to the floor. He wheeled to call to the two EMS men but they were so close behind that he bumped into them; they had dogged his heels like two eager puppies.

"Stu! Bud! Think you could grab ahold of that one and cart him in here? We got another emergency coming that's going to need that there examining table."

Ignoring Jonathan's protests, the two men hoisted the patient like a large bag of—well, manure. Stu, toting the front end, sounded peevish. "Emergency? How come we weren't called?"

The doctor was spreading a white sheet across the desk. "The deputies are bringing him in. Some kinda prisoner, I guess. Appears they must've shot him."

As they settled Jonathan on the hard desk top with his legs dangling off the end, he muttered under his breath, "Oh great. I'm dying and I have to relinquish the only decent place to lie down to a criminal."

There must be a lesson in that. Maybe he should look for the wisdom in the mundane; it was obvious that there sure as hell wasn't going to be any other kind. Perhaps he shouldn't try so hard to think. Maybe some things couldn't be grasped by thought. He saw a habit here, a childhood pattern: as the older sibling, he had been expected to relinquish, to make the sacrifice.

While the doctor arranged a well-worn corduroy chair pad under Jonathan's head, Stu's beeper went off. He grabbed up his phone and said, "Yeah, whataya got?"

Bud hissed, "Wouldn't you know? Always at meal times. Ever' gol-damn time! I swear to God, I'll meet my Maker waitin' at the drive-up window at the Taco Bell."

Stu's face grew serious and he turned his back on the others, uttering only hushed monosyllables. In a moment he faced around and drew a deep breath. "If that don't beat all. Doc, I got some bad news. Your business is commencing to stack up. We got to bring in another one. Maybe two. There's been an accident."

"Where 'bouts?" Bud asked, already starting for the door.

Stu hesitated, glancing uneasily at Jonathan. "Out at the airport. It appears that while Arliss was looking the other way, Sonny Baldwin done collided the hearse into an incoming plane."

21

At Miguel's frantic urging, Guayo Cutzal, now called Hector, ran with the heavy jug the last fifty yards back to the bus, arriving to find the *gringo* collapsed on the floor. He helped them lift the comatose man onto the seat and he and Miguel held him there while the woman drove to the next truck stop, several miles north of a place called Fort Stockton.

Hector remained hidden in the back among the chicken coops while the EMS team carried the *Anglo* off the bus, but once the woman called Elise drove off again, he moved to the front and sank in a pool of sweat onto one of the long bench seats, soon falling into an exhausted sleep. He couldn't remember when he'd last had a decent meal, and the long hot walk to the arroyo to fill the water jug had depleted what strength he had left.

But in less than an hour Miguel's peculiar brand of Spanish interrupted his dreams. Miguel spoke a slightly different dialect than that which Hector had finally learned to understand during the months when he traversed the country of Mexico to reach the States. Mexican Spanish was nothing like that spoken in his mountain village in Belize, and the Spanish of the New Mexicans and Texans was stranger yet. The *gringa* Elise's university Spanish was like another language. He had to focus all of his faculties to understand a conversation between Miguel and the *gringa.*

The old man was leaning near Elise's ear, shouting to make himself heard above the rattle and roar of the ancient engine. "I don't feel good about this," he was saying over and over. "Not good."

"About what?" she said.

"Leaving that sick boy behind. He will surely die now."

Elise didn't answer for several seconds as they bumped on down the highway toward a place Miguel had told him was called Sanderson. Finally she said, "You think we ought to turn around?"

"*Sí.* Or he will die. He needs to see *Tía* Carlota."

"Even if we went back, he probably wouldn't come."

"He will come. If he is conscious, he will come."

"But what if he's too sick?"

Miguel sounded impatient. "We have to try. That is our only duty."

She hesitated before she said, "I promised to deliver you to Crystal City so you would sign the release he needs."

"Give me the paper. I'll sign right now."

Abruptly Elise put on the brake and swung the bus in a wide arc, making a U-turn in the middle of the deserted highway. The maneuver was too taxing for the old tub: Hector heard a loud pop and recognized the sound of a belt snapping. Almost immediately after completing the turn, the bus lurched to a stop and died.

Hector sat up. "I heard a belt break. I worked in a garage in Hobbs. I know the sound."

The *gringa* sounded cool and collected, but Hector figured she just didn't want to alarm the old man. She fastened a veiled pleading gaze upon Hector. "Think you could fix it?"

He cringed inwardly, sorry he had mentioned having worked in a garage, when actually he had only cleaned the latrines and disposed of the dirty oil. "With what? We don't have no tools."

"Then I guess you'll have to go for help." She reached around for her backpack and dug inside until she came up with a pen and paper. She scribbled a few lines then handed the note to Hector. It was in English, he could tell.

"What does it say?" Hector asked, although he could not read in any language.

"It says: 'Broke our fan belt. Please send wrecker thirty miles south of Fort Stockton on Two-eighty-five. Bus full of valuable poultry in danger of perishing.'"

Miguel, leaning in to peer at the paper, snorted at the affront. "Poultry? What an insult to my birds!"

Hector tried to laugh, to join them in the charade that this was not a serious situation, given their depleted physical states. Still, he was the obvious one to go for help. He pointed to his knife, still resting on the dashboard. "I might need that."

Without hesitation, Elise handed it to him. "Just make sure you don't abandon us."

Remembering Miguel's promise that *la curardera* would help him get home, Hector said, "I'll come back, with help."

He got off the bus and headed at a trot down the highway back toward Fort Stockton, hoping to meet a friendly motorist who would give him a lift into town. To the east he could see machines like black grasshoppers dotting the desert, their heads bobbing up and down like burros on a mountain trail. Miguel had told him they were oil wells. So there must be people nearby. Surely they weren't allowed to pump the life out of the earth forever without someone coming along to shut them off when the oil tanks were full. Nobody could be that wasteful, that rich.

How ironic that, desperate as he was to return to his homeland, here he was heading in the opposite direction. With all his soul, he longed to look upon the face of his bride Chacach, who had given birth to his son, so the fortune teller had told him. Before he left home, he had promised to make enough money to send for Chacach and his mother and sisters, but life had been too grim without even a single picture of them, nothing to tie him to his homeland except the knife that had belonged to the father he barely remembered.

Now he must admit that he also left home for adventure, and to escape the heavy responsibilities their poverty exacted. He had envisioned a carefree life among the *caballeros*, drinking fermented mate and dancing in cantinas with tall women in low-cut blouses who leaned in close and rubbed against him and blew into his ear to bring his arousal. But God had punished him for his abandonment and his wicked thoughts.

Some days he would lie on his cot in the back of the garage, held in the grip of dysentery brought about, he was certain, by the fearsome and lonely night that had crept in and settled deep within his heart. Unable to work for weeks at a time, he had often had to burn the thorns from what little prickly pear fruit he could find, to keep from having to beg for food.

Besides, the fortune teller had told him that his mother was gravely sick; he didn't reveal to her that God was punishing him still. But unless *la curandera* could send him back home magically, it would be months before he could reach Belize, even if he didn't starve along the way. His fate seemed inextricably tied to Miguel.

He was barely out of sight of the bus when he heard a car approaching from the direction of Fort Stockton. Even from this far away, Hector could see the sun glinting off the lights atop the vehicle, marking it as a highway patrol or a sheriff's car. Instinctively he veered off the road and trotted toward a spindly mesquite, the only hiding place, hoping the occupants of the car hadn't spotted him.

But the officers must have seen him, for the patrol car slowed, then whipped across the road and came to a stop on the shoulder near him. Hector, crouching behind the mesquite, felt his blood bursting against his eardrums. He took off at a frantic gallop across the prairie, not daring to look back.

He heard a car door slam, heard the officer call out in Tex-Mex Spanish, "Wetback! *¡Álto!* Or I'll shoot!"

Hector's legs were still pumping when the bullet propelled him outward, lifting him off the ground. The crack of the pistol reached his ears as he was already crumbling to the earth. He was not quite sure why he flew forward, why, as if in slow motion, he seemed to lose all control and fall, for at first he felt only a slight stinging pain, felt a warmth spread from his bladder along his crotch.

As if it were happening to someone else, he saw Elise's scrap of paper fly out of his grasp and off onto the wind just as his head crashed against a large abandoned piece of oilfield equipment jutting from the sand like a maul of God.

22

As soon as that ominous report rocketed across the dry landscape like a cannon shot, Elise could think of little else. "Jesus," she muttered under her breath. "I hope Hector's not toast." After an eternity, she excused herself and walked several yards away from the bus across the blistering prairie to a clump of cenizo bushes, as much to relax her bravado as to relieve her full bladder. Ever since Jonathan's collapse, she had assumed the role of reigning elder, for no reason she could explain.

Except that she'd watched Miguel grow more ashen in the unrelenting heat and was struck by his fragility, his tenuous hold on life after more than nine decades that must never have been easy. Now, uprooted again, he must relocate to the household of an even older relative. It was possible that *Tía* Carlota didn't even know he was coming. What if she refused to take him in, him and his fourteen chickens? What would Elise do then?

Then there was Hector, desperate to reach Belize, to see his dying mother. With no money, and the entire length of Mexico to traverse on foot, how would he ever manage? He was still a boy, younger than she. He'd be eligible for Social Security by the time he got home. She almost felt responsible for getting him there. Responsible for a piece of toast now, maybe.

A half-hour earlier an old Impala crammed with Hispanics headed toward Sanderson had stopped and asked Miguel if he needed a ride into town. Of course Miguel refused: even if by some miracle he could have squeezed in, he couldn't leave his cocks to fricassee in that ungodly tin can. Besides, he would never go off without Hector, who went in the opposite direction in search of help. Elise couldn't accept a ride, having promised Jonathan she wouldn't leave Miguel's side until he signed the release. Now she admitted that she couldn't leave him under any circumstances. So they were both stuck here with this crapped-out steaming carcass, shriveling into two pieces of jerky while they waited for help. Man! Did everything have to remind her of food?

She squatted behind the scraggly bushes and glanced at her watch, trying to remember how long Hector had been gone. Had it been only an hour? It seemed much longer, and the more time that passed, the more she wondered about the loud crack they'd heard when Hector was barely out of sight. Miguel had started and whispered, "Gunshot." But she assured him that it was probably a backfire.

Miguel wasn't convinced. "There are lots of crazy hunters out there who'll fire at anything that moves."

"That wasn't the sound of a shotgun," she said. "Even I know that. Maybe it was something out in the oil field."

He shook his head and went back to check on his cocks. But now she wasn't so sure about the sound, especially since no backfiring automobile ever appeared.

It would be hours before they could presume that Hector had arrived safely. They couldn't be more than thirty or forty miles from town, but unless Hector caught a ride, it might take him several hours to reach Fort Stockton. If he didn't collapse into a puddle of melted lard first. And if he did, they'd all be meat loaf in another hour.

In resignation, she trudged back to the bus, mopping her forehead. At least she was still sweating. A sign of heat stroke, she knew, was when there was no perspiration. But she needed to conserve fluids, quit sweating, quit peeing. Slow down. Well, there was no hurry. She mumbled, "You're not sure you have anyplace to go, either, sport."

There. Now that she'd said it, the band around her chest loosened, at least for the moment. So there it was in the open: she was scared spitless to get to Uvalde, for fear her dad wouldn't acknowledge her. And if he didn't, she wasn't sure she could bear it.

How dorf-brained not to have called ahead. She kicked at a pebble, sending up a plume of dirt. Still, it wasn't too late; she could phone him from Sanderson and say something like, "Hey there! This is the daughter you never knew you had."

No, he might hang up. Better to begin with something about her mom: "Remember Cherilita? She's broke and trying to pull her career out of the toilet. So she's kissed her kid off." No, he'd probably be smegging glad to hear bad news about Salome.

"You don't know me, but...Mom told me to get lost, make my own way. But I don't know how." No, why should he care?

"Look here, you're my dad and I've got the DNA to prove it." No, too confrontational.

"Dad, I've got no place to go. I need a home."

I need a home.

The old man was sitting on the bus's second step, blocking the doorway. He looked even more tired and shrunken than when she'd left him; the heat was beginning to tell. When she was almost upon him, he placed his hands on his bony knees to push himself, painfully, to his feet. She could see the effort it cost. She didn't particularly want to get back on the bus so soon, but there was nothing else to do. Maybe she would take a long nap, to kill the time, conserve energy.

She passed him without meeting his eyes and climbed aboard. He said, "That is not the face of a girl anxious to see her father."

He could not see the pounce of tears which she quickly swiped away. She swung into the bench seat next to the door and lay down, then said, "Have you ever considered what you'll do if your aunt doesn't want to take you in?"

She'd forgotten that he was hard of hearing. He climbed the steps and sat down across from her. "¿Como? What did you say about my aunt?"

"Does she know you're coming?"

He shrugged. "Maybe. She is *la curandera*. She knows many things."

"But you haven't told her, have you? That you're moving in, chickens and all?"

He regarded her with amused pity. "That is the difference between us. My family would never turn a relative away. It is our duty to care for one another."

176

"Even if you don't like each other?"

"Even if we don't know each other. Blood is blood. Besides, it is our duty to like each other."

She clasped her hands across her middle and studied the ceiling, dented by a tall hard-headed Baptist, no doubt. "What if someone came to your door claiming to be your daughter, and you didn't even know she existed? Would you really take her in?"

"Oh yes."

"Even though she might be a fraud?"

His tone suggested an element of resignation. "Who could say, for sure? She might be mine."

She faced him and glared in disbelief. "Get out! A strange woman, sponging off you? You're not even that fond of women anymore, I take it."

A squabble erupted among the cocks. He got up and shambled toward the back, mumbling, "Well, if it were a son...."

Elise sighed and closed her eyes. The lids felt very warm. "Yeah, that's how I figure *my* dad'll react, too."

Maybe she wouldn't identify herself—just ring his doorbell, meet him face-to-face, then say she had the wrong house if he looked even halfway hostile. Maybe she'd leave without ever telling him and drive the bus back to where her VW crapped out, see about getting it towed. She could always go back to Boulder and crash with Jennifer until she could find a job. Yes, Jennifer would be the obvious choice: she'd be in school forever at the rate she was going. She'd probably be so stoned, she wouldn't notice Elise was there for a couple of days.

A great welling sadness filled her whole body, swelling behind her eyes until they hurt. Outside of Jennifer and a couple of other classmates, she had no one. Her mother had cut the cord with great finality. It wasn't the first time Elise had seethed with hatred. She'd been dumped more often than nuclear waste by that bitch.

Miguel returned to the bench across from her, whistling softly so that she would know he was there. She said, with some irony that she didn't expect him to discern, "Looks like we've been abandoned."

"Ah. Then everything is as it should be," he said in a small dry voice.

Maybe she had misunderstood him. She turned onto her side, propping up on one elbow so she could study him. There were dark cavities around his eyes. He looked like a flaming cadaver. "What do you mean by that?" she asked.

"Being abandoned is part of our natural state. That's the way of life."

Her mouth was so dry it was difficult to speak without clacking. "How do you figure?"

"Didn't God put us here and abandon us, without even a guarantee of immortality? Later—or sooner—our parents abandon us and we must learn to fend for ourselves. Then lovers leave or die. Children can't wait to get away. Finally we are alone to settle the score, and we realize we have always been alone."

She frowned. It didn't make sense, but it seemed terribly important that she understand before—Lord, the old guy might keel over any minute. "What score is that?"

"The score with God for stacking everything against us, so we always know whatever we do is futile. Because in the end we are going to die, and all the people who knew our name will die, and what we build will crumble into dust. So we try to settle our grudge with God—or the whole universe, whichever is bigger." He paused and grinned, his black eyes gleaming and sharp. But she sensed his bitterness as he added, "It is a very uneven contest."

Now she felt worse than ever. "Well thanks for that. You're sure a little ray of sunshine."

"But being abandoned is a good thing, *chica.* It makes you strong. All strength comes from abandonment."

"Strong for what?" She flopped onto her back, dismissing him. "So we can die with muscles?"

"Well...that, too—but mostly, strong so we can live."

She snorted. "What the hell for?"

She imagined that he was shrugging again because his voice sounded light, playful. "What else? For one thing, for cockfights!"

A sudden breeze whipped needle-like mesquite leaves against the bus and sent a cloud of sand through the windows. Miguel pointed. "See? Even the wind is dancing."

Like Shiva dancing, she thought. No need to mention it to Miguel; he'd probably never heard of Shiva. The stifling heat was getting to her, and her mouth was full of grit. She felt languid, dizzy. But she forced herself to continue, as if only the talking kept them alive. "What's this about no immortality? Don't you celebrate the Day of the Dead, when everybody comes back?"

"Yes. But the dead are always nearby. We can talk to them, go out to the cemetery after mass sometimes, take a picnic lunch and catch them up on the news. And once a year, when they return for us to honor them, we feel very close. But they are still dead. Dead is dead."

"Which means what?"

"Dead people don't play anymore, although once in a while they play tricks. Mostly they quit playing when they die. If you want to play, *chica*, you have to do it while you are alive."

Elise thought about Jonathan. "I don't think Jonathan knows that. I don't think he has ever played." The sweltering air pressed in on her, and she heard her heart pounding, like an executioner's drum. "Now he'll probably never have the chance."

The old man's voice was wispy, as if it cost great effort to speak. "We are his chance. We need to hurry back and get him."

"Yeah, sure," she said. "Why didn't I think of that?" Laboriously she pulled herself up and peered glumly out at the dancing dust toward the direction where Hector had disappeared. If help didn't come soon, she and Miguel and all fourteen chickens would be pickled in their own brine.

23

Just as the EMTs started out the vet's door, Jonathan heard a patrol car, sirens blaring, pull up in front and screech to a stop.

"Damn melonheads!" Stu said. "They're blocking our vehicle. The whole of by-God Pecos County to park in, and they have to—"

The ever practical Bud seemed in no hurry. "Let 'em unload the patient first." Jonathan suspected neither man wanted to miss getting a glimpse of the gunshot victim.

The IV had revived Jonathan enough to raise his level of outrage at being summarily relegated to the top of a hard desk. Where his legs hung off, the desk edge bit into the backs of his thighs and was already cutting off circulation. The buttons on the old corduroy chair pad dug into his head every time he tried to turn to see what was going on. The EMTs lounged against each side of the doorway, watching the proceedings.

Two uniformed deputies half-carried, half-dragged the screaming prisoner through the office and flung him onto the examining room table like a slab of meat. The patient's yowl of excruciating pain shot through

Jonathan like a bullet. From the greetings exchanged between the EMS and the officers, he surmised their names to be Lon and Don. The patient's name was apparently Sorrydumbasssonofabitch. The narrow door opening partially blocked by the EMS men prevented a view of the man's face, which Dr. London described in graphic terms. "That's one godawful bloody mess. Chewed up like a bobcat got aholt of him. What'd you go and shoot him in the head for, Lon?"

"I didn't," Lon said. "I shot him in the back. That's what the sorrydumbasssonofabitch is caterwauling about. You got him lying on his gunshot wound."

"Well, soon as I get a compress on this frontal laceration, you can flip 'im over. How'd he get this nasty head wound?"

"Fell on something rusty."

"Then he'll have to have a tetanus shot, too."

Jonathan winced as the man screamed when he was manhandled into a new position. The poor devil's cries sent a wave of nausea through Jonathan and the man's agony resonated with his own. But the patient's writhing impeded the doctor's attempts to cut off his clothing and examine the wound to his backside.

Lon yelled, "Keep still, you dumbasssonofabitch!"

His partner said, "Doc, can't you do something to put this bastard out of his misery?"

"Hard to say," London said. "This isn't a horse. I can't just shoot him." He laughed at his own witticism while the patient bellowed louder.

Unable to shut out the noise, Jonathan stared at the water-stained acoustical tiles overhead and asked,

"Whatever a man has done in his life, doesn't he deserve a better end than this?"

Stu turned around. "Huh? You say something?"

Jonathan realized that he had spoken aloud and that he had been praying to a circular spot on the ceiling that resembled, in his mind, a great pendulous breast. He said, "Yeah. Move over, so I can see."

Stu and Bud stepped aside, and Jonathan saw London calmly fill a syringe and move to the table, once again obscuring Jonathan's view.

The doctor turned to Lon. "Grab him by the scruff and Don, you hold his hind legs while I put this into the loose skin of his back—"

"Like a housecat?" Lon said.

The doctor seemed to think better of it and said, "Yeah. Guess I can just use his shank."

The shot had the desired effect of calming the patient to a whimper, enabling Dr. London to work on the wound. At length Jonathan heard the plink as something hit the instrument tray.

"There's your bullet," London said. "This fella must've done something right. It deflected off the knife in his pocket and just barely embedded itself in the fatty tissue of the gluteous maximus. It'll just require a couple of stitches."

Lon yelled, "You hear that, you sorrydumbass bastard? Your knife saved your sorryass hide. Now you can join all the other sorry dumbasssonofabitches—"

Immediately the sedative seemed to wear off. The man cried out, "*¡El cuchillo de me padre está arruinado!*"

Jonathan knew the voice at once. He leaned up on one elbow and called out, "Hector? Is that you?"

The man's voice registered incredulity. *"¿Jefe?"*

The officers apparently noticed Jonathan for the first time. Lon stepped to the doorway, eyes narrowed. "You know this man?"

Jonathan ignored the question. Again he yelled at Hector. "Where are the *señorita* and Miguel?"

Hector jabbered something that Jonathan couldn't understand. He asked Lon, "What did he do?"

"Didn't halt when I told him to."

Jonathan felt his ire building. "Is that *all?* So you shot him in the *back?*"

Don peered into the room, and the two officers glared down on him. Don said, "You been harboring illegals, mister?" while Lon turned to the doctor and said, "Who is this yokel?"

"Name's Tyler," the doctor said. "Big shot from up north."

Bud put in, "Got his own airplane that's too big to land out on Arliss's strip."

Stu added, "Got his own pilot, too."

Don's squint swept Jonathan from head to foot, darkening with menace. "What are you? Some kind of fancy-ass drug runner?"

London stepped in and caught Don by the arm. "Ix-nay. This man is one of the Fortune Five Hundred, or somethin' like that."

Don shrugged off London's hand. "Oh yeah? Then what's he doin' lyin' on your desk like a blotter?"

Bud said, "Whyn't you tend to your own beeswax and one of these here days when you get old enough, we'll explain it to you."

"Yeah," Stu said. "Lissen to him talk. Ever hear a drug runner talk like that?"

For once Jonathan felt gratitude to the EMS men for bringing a glint of respect to the officers' eyes. He went on the offensive. "Is this how you treat people? Shoot them in the back for no reason?"

"Like I said, he was running—"

"Is running an offense? He wasn't running from the scene of a crime, was he?"

"No, but technically—"

Don spoke up. "We know an illegal when we see one. And after going through his pockets—"

"Did he give you permission to go through his belongings? Isn't that illegal search and seizure?"

The men exchanged glances before Don hitched up his trousers and took a menacing step forward. "Look, mister hotshot. We're in the business of protecting our law-abiding citizens, not making nice-nice for somebody—I don't care how rich he is—who hires a sorry illegal dumbasssonofabitch from Guatemala who takes food out of the mouths—"

Hector spoke up weakly, "No Guatemala. Belize."

Jonathan was seized with inspiration. "Officer, since when does someone with diplomatic immunity have to produce proof of citizenship?"

The officer's Adam's apple bobbed with his audible gulp. "Whassat about diplomatic immunity?"

For the first time in months, Jonathan was beginning to enjoy himself. Adrenalin gave him the strength to sit up. "This is Hector Mendoza, the son of Belize's—" He paused, uncertain whether Belize rated ambassadorial status. He cleared his throat and plunged ahead. "—highest ranking diplomatic official. He is my guest until he can return to his country to—attend the wedding of the—president's daughter. Just what were you planning to do with him?"

Too late he remembered that Belize had no president, but a governor general appointed by the queen of England. But maybe this bunch wouldn't know the difference.

Dr. London, who had bandaged the patient's backside and turned him over to clean his facial wound, said, "I know the answer to that. They would've loaded him in a bus and dumped him across the Rio Grande at Piedras Negras or Ciudad Acuña without a dime in his pocket."

Again Hector moaned, "*¡El cuchillo de mi padre está arruinado!*"

"What's he saying?" Jonathan asked. "Is he talking about a girl and an old man?"

"He says his father's knife is ruined," Bud offered. "Sounds to me like his father's *dead* already."

Jonathan thought fast. "True, true. The...highest ranking diplomatic official from Belize is actually... Hector's mother. She's waiting back in San Antonio while my pilot comes for us both." Suddenly a light dawned. "Good lord! You don't suppose that ambulance ran into—"

Stu and Bud seemed to come to. Stu said, "Hey Don, get your damn squad car outa the way! We got another emergency to bring in from Arliss's airstrip."

As Don followed the EMS men outside, he said, "Whyn't you say somethin'? What's the matter? Sonny

Baldwin been suckin' too hard on the fruit of the vine again?"

Lon snorted. "Don't you know nothin' about horticulture? Tequila don't grow on vines. They squeeze it outa cactus."

Jonathan called to the doctor, who had returned to his patient. "What's the chance of that being my pilot's plane the ambulance hit?"

"I'd say pretty good, since Arliss might not get one plane out there a week—what with all the regular airfields we got in this county."

He faced around with a sour expression. "Meantime, if this boy's fixin' to see his mama, you might want to clean him up some first. I've smelt polecats sweeter."

He stepped in and bent close to Jonathan's ear. "And if he isn't about to see his mama, I best not know. Got it?"

"Gotcha."

24

Over Jonathan's weak protests, the doctor and the two DPS officers shoved the desk against the wall so that Jonathan would not roll off when they laid Hector beside him, thus clearing the examining table for the incoming patients from the plane and hearse wreck. Outside the window beside Jonathan's head, he could make out a dog's bark growing nearer. The doctor muttered something about almost forgetting about his three o'clock.

Hector, who had inherited Jonathan's corduroy chair pad for his head, appeared to be in intermittent pain. He kept writhing against Jonathan, pushing him farther into the wall and its two slatted-blind windows. The sun had baked into the slats so that they almost burned his arm, and the afternoon's heat radiating from the windows soon sheathed his body in sweat. In addition, Jonathan was aware that the vet's complaints about Hector's appalling odor were not exaggerated.

He shuddered in revulsion and wondered what had possessed him to save this alien worm from instant deportation by the officers. Possibly his own deteriorating physical condition was affecting his ability to reason. For all he knew, he could be protecting a murderer. It was entirely conceivable that Hector had slit Elise's throat and taken her money, then abandoned the bus and its contents in a ditch. He didn't share Miguel's faith in Hector's innate goodness, and he had the knife prick to prove it. Unconsciously he reached up to his neck and fingered the wound.

Hector, noticing the action, stopped moaning long enough to point to the prick and say to Jonathan in apparent sincerity, *"Lo siento, jefe."*

"Yeah, sure you are....Now what did you do with Elise and Miguel?"

Hector obviously recognized the old man's name. He lifted his head from the pad—Jonathan considered quickly whisking it from under him—and rattled off a saliva-slinging explanation of which Jonathan recognized only the name "Miguel". A riot of sensations assaulted Jonathan's olfactory system, almost pushing it into overload. It was hard to decide which was worse: the Belizean's rancid breath or the redolence of his unwashed body.

Jonathan wiped Hector's spit from the corner of his eye and called to the retreating officers, "Tell him to be still, will you? And ask him where's the bus."

After a brief exchange with Hector, Lon said, "He says the bus broke down—fan belt, he thinks. They sent him into town for help." He paused while Hector rattled on. "He says he can't be still unless the doc gives him something for the pain."

At that moment the door opened and, without ceremony or a decrease in pace, a stout woman led a large yellow lab past the desk and directly into the examining room. Dr. London, who was readying the table for the dog, called out to Jonathan, "I can't give him anything else because of his head wound. He'll just have to tough it out until we're sure there's no concussion or neurological damage. Sorry I can't be sure about that. You don't see an MRI or CAT scan machine anywhere abouts, do you?"

The woman's chortle was accompanied on the inbreath by a snort. "Every vet should have a CAT scan."

The doctor turned his attention to her. "Need anything besides just his yearly shots, Nancy?"

The woman, who was out of Jonathan's range, said, "Nothing but a ring-side seat to this zoo you're running today."

"No kiddin'! Doc Barnes picked a heck of a time to have a heart attack," the doctor said glumly. Jonathan surmised Barnes was the nearest bonafide M.D.

The telephone rang somewhere under the desk. Both officers scrambled underneath to find it. Ron came up with it and called out, "Hey Doc, Thelma Cantrell's prize setting hen—that she's entering in the Houston Livestock Show? She's losing her feathers and breaking out in bumps."

London sighed audibly. "Better tell her to bring 'er on in."

When he hung up, Ron turned to Lon and said, "Gonna get crowded in here. Maybe we ought to get on the road and see about that broke-down bus."

Without thinking, Jonathan raised up and said, "No!" much too sharply. The bus did not look like the conveyance of a diplomat's son, and Elise wouldn't know to corroborate his story about Hector's recent elevation to diplomatic status. As the officers eyed him curiously, he sank back against the hard desk and gave them a wan smile.

"Could you just stay here to—uh—translate? Anyway, it could be my pilot whose plane was struck. And if the hearse is damaged, we may all need some transportation back to that bus."

The officers exchanged glances. "Well...I don't know...."

"Your help would go a long way toward mitigating the need for an investigation into how you happened to shoot the Belizean diplomat's son in the back," Jonathan added.

The dog let out a yowl and Jonathan heard a splattering noise.

"Jeez!" Lon said. "The dog's pissing all over the table."

Ron said, "Dog that size can sure turn it out. Looks like Niagara Falls."

When the huge dog had finished relieving himself, Nancy and Dr. London lugged him down from the table. She said, "Sorry about that, Doc. The shot must've scared him. Want me to stay and help clean it up?"

"Naw. Goes with the territory."

"Why don't I just pay you later?" she said.

Jonathan bellowed, "Pay him now, lady! You might be dead tomorrow." Then he wondered where all that passion had come from.

Lon said, "Yeah, pay him now, Nancy. It's the least you could do."

"Well!" the woman said. "I just never!"

After she was gone, Dr. London went to work with a mop and a roll of towels while Jonathan listened as distant sirens grew steadily closer. He prayed the plane had been someone else's. "Better hurry," he called. "They're coming."

The doctor muttered, "How did I ever run this office without you?"

Jonathan looked over at Hector, whose head was swathed in gauze. The young wetback was now lying quietly on the coveted corduroy chair pad, *his* corduroy pad. What strange quirk of karma had led him to this wretched hot desktop, crammed against a smelly little alien, his only hope of rescue probably dashed by some jerk named "Sonny"? Was this where he was destined to breathe his final breath? He realized his breaths had become more and more shallow, and with a concerted effort, he forced himself to take several long, deep gulps of air. God, how he wanted to live! But not necessarily on this desktop.

The sound caused Hector to turn toward him, concern glowing in his warm dark eyes. "*No se muera,*" he whispered. "*Espere a la curandera.*"

Jonathan nodded, knowing instinctively what Hector meant. *La curandera* was his only hope. Even if she couldn't cure him, surely she had lived long enough to be able to tell him what this life was supposed to be about. Just the sound of her name had taken on a magical quality, as if possibly just repeating it could heal. He sucked in deeply and repeated, "*La curandera, la curandera....*"

The rapid intake of oxygen began to make him dizzy. He closed his eyes and stored his strength, barely aware that he was dozing off.

The commotion of the gurney being wheeled past his head into the next room roused him. Without opening his eyes, he recognized Stu's Hoss Cartwright voice. "We got 'em both. We left Sonny in the EMS truck for the time being. He's so tanked up he's in no pain, although it appears he may've boogered up his kneecap. The main damage is to the plane. The collision sheared the tail clean off. Didn't do the hearse any good, either. The front end is scraping the ground."

"Hm. Maybe you ought to call Old Man Baldwin," London said.

"We did already. He'll probably show up directly."

The doctor turned to his new patient. "So who's the Arab?" He leaned down and yelled, "What's your name, fella?"

"Arpad Patel," the patient said in a formal tone, as if he were being presented at court. "I am Indian."

"Arpad!" Jonathan called weakly. "I'm in here! You hurt?"

The doctor's voice was sharp. "Whyn't you let me take this case, Tyler. Then you can have the next one. Now what've we got here? Is it your shoulder?"

"Perhaps." Arpad's always correct demeanor was being taxed by severe pain, Jonathan could tell from his voice's thin, reedy quality. "It may be dislocated."

"Let's have a look—oh brother! Yep, she's out of whack, all right. Anything else? You bump your head or take a control knob in the balls?"

"I...don't know..."

Jonathan couldn't stand it; the pilot was obviously in great distress. "For God's sake, give the man something for his pain!"

"Now looky here, Tyler—" the doctor began.

The office door opened and a breathless woman stumbled across the threshold, a bedraggled chicken nestled in the crook of her arm. She nodded to the officers. "Hi Ron, Lon. I rushed right over." She glanced at the two men on the desk. "Oh lordy! Business stacking up?"

Lon gestured to one of the chairs against the far wall of the small office that obviously doubled as a waiting room. "Not really," he said. "Doc can probably squeeze you in before he gets around to Sonny. He's sobering up in the EMS vehicle, according to Bud and Stu."

Ron added, "The Old Man's on his way. That oughta sober him up a right smart."

Dr. London called out, "Be with you in a sec, Thelma...soon as I X-ray this shoulder."

Jonathan stared at the ceiling and considered the irony as his outrage mounted. He raised up on one elbow and yelled to the doctor, "My God, do you realize that everywhere I turn, it's another freaking chicken? The whole world stands still for chickens, while I'm lying here—"

The doctor motioned to the two officers with an exasperated wave. "Okay, that's it! Would you gentlemen mind shutting that door on your way out?"

"Sure thing," Lon said. And before Jonathan could protest, they had closed the door to the examining room, opened the office door, and walked outside, leaving him sweltering in the box of an office with Hector, Thelma, her hen, and, he figured, about half an hour's worth of life remaining.

25

While the veterinarian attempted to manipulate Arpad's dislocated shoulder back into position, the telephone rang several times, jarring Jonathan from his pensive, glucose-starved self-analysis. Each time, Stu came into the office to answer it, deliberately closing the examining room door behind him and affording Jonathan no view of the doctor's progress.

He surmised that several of the calls had to do with him, and he thought it wise to feign sleep so as to afford the EMS more privacy to discuss his condition freely. In this way he hoped to learn something about his own prognosis, and at the same time avoid speaking to his wife or his physician.

One of the callers was obviously Sarah. Stu's Bonanza intonation softened, taking on more deference than Jonathan thought necessary. He heard Stu assure her, "His vital signs have strengthened and stabilized, and he's resting comfortably—well, relatively comfortably. No ma'am, I wouldn't wake him if I were you. Soon as the doc pops the pilot's shoulder back in place, the three of them will be on their way, somehow or other."

He paused, then answered her question, "The third one's the ambassador's son. He'll be traveling with them, I guess."

Jonathan smiled secretly. Nothing pleased Sarah more than diplomatic ties.

But he could still think of no good reason to return to Sloan Kettering. Sarah wouldn't care one way or the other, once she was sure their estate was intact. And he had seen all he wanted to of her many years ago; in fact, just talking to her would doubtless shorten his remaining minutes on earth. In the back of his mind, for several years at least, he realized that he had hoped that someday he would be able to have a life without Sarah. If that was not possible, at least he could have death without her.

Anyway, he figured that if he learned the mystery of his life, it would be at the price of whatever innocence he still possessed, and he wanted to be free of outside influence.

But as he mulled it over, he wondered if the only real influence he had ever had was his own, despite that he used to blame his parents, and later Sarah, for regrettable decisions he made. Apparently he'd been over-long in accepting this responsibility: Julian Barnes claimed that after the age of twenty-five, you could no longer blame your parents for your life. Jonathan had shrugged off those words when he read them; then why had they stayed with him so vividly?

When he was a boy, he sensed a unique destiny of greatness—at something—that he was meant to fulfill. Now he felt cheated of this promise, and he clung to the stringy hope that somewhere, Someone Up There or Out There would not let anything happen until his destiny was complete. Still he couldn't put from his mind Updike's remark about quickly becoming history while waiting to be news.

He shifted uneasily on the desktop, frowning. Too much thinking led to grave misgivings at the cost of his tranquility. Better not to think at all. In the past twenty-four hours events had been coming too fast. He seemed to have embarked on an accelerated journey, a sort of forced-march evolution where he spun through experiences that occurred so spontaneously and rapidly that even his identity was beginning to shift. He wondered if this was what ancient mystics called "the quickening."

Suddenly he could no longer get his breath. Clutched by panic, he scrambled upright and, eyes bugging, made frantic gestures toward the woman with the chicken, who responded by screaming at the EMS men.

"Hey, this guy's going ballistic! Better come quick!"

After what seemed like only moments of blackness, Jonathan regained consciousness to find himself once again hooked up to oxygen. He turned his head slightly to find Hector's blackhead-infested nose only inches from his. Apparently being at death's door hadn't rated him even one more inch of desk space. Or the coveted chair pad.

"You better now?" Stu yelled at him, inches from his face.

Bud said, "Yeah, he's pinkin' up."

Jonathan had come to with the realization of something he must not put off any longer. He pulled the oxygen mask away and said, "Ask Doc—get cell phone cord." Before they could suggest that he just use the doctor's phone, he gasped, "Need number off—rapid dial."

The cord was produced and miraculously it could be attached to his phone, which Bud then held against Jonathan's ear, after having been instructed which button to push to reach Bett's voice mail. After a few rings Jonathan heard her beeper message, and the sound of her throaty voice swamped him with fresh guilt. He was relieved that he wouldn't actually have to speak to her; he wasn't *that* brave. Once he returned the cord, she wouldn't be able to reach him. And he knew she would try frantically, poor kid.

He felt self-conscious about talking in front of Bud, so he motioned him away and, trembling, took the phone himself, turning to face the window blinds, and speaking in a breathless mumble.

"Betts—May not make it back...unless a miracle happens. If not, I want you to know I've used you, screwed you over. Sorry." He fell back, spent. Poor Betts. It would break her heart. But the confession lightened his burden. And it might not come as a news bulletin to Betts. This just in: Man screws paramour.

After he hung up, the woman named Thelma who held the mangy chicken on her lap said, "Would one of you all bring me some tissue? Harriet has dookied on my jeans."

Bud left and when he returned with a roll of paper towels, she asked, "How much longer until—"

"Doc and Stu are trying to pop that sucker back into this Indian fella's shoulder socket. Doc says the angle's different than on a cutting horse. But if they succeed—"

The telephone jangled again just as several voices in the examining room whooped in triumph. Jonathan heard Arpad's muted grunt of pain, the doctor's "Bingo!" and Stu's "Way to go, Doc."

Bud picked up the phone, then called, "It's Kelvin Baldwin. Wants to know about Sonny. More to the point, he wants to know how's the hearse. Shall I tell him?"

"I'll take it," London said, coming into the office. He nodded to Thelma and her hen, then addressed Bud in a loud whisper. "How's he doing?"

"Color's good," Bud said. "I think he was mainly just dehydrated from being stranded out in that old bus—"

"And this Belize guy?"

At the mention of Belize, Hector stirred against Jonathan. "¿Cómo?"

"Shut up!" Jonathan growled, fearful that Hector, unaware of his exalted status, would give the lie away.

Bud answered Hector in pidgin Spanish as London took the phone.

"Kelvin? Where's your daddy?"

London turned to the others and said, "Old Man Baldwin's about to have apoplexy. At least we won't have to deal with him."

Bud said, "Not unless he has a stroke. He could, you know, the way your luck's been runnin' today."

London rolled his eyes upward and spoke into the phone. "Yeah, your baby brother's having to wait his turn in the EMS truck....Nothing that a few hours' sleep and a gallon of coffee won't cure. And maybe a whole new kneecap. But from what I hear, your hearse is going to need a spell in Intensive Care."

Jonathan tuned him out and returned to reciting his own private litany of despair. He decided that desire was at the root of his present suffering, but if he didn't give up suffering, he wouldn't have to give up desire. And he did so want to hold onto desire.

Maybe, he thought, the only desire he would have to give up was the desire to be taken care of. This interlude on the desktop might then be perceived as only a liminal one, a threshold experience before he stepped into something different—not better, necessarily, just different.

"Your main problem is all these important passengers he was supposed to pick up," London was saying. "We got us a wounded ambassador and a billionaire that's low sick and his pilot that I just fixed a dislocated shoulder on."

He paused, and the receiver crackled with excitement. "Name's Jonathan Whitley Tyler IV. Fella from back East."

From across the room Jonathan plainly heard Kelvin's voice. London said, "That's the one. Cover of *Forbes*, huh? I might've known if he had money, your daddy'd of heard of him."

When he hung up, he said, "Kelvin's on his way with the limo. The Old Man told him to drive you all over to San Antonio himself."

Stu chuckled. "Guess Old Man Baldwin's good and pissed at Sonny."

"He's more than that," the vet said. "The Old Man's got visions of being sued out of his socks. He told Kelvin to load that limo with bootleg champagne if necessary and everything that Kelvin's wife's been fixing all day for the Rotarians."

Stu said, "Her being a caterer, that could be a right fine feast."

"The Rotary Club may be a little shy of supper tonight," London said, "but Old Man Baldwin can only kiss one butt at a time, and right now the Rotarians are going to have to stand in line behind Mister Tyler here."

Jonathan had been thinking about what to do, about how to command at least a shred of moral verve if this really was to be the end. Without opening his eyes, still conserving every dram of energy that he could, he said, "In that case, call him back. Tell him—bring a tow chain."

26

On the highway

"It wasn't supposed to happen this way," Arpad said for the twentieth time. "I meant to take care of you. At least let me help you into the limo."

Jonathan didn't want to get back in just yet. He wanted to stand around on the highway with the others and watch.

Kelvin Baldwin's legs protruded from under the front bumper of the bus. His black shantung trousers had hiked up, revealing midcalf black silk stockings with clocks on the sides, the kind Jonathan's grandfather had worn. A layer of reddish dust had already attached itself to the toes of his black patent undertaker's shoes. A disembodied voice drifted up from beneath the bus.

"I'm not dressed for this."

Jonathan, supported by Hector and Arpad—alias the Halt and the Lame—had downed one flute of champagne on the drive from London's veterinary clinic to the site of the broken-down bus. It was his first fluid by mouth since breakfast, discounting the chicken water that had been forced down him following his initial collapse. Although the EMS intravenous feeding

205

had restored his electrolyte balance, the champagne did more to revive his *joie de vivre*. When their limo reached the old bus, he had insisted on getting out to supervise the attachment of the improvised tow chain. Elise stood by as well, having been introduced to both Arpad and Kelvin. But Miguel was nowhere to be seen.

"He insists he's going to ride home with his chickens," she explained.

"Nonsense," Jonathan said, surprised at the strength of his voice. "He needs food, drink, and air conditioning. I don't want to be responsible for another death."

Arpad growled into his ear, "Careful what you say, chief. Lawsuit alert."

Jonathan turned to Hector, whose head bandage had slipped down over one eye, and issued orders as if the young Hispanic could understand. "Go get Miguel. Tell him he *has* to ride in the limo. Those cocks'll be fine without him."

Miraculously, Hector appeared to comprehend. With one protective hand over his wounded backside, he hobbled to the bus and climbed aboard. Elise moved to Jonathan's side, placing an arm around his waist to steady him.

"I don't need all this," Jonathan said, but he made no effort to disengage from his two supporters, even though the heat of their bodies only added to the sticky discomfort from the blazing sun.

Kelvin's muffled curses were punctuated by the sharp clang of metal against metal, as he apparently used a tire iron to beat the chain into submission. "Goddamn undercarriage isn't built for this!"

"You can make it work," Jonathan called cheerily. He turned toward Elise, slipping an arm around her shoulder and giving it a squeeze. "I bet you haven't had your champagne today."

She brightened. "Can't say that I have. Got any food in there?"

Despite what must be a painful shoulder, Arpad gently turned them and steered them, like a pivoting chorus line, toward the limo. "The chief wouldn't let us eat until we got to you and the old man. Now perhaps he'll—"

Jonathan balked, looking back toward the bus. "We have to wait for the others."

Elise left them and ran back to yell into the bus's doorway. In a few seconds, the two Hispanics appeared. When Hector attempted to help Miguel down the steps, the old man jerked away and snarled something that sounded like a curse. Hector grinned, shrugged, and limped over just as Kelvin emerged from beneath the limo and scrambled to his feet.

The mortician attacked the dust on his trousers and shirt with vicious zeal, then, in a failed attempt to resume an air of prosperous distinction, retrieved his suit coat from the limo and put it on, despite that his white shirt was soaked with sweat. Jonathan noted that Kelvin was a little inclined to stoutness, due, he hoped, to his wife's cooking of which they were about to partake.

The passenger side of the limo's front seat was stacked with deli trays covered with clear plastic lids. As soon as all five were settled comfortably in the rear, Kelvin, plastering on an ingratiating smile like a game show host, began removing the tops and handing the trays to Elise, who passed them around.

"Deviled egg?" she said, offering a tray to Jonathan.

"Can't," he said, at the same time accepting a second flute of champagne from Arpad. "All that cholesterol."

"Hold it," she said. "I thought you were dying."

A pain, quick as a fish, darted through his chest: a silvery glint, always gliding silently deep in his gut, only occasionally flashing to the surface of his consciousness. "Oh yeah. It keeps slipping my mind."

He took an egg and popped it into his mouth. It tasted divine: a hyperbole his wife Sarah would use. Only this time it was oddly appropriate, even profound. The egg: promise of new life, except that this one had been tampered with by the devil. And it tasted, not hellish, but divine.

When everyone in the party held filled flutes, Arpad cleared his throat and said, "Perhaps we should *all* toast to living as though we are going to die."

"Hear, hear," said Kelvin, who stood at the open door with a raised glass.

Elise frowned at him. "Should you be drinking that? Aren't you supposed to drive?"

The mortician, who had just taken a healthy mouthful, swished it around in his cheeks and spat it onto the ground. "Just cleansing the breath," he said with a lame grin. "It makes a great gargle." With a martyred expression, he poured out the remains of his glass and dropped heavily into the driver's seat. Under his girth, the leather seat whooshed like a whoopee cushion.

The pane between front and back had been lowered so that the passengers could have free access to the food trays. Elise bent through the opening for refills, and at the sight of that perky little butt waving in their faces, all voices stilled, all mouths fell agape in silent appreciation until she backed down into her seat.

The limo slowly bore its great white burden off the shoulder and lumbered onto the highway and made a wide U-turn, heading south. As the old bus bumped onto the pavement and fishtailed wildly across the median, Jonathan fancied he heard a squawk or two. But he thought it wise not to mention it to Miguel, who had resumed an animated conversation with Hector in which Jonathan recognized the word "tequila."

They all settled back with barbecue ribs, while Arpad filled their glasses once more. Elise smacked on her fingers and glanced out the window. Through the tinted glass, the landscape appeared bleak and somber.

"Bugger!" she said. "Is this the promised land I've been trying so hard to reach?"

"All promised land is wilderness," Arpad said in the sober tone of a yogi. "Didn't you know that?"

"Wait!" Jonathan said. "That was deep! Who's got a pencil? I need to write some of this stuff down."

"Why?" Elise asked. "So you can look back over it in the years to come?"

Jonathan thought about it. He was used to cataloguing and filing, not memorizing. He said, "Pass me another deviled egg." While he waited, he sucked the grease from a rib and repeated to himself, *All promised land is wilderness.* But it seemed such a formless concept, and he knew that what is formless cannot be held onto, or committed to memory.

Miguel, who had ceased his dialogue with Hector and was listening intently, addressed Jonathan, then motioned for Elise to translate.

"He says the desert fills men's minds with visions. I'd say hallucinations," she said. "As far as I'm concerned, this has been the longest day on the face of the earth."

Food and drink were mellowing the crowd. A smile touched the corners of Arpad's mouth, and he said, with the intonation of a philosopher so that it was hard to tell whether he was serious or not, "Time is relative. We judge the degree of speed by the intensity of forgetting. Anyway, time is never an enemy to be conquered; it is a mystery to be contemplated, and it is circular, cyclical, not linear."

"Cool!" Elise nodded thoughtfully and folded her legs onto the seat Indian fashion. "I remember the Lao Tse quote about soft overcoming the hard and slow overcoming the fast."

Arpad leaned past Jonathan and freshened her drink, looking deep into her eyes. Jonathan might as well have been a post. Now Arpad's tone became hushed and conspiratorial. "If we remain together long enough in this car, our rhythms will become entrained. We will become in sync, like the tides, or atomic particles."

Jonathan recalled having read that pendulum clocks, placed side by side, will eventually begin to swing in unison, keeping time together. He would try to think about this later.

But not now. The rich food and drink was not setting well; suddenly he was very full and too warm. By the time the chocolate éclairs came around, he felt queasy and turned away, unable even to look at them. "I wish I had a glass of plain water," he said, stunned that his voice had grown weak again.

The others stopped talking and looked alarmed. Elise called to Kelvin, "He needs water, quick!"

Kelvin glanced in his rearview mirror. "What am I, the Ozarka man? I've already got her floorboarded. This is all she'll do. But we'll be in Sanderson any minute."

"Well, goose it some more!" Elise screamed.

Miguel, sitting on a jump seat, took one frightened look at Jonathan then slid onto the floor and, kneeling, began praying. He turned and pulled Hector down as well, and in unison the two rattled off some ritual prayer that Jonathan figured must be the Hail Mary. He hoped to heaven it worked—and quickly. He sank back, eyes fluttering, and willed himself not to pass out again.

As if Jonathan were nowhere around, Arpad said, "I knew this was crazy. I should never have agreed to it. I should've taken him directly back to San Antonio and flown him home, and to hell with the chickens and all the rest."

He whipped out a handkerchief and drenched it with champagne before handing it to Elise. She sat on her haunches beside Jonathan and bathed his forehead. It felt good. But his nausea was rising, warm and suffocating.

He said, "Do my neck."

"Huh?"

"My throat. Put it on my throat. I think I'm going to—"

"Oh my God, open the window!" she yelled. "He's going to hurl!"

They scrambled to get a window down, but it was too late. The contents of Jonathan's stomach spewed out in a wide arc, spraying them all. A large glob flew past Miguel's ear and attached itself to the back of Kelvin's neck, just above the collar of his black shantung jacket. Even as he wretched, Jonathan watched with fascination as the blob gradually slid down beneath Kelvin's collar and out of sight, leaving a red trail.

He hoped to God it was barbecue sauce, not blood.

As the ooze made its way down his back, Kelvin hit the brakes, and the trailing bus crashed against the rear of the limo. The collision threw Jonathan and the others off the seat. He found himself face-down on the floor, wallowing in his own vomit. If this were a heroic quest, he would have descended into Hades. Only there was no demon to grapple with, no antagonist to best. Life was nothing more than a series of mortifying, degrading anticlimaxes, gradually petering away into nothing.

27

While Kelvin surveyed the damage to the rear of the limo, Miguel and Hector leaped out and boarded the bus to right the crates and calm the birds. Elise and Arpad purged themselves and Jonathan of the more offensive chunks of recently tossed clabber, using champagne-soaked deli napkins and a T-shirt from Elise's backpack. With the excitement of the crash, Kelvin had apparently forgotten that he too wore bile down his back, and none of the others seemed inclined to remind him of it.

Arpad got out to look over the situation. With his assistance, punctuated by several "freakin' idiot"s, Kelvin gradually deduced a flaw in his tow engineering. He announced, loudly enough for those in both vehicles to hear, "Somebody's going to have to ride in the bus and work the freakin' brakes."

Elise was sent back to translate the message to Miguel and Hector, who between them decided that Miguel would sit behind the wheel. The party was not cheered by the prospect of a ninety-seven-year-old bus driver, so short that he could barely reach the pedals. But Hector's head still throbbed, only one eye was visible, and he was too full of pain-killer to be reliable.

Jonathan viewed the happenings as from a great distance. With all his soul he longed for a drink of water, and for water to wash the sticky champagne from his head and neck. He lay back, sucked dry of energy, and waited for Kelvin to get underway.

As soon as they were on the road again, Arpad said, "That settles it. When we get into Sanderson, we're going to ditch that bus, and Kelvin and I are taking you back to San Antonio. We'll pay someone else to haul the old man and his precious chickens the rest of the way."

Jonathan pushed himself up, ignoring the buzz circling in his head. He meant to yell, "No!" but it came out a ragged whisper. Then he fell back, depleted by the effort.

Arpad said, "The signed release be damned, chief. It won't matter a whit to you when you're gone."

Elise said, "Miguel has already promised to sign, but I don't think Jonathan cares about the release anymore. He just needs to get to Crystal City."

"For what reason? Surely there's no doctor there who—"

"To see *la curandera*," she said. She turned to Jonathan. "Am I right?"

Grateful for her perspicacity, Jonathan closed his eyes and nodded, no longer caring what Arpad might think about such a foolhardy venture. He could imagine his pilot's look of incredulity, if not outright disgust. He had long enjoyed Arpad's worshipful attitude, but now that would be gone forever. For Jonathan, forever probably wouldn't be much longer.

Elise went on. "Well, wouldn't you, if you were Jonathan? I mean, what has he got to lose now? He already looks like something materialized from ectoplasm."

Guida M. Jackson

She patted Jonathan's arm and snuggled against him, whispering into his ear. "Just kidding. And don't worry about me going to Uvalde. I'm going to stay right by your side from now on. After all, if I don't, who'll translate for you?"

Warmed by her sour-smelling closeness, even in his desiccated state, he saw seduction as a grand art in which prolonging for as long as possible a state of arousal would make the final culmination sheer unbearable bliss. He patted her knee and sighed acquiescence, although realizing the need to offer at least a token protest. "But your dad...."

"I can meet him later. Anyway, I may not like him as well as you. Maybe I'll just adopt *you* as my dad. You can't be more than a couple of years older than him."

Jonathan winced and opened his eyes to reality. "Oh great. I didn't need to hear *that.*"

She sat up and moved away. "Hey! *Surely* you didn't think that I meant that you and *I*—"

He batted her words aside. "No, no. Of course not. But to be turned down like a bedspread...."

"I mean, you're *married* and *old* and—man, get a reality check!"

"Yeah, yeah," he said wearily, shutting his eyes against her indignation. "I just did. In spades."

"I mean *look* at you! Your hairline's receding, and—"

Arpad, he of the great mane of black hair, cut in. "He gets the point. We all do."

She sank back and, suddenly appeasing, said, "Of *course* you are attractive, I didn't mean to imply....You're

215

not geezerish yet, not toad bait. You sort of have a decent physique—semi-tight abs and tush. You can probably still get it up once in a while, I bet."

Jonathan, eyes still closed, smiled to himself and thought about Sarah, who would doubtless disagree with her. Betts, on the other hand....Surely Betts wasn't faking.

"Anyway, you are *definitely* too young to flat-line it." She picked up his flaccid hand and squeezed it. He made no more effort to respond than a mummy trapped in its winding sheet.

Betts: he'd all but forgotten about her, as if the meager crumb of a voice-mail message he'd left on her pager would suffice to dismiss his obligation to her. He ought to do more, but what? Now he wondered why he had ever lusted after her. A week ago—or maybe only yesterday—he'd thought he couldn't do without her for more than a week or two at a time. Now he could scarcely recall her face. He could conjure up the feel of the luxuriant red hair that he used to love to bury his face in. By now it was probably dyed, if that mattered. Betts was nearly his age, so surely she didn't consider him old. Surely.

What had kept their passion alive for decades was its clandestine nature. If he'd married Betts, by now they'd be as stale as month-old bread. There was a lesson in there somewhere, but it was probably too late to learn it now.

As they reached Sanderson, Kelvin pulled into a service station so they could wash, and so that Jonathan could have the drink of water he craved. Arpad helped him to the men's room, even sponged him off. He drank eagerly, then motioned for Arpad to help him back to the limo. He must make every moment count. There was so much he must do, so much he wanted to understand.

"What you said about all promised land being wilderness…"

"Oh. Yes. Think about it." Arpad settled him on the back seat and, using paper towels from the rest room, continued to clean the interior. "We envision a city paved with gold, but when we arrive, there is nothing but uncharted land—potential, you might say. That is how it must be, for the promised land of one would not please anyone else. Even if there were a great city, it would never be the city of our dreams. It would be a different kind of wilderness: one just as fraught with danger and untamed forces. So we must create our own promised land from the wilderness at hand."

He left to deposit the towels in a trash receptacle, returning with an even larger stack from the rest room. Jonathan watched impassively as he worked, feeling only vaguely guilty about the mess he'd made. Something like an errant family pet, who'd made no-no on the carpet. Finally he said, "I thought you meant something different…about the wilderness."

Arpad stopped working, an amused light playing in his eyes. "Good point. You're thinking that all ascetics retire to the isolation of a barren wilderness to seek enlightenment, right?"

"Something like that."

"So there must be great value in the act of deliberate deprivation, in adapting oneself to the starkness rather than trying to change it. It bears thinking about."

Not that there would be time for thinking. Now that he had access to Arpad's battery, Jonathan asked for his briefcase containing his phone. He must try to reach Betts again and tell her goodbye, soften his earlier message left on her pager. He'd been too abrupt. What could he have been thinking, blurting out that he'd only been using her? Was that supposed to cause her to grieve for him when he was gone, to splash tears of remorse upon his coffin for not having treated him better? Lord, where was his high-priced image-builder when he needed him? He owed Betts an explanation, an elaboration, some embroidery work. That much, at least. Maybe he even owed her money.

In the past he had been careful never to leave his personal digital phone bill where Sarah might see it, and he had never called Betsy on his home lines. But if he died now before getting back, Sarah would find out, anyway. The rent on the New York *pied-a-terre* would come due and his secretary, who handled it instead of his business manager, would want to know what to do about it.

Now that he thought about it, there were a dozen loose ends concerning Betts that would surface when he died, things he might eventually have obliterated once the affair ran its course. Why hadn't he been more discreet all along? Had he deliberately meant to wound Sarah? With a deep pang of regret, he realized afresh how many ways he had used Betts, often feigning lust even to himself. It had been boring and pointless to a fault: his marriage, his career, his casual liaison, his whole life. Now he had so little time to make something, *anything* matter.

And yet, he still felt pleasantly unsettled by Elise's recent closeness, and it occurred to him that living in a constant state of arousal might be life-prolonging. He must endeavor to remember this. Maybe he ought to buy some magazines, or search the porn sites on his TylerGiz.

When Arpad left him alone in the limo, he pulled out the phone and stabbed at the number. As it rang, he muttered, "Not my life. Not my life. Boring, maybe, but not pointless. Please, God or Whoever, not pointless." He had to connect with people while there was still time. Become entrained, like menstruating women, or pendulum clocks. Use other people's rhythms to bolster his own failing ones. Connect.

He ought to find a way to make things right with good old Betts. She might feel better to know that she wasn't the only person he'd merely used. Using people was his life pattern. She mustn't take it personally. She would be crushed at first; it would break her heart. But in the end, possibly she would be able to see the wisdom of forgiving him, for her own peace of mind. They would connect again, on a strictly platonic plane, become synchronized....

The phone stopped ringing but Betts didn't answer. Instead he heard a vaguely familiar recorded voice: "Hi. We're not home. Leave a message."

But it wasn't Betts's voice; it was a man's.

28

The sun hung a few degrees above the earth's western rim as they began the journey's final leg, but for a brief period the afternoon heat, bearing into their tinted windows at a dead horizontal, penetrated their lurching crate with bullet intensity.

Because Miguel must direct them to his aunt's house, Arpad, looking sorely troubled, had relieved him behind the wheel of the bus, with Hector still riding co-pilot. In the limo, Miguel and Elise sat behind Kelvin while Jonathan lay across the back seat, holding the phone against his chest. Outside, the scorched landscape, gradually shrouded in long shadows, slipped by with unerring sameness.

Miguel said something to Jonathan which Elise translated. "He says Hector's worried about what's going to happen to him."

For the moment, Jonathan's voice was strong. "Barring his miraculous transmigration to Belize by Miguel's aunt, my pilot will fly him home. Tomorrow. Soon as they get back to San Antonio. Don't worry. There are ways. Arpad knows them all."

"Arpad's dragging ass as if his finger was on the doomsday button," she said. "I doubt he'll leave you alone that long."

"I won't be alone. I'll have Miguel and his aunt. And you."

But not, apparently, Betts, even if he lived. He'd recognized the voice on the recorder. It was Barry Lindsay, a client of hers he'd met at her apartment when he dropped by unexpectedly several weeks ago. Later he'd spotted them together in an out-of-the-way supper club Sarah wanted to try. Sarah insisted on speaking to Betts, whom she knew only slightly, and to Barry, whom she knew as well. How, he wasn't quite sure.

At the time Jonathan wondered if Sarah had somehow guessed about his own liaison with Betts and staged the meeting. He even wondered if Sarah had arranged to introduce the two. Such was the level of his own self-absorption, he decided.

Later, when Betts assured him the dinner with Barry was strictly business, he quickly dismissed it from his mind. So much for inflated egos. Now he felt cuckolded. Would she still have betrayed him if she knew he was dying? Or had she intuitively known and written him off weeks ago? He couldn't imagine what either his wife or his mistress was thinking. He didn't know either of them. No more than his father had known his mother.

He ought to call his father since his time was growing short, although now that he'd had a long drink of water, he felt much better. It was impossible to imagine that he wouldn't be around for a while to come. Still, there would be a certain morbid satisfaction in confronting his father with his imminent death. It was difficult to get the old man's attention on a subject other than money or mergers or deals.

He only regretted that he couldn't be there in person, to see his father's face when he delivered his farewell address. The elder Tyler would be flustered, mildly embarrassed, confronted with a situation over which he had no control. He would be terrified at the intimacy such a moment demanded. Jonathan would almost forfeit an hour of his life to witness his father's discomfort. But then, he himself lacked the courage for such a confrontation.

He glanced at his watch. His father might still be at his office, or at his club. Either way, the old man's long-time secretary Geneva would be able to reach him.

He should have the number of the private line in his phone, but since he did not, he had to endure the tedious voice mail announcing normal business hours. Damn. His own secretary usually got his father on the line. He didn't even know his extension. He punched in "Operator" and waited a long time, listening to Barry Manilow music, before being connected to Geneva.

The secretary's hurried tone gave him to understand it was after hours and she was just on her way out. "Did you forget? He and Mrs. Tyler won't be back in the country until the fifteenth."

Jonathan, feeling testy from the overload of Manilow music, was in no mood for niceties like apologizing for the inconvenience. "Check his itinerary and tell me where I can reach him," he said curtly.

He heard the briefest of exasperated sighs and imagined her slinging down her bag and rebooting her computer. After a few minutes she said almost triumphantly, "Afraid you're out of luck. They're in

Angkor Wat, but before you could get a call through, they'll be gone."

With a streak of perverse pleasure, he said, "Then deliver this message when he gets back: Your son tried *desperately* to reach you *one last time.*"

"Excuse me. Did you say 'desperately'?"

"That's right. 'Desperately' and 'one last time' are the operative words. Be sure to get them down."

He was almost chuckling as he hung up. His father would be wrung with guilt because his dying son had been desperate to talk to him. Doubtless this latest trip was another brainchild of Shirley, the new twinkie wife, the second young thing to hold the title since his mother's death. Shirley must lie awake at night figuring out new ways to spend the old man's money.

He glanced up. Elise, watching curiously, said, "Bad news?"

"You mean worse news than that I'm dying? No news at all would be more like it." He sat up and tossed the phone aside, motioning for her to move over beside him. He picked up her hand. It felt cool and smooth, like the skin of a newborn.

"Didn't you tell me that you started out majoring in psychology?" he said. "What do they teach you about people who are congenitally unlucky in love?"

She shrugged. "I wouldn't know. The whole therapy bit is barf-inducing. That's why I switched to physics. I only started out in psych because I was fascinated by the name psychology, a combination of 'psyche' and 'logos'. Literally it means 'the spoken word of the soul.' *Quel* perversion!"

Again, Jonathan's inclination was to reach for a pen and write it down. There was so much to remember now.

"What the ninnies taught was anything but the spoken word of *my* soul," she said, pale eyes glinting their disgust. "So I tried to block out the babble. Anyway, to answer your question, I don't believe anybody's unlucky. Not all of the time."

"So you're one of those perpetually sunny California girls. How do you reconcile all that positiveness with the physics principle of entropy? Doesn't everything ultimately self-destruct?" He was baiting her for no other reason than to grasp for a string of hope that had some scientific credence. Or maybe he was only trying to connect.

She answered immediately, as if it was a matter about which she'd already given considerable thought. "I'm not so sure. If entropy and disorder are really the rule, why does life flourish, y'know?"

He mused, almost gleeful, "True!" He thought for a while before continuing. "It does appear that living systems have kept *progressing* since the beginning. They've kept evolving into higher and more complex forms. The spiral of life definitely seems to be upward."

She turned toward the window, disengaging her hand from his and gesturing outside, where only a few desert flowers freckled the grey earth. "See what looks like bare land? I've read it used to be an ocean, filled with living things. Even now it's teeming with life, all kinds of critters and plants we can't see. But when it rains, within hours it'll be covered with blooming wildflowers that spring up out of nowhere."

He felt like a student in the presence of a much older, wiser person as she went on. "There's order out there. Living systems constantly renew themselves and regulate things to maintain their integrity. And that's not all."

He leaned in closer and again reached for her hand, drawing a circle in her palm with his finger. "What else?" It took all his will power to focus on her discourse.

"Even the most primitive forms are forever pushing against their own nature, trying to burst out, become something higher."

"But ultimately all is chaos," he insisted. "I've read—"

"Yeah, but chaos doesn't lead to the death of a system. What happens is, everything gets turbulent and breaks up, like a glacier calving into warm water. The system lets go of its old form and regroups so it can cope with a changed environment. Even though the glacier looks solid and sedentary, it's been inching along. Nature won't let anything stay in one place."

He listened in spite of himself. "It's all movement...."

She nodded. "All Shiva. Think of chaos as just the source of creativity."

As if a light bulb had come on, she sat up facing him and tucked her feet under her again. "Or—How about this? It's more that everything happens on the edge, you know, the threshold—just where order meets chaos. There's that tension there...."

She stopped and cackled. "Whoa. I'm in over my head. Sometimes I'm so smart I don't understand a word I'm saying."

But she couldn't seem to let it rest. She backpedaled. "It's more like, chaos is the artistic temperament of the gods."

"Is that what they teach in college these days?"

She shot him an angry grin. "You've got a smart mouth, Tyler."

In the silence that followed, she looked down at the phone. "Did you reach your party?"

"Not really." He thought about Sarah and picked up the phone again. Sarah: who would wear dark glasses to his funeral to hide a twinkle of glee. Maybe he would irritate her with the news that he wouldn't be coming back to the hospital, ever.

He speed-dialed his home and the houseman Peters answered. "She left less than an hour ago for Scottsdale. It was her week at the spa and she said she couldn't cancel because reservations were too hard to get. Do you have the number?"

From past experiences Jonathan knew that personal calls were discouraged at the spa that Sarah frequented, to lie in expensive mud and then get massaged with hot oil by an ex-Mr. Universe. A woman's first duty is to her masseur.

Anyway, he didn't actually want to talk to her. They had managed nicely for years dove-tailing their time at home so as to miss one another.

No wonder she had been so anxious for him to return to attend to domestic problems, so she could go off guilt-free and nuzzle a mud-covered dildo in the privacy of her own tub of goop.

Belatedly he thought about his two errant sons. "What about the boys? Did you get Chip out of the detention center?"

"It took some doing; they wanted to keep him overnight. But I managed to take care of it. He's in his room, online."

"Call him to the phone."

Peters hesitated. "It might be best to dial him direct. Master Chip gave me instructions never to speak to him again."

"Bull! Go tell him I said to pick up."

"He said he would break my fingers," Peters said. "If you haven't noticed, sir, Master Chip has grown into a strapping young man. He could do more than just break a bone or two."

And Sarah had gone off and left him. Doubtless she, too, was afraid of confrontation; lately Jonathan had to admit a reluctance to cross their younger son himself. There was an unpredictable edge about Chip that was intimidating. Well, later he'd call the boy. After he'd rehearsed what to say.

He changed the subject. "What about Whit? Where is he?"

The houseman cleared his throat. "I—ah—couldn't say, sir. He drove off yesterday with a group of friends and didn't come home. He left a number where he could be reached, but there's been a digital overload...."

Jonathan felt blood surge to the top of his head. With a curse, he cut the connection, rolled down the window and sent the phone sailing across the desert. "Screw the whole bunch of them. And screw progress! Progress and death—are they both inevitable?"

Elise gasped. "I sense we are getting a mite testy."

"I hate these damn digitals that let us keep constantly in touch! I hate technology. I hate my family. I hate my life!" Even as the words escaped his lips the truth struck him as awesome.

He looked at her, wide-eyed. "Did I just say that? But I *don't* hate *life*, just *my* life: the way it is." He was beginning to think that the whole first half of life is a gigantic mistake, as necessary as it is unavoidable. The task of the second half of life is to recover from that mistake. Only in his case....

"Whatever you give your attention to gives its attention to you," she said, grave and straight-faced as a sphinx.

"What's that supposed to mean?"

"Could be you're *willing* death as a way out, huh? Or not out, maybe: up. Maybe you're trying to find a way to reemerge in a form better suited to your environment.... Only you hate your environment, too. Right?"

He was still marveling at his blurted admission. Now a new insight surfaced. "I've heard that in quantum theory, when these 'new forms' or mutations appear, they do it all at once. One minute they're one way, then they vanish—they take a quantum leap—and reappear in their altered state."

"Something like that. Spooky, huh?"

"So when they disappear, during the leap, what actually happens to them? Are they in a sort of vacuum?"

She grinned and blew upward at a wisp of bangs. "You want me to give the vacuum a name, don't you? Like, the afterlife maybe?"

He felt insulted. She was trivializing his need to know. "I just want to understand where something is that's here one minute and then gone and then here again in a new form."

"Well…on a quantum level, there's a kind of sea of negative potential energy. That's the vacuum. Under certain conditions, particles can just pop into existence out of this void. And I guess they can just as easily pop back into it."

"Let me get this straight," he said. "If a particle can pop into being, it must have been *something* in the void, like an embryo or *something*."

"It wouldn't be a void if there were something in it."

Against all reason, he wanted something to be in the void.

"It was a virtual particle, like a pattern, maybe," she said. "In our so-called 'real' world we have all these electrons spinning around. That's what everything's made of: sort of spinning nothings, really."

She squeezed his thigh a couple of times. "You feel solid, but all you are is a lot of spinning energy."

"Some energy is more fetching than other energy," he said, warmed by her touch and, apparently, by her pheromones. He could feel himself swelling, coming to life. How long had it been since he had made love?

"And in their mirror world," she continued, ignoring the come-on, "the negative energy world, the vacuum, we have their soul mates, the virtual electrons that don't really exist, as we think of existing."

He doubted that he could extrapolate an ongoing life for himself out of quantum theory. But she seemed to read his mind.

"If we back off from this far enough, maybe the big bunch of spinning electrons that is Jonathan has a mirror image of virtual electrons in the vacuum, and that's what? Your soul? That's what you're thinking, isn't it?"

"Of course not!" But secretly he wondered if his death would be nothing more than popping back into a field of negative energy. He added, "They can't really know all this for certain."

"Who? The physicists? No way. All that quantum physics has proven is that we live in a world that's ultimately mysterious and unknowable."

It was not what he wanted to hear. If he was going to die, dammit, he wanted answers.

"Anyway," she went on, "it's impossible to know for sure what happens at the subatomic level. The observer, by the very act of observing, interferes with what he's trying to see. And more than that: he actually participates in creating what he observes. He changes the course of electrons by looking at them."

While they talked, the sun had set, and night gradually closed the limousine in an invisible void. Jonathan stared out into the blackness, wondering if the Ultimate Vacuum looked like this. "So everything comes from the invisible. It's the sole cause of that which is visible, you might say."

"Apparently," she said. "So we'd better trust the invisible above all else. Anyway, I have a theory: when we die, if we're good, we go to Oregon."

"And if we're bad?"

"Where else? Kansas."

He looked over Kelvin's shoulder at faint dots of light ahead. "What's that, Kelvin?"

"Crystal City, about ten minutes away. But Miguel says his aunt's place is some distance south of town. Better wind up all that philosophizing so the lady can translate his directions."

Kelvin paused, then added, "I've heard about that famous *curandera* all my born days. Never thought I'd actually see her with my own eyes. It's like getting to see Kalista Flockhart."

29

Arpad had developed the habit of glancing at his watch to check, not the hour, but the date. Soon hours would begin to matter again, but at the moment, his life and Jonathan's could be measured in days: three, four at the most. It seemed prudent to remind himself frequently.

From his position behind the wheel of the bus, he glared into the mirror at the reflection of Hector, who had complicated their lives and their deaths immeasurably. It appeared likely that Jonathan would require him to fly Hector back to Belize; he had indicated as much in a hurried aside earlier in the day.

That meant another revision in plans. Because of FAA regulations regarding sleep, even a turnaround flight would eat up a couple of days.

Then there was the matter of his co-pilot Wheeler, whom he couldn't take down with them to their deaths. Silently he cursed that bumbling sot Sonny Baldwin, whose hearse had disabled his plane. The little rented Cessna would have worked. He could have kamikazed into the desert with almost certain mortal results. Not as foolproof as a dive into the ocean, unless the plane exploded on impact, but it would have been over without all this.

233

Now, Wheeler's presence on the return flight to Boston precluded taking a detour due east from San Antonio for a dip into the Gulf of Mexico.

He sighed heavily. Dying was so much harder than most people imagined.

***

Over Miguel's protests—he was anxious to get his fighting cocks out of the bus—the group decided to stop for supper on the outskirts of Crystal City. Kelvin selected the restaurant on the basis of parking space for the limo and bus along a side street, under the crass eye of a street light swarming with suicidal flying insects.

"Hope everybody likes Tex-Mex," he said, switching off the ignition. "Wouldn't matter. I doubt if you'll find much else to eat in Crystal City."

"What about that billboard at the city limits?" Elise asked. "'Spinach capital of the world.'"

"Oh yeah. They're famous for having a statue of Popeye in the town square," Kelvin said.

Jonathan could scarcely conceal his disappointment. The name Crystal City had conjured up the Land of Oz or at the very least, Disney World. A place where magic was a matter of course. He must be even sicker than he realized. All he had seen was the admonishing finger of a lone church steeple that promised no miracles, no magic. Eternal damnation, more likely.

A gloomy Arpad appeared at the door to assist Jonathan. The South Texas night concentrated on a breath. Jonathan leaned heavily on Arpad and took

Elsie's arm as well as they headed for the entrance. His strength ebbed and surged. At the moment it had waned so as to make walking difficult. He was aware that in his stained unkempt clothing he did not cut a dashing figure. Maybe he would be denied admittance.

It was a somber group that shuffled into the restaurant, and the decor did nothing to cheer them. The ceiling was decorated with tiny twinkling Christmas lights and several badly faded piñatas shaped like of bulls or roosters. The menu was written on a blackboard on the back wall. They took a table for six; Jonathan and Miguel at each end with Arpad and Elise on either side of Jonathan and Hector and Kelvin next to Miguel. The juke box blared a hot throbbing song by Selena, so loud they had to shout to be heard. An elderly Hispanic waiter with a Bull Durham tab dangling from his shirt pocket took their drink orders: Coronas all around.

While they waited, Jonathan, as much to bolster Arpad's flagging spirits as to impart information, said to him, "It's also famous as the home of *la raza*. Ever hear of it?"

Arpad shrugged, disinterested, but Miguel perked up and nodded gravely. *"¡Sí! La raza unida."*

Jonathan explained. "A political action group. Pretty powerful at one time. I heard about it from Doss back in Roswell."

While their beer was being served, Miguel spoke rapidly. Elise translated, "He says it was formed by José Ángel Gutiérrez, a doctoral student in political science at UT. They began by literally taking over all this town's public offices in the seventies."

She laughed wryly. "Here's an anomaly: He says Gutiérrez's grandfather has a restaurant in Hebbronville called 'Frank's Place' where women aren't allowed to this day. They can buy enchiladas to go, but they can't eat there."

Kelvin lifted his mug in a toast. "Here's to keepin' 'em barefoot and pregnant." He leaned over to Elise, sitting beside him. "Just kiddin', doll face." In turn, she regarded him as if he were a scabrous lesion on someone's backside.

Jonathan glanced at Hector, sitting on Arpad's left. He hadn't said a word since he got off the bus, hadn't even evinced interest when Miguel spoke. He looked peaked and blotchy, and his forehead bandage had begun to seep.

"You okay, Hector?" he asked.

Hector shrugged. "*Sí.*" But he didn't say it with conviction. It was always problematic as to how much English he understood.

Arpad, looking particularly frazzled, as if he had been wrestling with a grave decision, said, "Maybe we ought to just get a room for the night."

"No!" Hector said, then lapsed into Spanish.

"He wants to see *la curandera* tonight," Elise said. "To find out how his mother is."

Jonathan wanted no one to interfere with his own interview with Miguel's aunt. "Remind him he'll be with his mother tomorrow. Day after that at the latest."

"Not really," she said. "It's a long walk to his village in the Maya mountains from Belize City. Hector says he lives down south and inland, miles from even a dirt road. Anyhow, if your mom was sick, you'd want to find out about her soon as possible."

Jonathan conceded, then marveled at the faith they had all come to place in the powers of the ancient healer. He glanced from the battered Hector back to Arpad, who must be hiding his shoulder pain with super human will power. As the music changed to a melancholy number that at least allowed them to talk without shouting, he said to Arpad, "But your point is well taken about spending the night here before going on. You've both had enough trauma for one day."

Kelvin half rose from his chair. "Hey! I oughtta have some by-damn say about this. *I'm* the one providing the transportation—oh and don't forget all that Rotarian food. I'll have a hard enough time explaining that to the wife without having to explain not coming home tonight."

Elise gave him a punishing nudge with her elbow. "Ten minutes ago you were slobbering all over yourself about getting to see *la curandera*."

"Yeah, *see* her, sure. I'd like to watch her do just one little miracle—transport the half-breed back to Central America or heal Mr. Tyler there—if she can really live up to her reputation. But that oughtn't to take all night. We could still get on the road by about eight."

Absently Arpad dipped a tostada into the salsa and spoke as if he were talking to himself. "The difficult may take only a short while, but the impossible may take a little longer."

Elise leaned over to whisper to Jonathan. "Arpad's a dish. Unattached?" To which Jonathan only frowned.

The waiter brought six Tampico Dinners. Jonathan examined his plate and decided that Fate had decreed that he must raise his lifelong cholesterol titer to astronomical heights before he died. The marvel was that he felt like eating at all.

Kelvin drained his mug and waved it to the waiter for a refill. "And another thing," he said. "I'm needed back at the mortuary. Somebody might of died by now."

Arpad glowered at him. "Then too, you might just want to engage an attorney, on behalf of that sorry-ass brother who crashed into my plane and dislocated my shoulder."

Kelvin stuck his finger into his guacamole and smiled wanly. "How's your beer holding out, ole buddy?" He called over his shoulder to the waiter. "Make that two Coronas…*dos*."

Miguel, who had begun shoveling in the food without let-up, glanced around and commanded, "*Cóman*." He circled his fork around the table. "*Todo*. Eat."

"He's right," Elise said. "We need to quit yapping and get on with it. His aunt's an old woman. She probably crashes by sundown." She muttered close to Jonathan's ear, "Here's a happy thought: what if the old gal refuses to take him in?"

"Don't even think about it," Jonathan growled.

"Or the birds? What if she balks at having them on the place? I know *I* sure as hell would."

"You take away his birds, he goes, too," he said. "But don't forget, they're a source of revenue. They're rent money."

She shuddered. "I've never seen a cock fight. It must be bloody awful." The thought appeared to take her appetite. She put down her fork, pushed her plate away and dabbed her napkin to her lips. "But as for *la curandera*, I'd like to get a crack at her, myself. Just for a minute."

"What for?"

"Advice, I guess. On what a twenty-two-year-old says on meeting her father the first time."

He reached for her hand and squeezed. "You'll be fine. Who wouldn't be glad to see you?"

"Just the same, the closer I get to Uvalde, the longer I want to postpone it. Don't know why I thought this was such a hot idea, except that I'm a homeless waif. Maybe I should ask *la curandera* how old you can be and still be considered a waif." She tried to remove her hand from beneath his, but he held tight.

He said, "Let's look at it rationally. What's the worst that can happen?"

Her small face grew pinched as she stared off beyond him and tried to imagine. "He could slam the door on me, not acknowledge me at all."

"And that would hurt? Be honest, now."

"Of course it would hurt. To be rejected?"

"By someone you've never met? How can he hurt you?"

The pale eyes filled with sudden tears. "How could you ever understand? You've always had someone to belong to."

He pressed her hand one more time, then let go. "Maybe I understand better than you realize."

Why, considering how little people seemed to care, was he so anxious to preserve his worthless life? Maybe *la curandera* would have the answer to the riddle of his misery. She could possibly either give him a reason to live or a reason to die.

With some misgiving, he stood unsteadily and looked around the table. "Seems we're all agreed about seeing *la curandera* tonight. So let's do it. Some of us are not getting any younger."

Or older, he thought with a thrusting pang of sorrow.

30

Miguel threw a fatherly arm around Hector's shoulder as he headed toward the bus. "You gonna be okay with me going in the limo, *amigo*, so I can show them the way?"

Hector gave a disconsolate shrug. Miguel understood. So much was riding on *la curandera,* who was by now very ancient. Hector probably had grave doubts about her powers.

As they paused at the foot of the bus steps, Miguel cast a swift sidelong glance at the young alien, whose own eyes focused on the ground. "Don't worry, man. She'll help you."

"But she maybe cannot help my *madre*," Hector said. "Not if *Mamá* has *susto.*"

Susto. Miguel sucked in his breath. Separation of soul from body. Certain death. He mumbled, "No, man. She couldn't have *susto.*" But he didn't sound convincing, even to himself.

"A fortune teller in Hobbs told me that what I learned as a *chico* is true: a mother is connected to her son for her whole life by his umbilical cord that she buries in her back yard. If he leaves home and don't come back for a long time, she will get *susto.*" Hector swiped his nose on his sleeve and looked away.

Miguel had no wish to embarrass him. "Wait to see what *Tía Carlota* says." He clapped the boy on the back and turned toward the limo, leaving Hector to board the bus.

Miguel lingered beside the limo door, waiting for the others. He surveyed the familiar landscape with the same disinterest he'd felt toward the grim surroundings of the New Mexico gravel pit. His own reaction, or lack of it, surprised and dismayed him. He had expected, had hoped, that the torpor that had all but sucked the life from him, that had grown like a tapeworm in his bowels for years now, would vanish once he returned home. But now it occurred to him that Hector may have named *his* malady. Except for his nephew Ramón and his beloved fighting *gallos*, he had lost all connection to earth besides *Tía Carlota*. Soon she, too, would be gone. With no tether, and not a single cause to believe in, to work for, there was nothing to hold him.

Susto. If he had *susto*, he might as well lie down and die this night. But he was not prepared.

He could not remember the last time he had been to Confession. He should confess what a poor family man, bad provider, he had been. It shouldn't happen this way, but he had lived too long already. On his death bed, he should be surrounded by his sons, with a circle of grieving tear-streaked women standing in the background while the priest administered last rites.

But he had outlived the women, most likely, and he had never known his children. Ramón had been more of a son than any of his real sons, and now maybe Ramón would never return to him. No brothers or even sisters or daughters remained. There once had been some cousins down the road from *Tía Carlota*'s house, but maybe they, too, had died by now. There would no one to mourn him.

Yet even that knowledge failed to stir him. His heart had grown hard as a mesquite knot. He felt...detached: a sure sign of *susto*.

As they neared the house of *Tía Carlota*, Jonathan heard Kelvin mutter, "Whoa! This is spooky."

Jonathan and Elise leaned forward and tried to see. Miguel, who had moved into the front beside Kelvin, was pointing and talking with a new animation.

Kelvin said, "It's like she knew we were coming."

Through a thicket of mesquite, a small frame house hove into view, caught in the headlights. A dim bulb in the sagging porch ceiling illuminated the silvery head of an ancient diminutive woman waiting, hands folded in an implacable bow before her.

As soon as Kelvin maneuvered the narrow approach and pulled to a stop with his trailing burden, Miguel jumped out. The old woman held out her arms as he called, "*¡Tía! ¡Estoy a casa!*"

While they embraced, Miguel's aunt rattled off a wispy-voiced greeting, which Elise, head stuck out the window so as to hear, tried to translate. "She's been watching for us for hours."

"In-by-God-credible!" Kelvin said.

The healer listened with intense concentration as Miguel apparently described the various reasons that they had all come. Finally she interrupted and began issuing orders, pointing toward the side lot where an old shed leaned inside a chicken-wire pen.

Miguel trotted back to the limo and pulled the much-creased release form from his pocket, handing it to Jonathan through the window. He spoke to Elise, then headed off down the road.

Jonathan said, "Now where in hell is he going?"

"Apparently a cousin lives in the nearest house down the way. He's going to get help unloading the chickens."

La curandera beckoned toward them and called in perfect English, "Come in, come in."

They climbed out slowly. Even as his physical strength surged, Jonathan felt sudden reluctance, and he sensed shyness in the others as well. Hector hung back behind them as Jonathan pushed Kelvin into the front. "Well, go on; you were so anxious to come out here and see a miracle."

La curandera's chin jerked up and he wondered if she had heard him and presumed that he was making light of her abilities. To allay this impression, he tottered forward and put on his most gallant smile. He caught her flickering sweep of his tremoring frame before the intense black bean gaze locked onto his.

"*Señora Rulfo?* I'm Jonathan Tyler. This is Elise Harwood, Arpad Patel, and Kelvin Baldwin. And back there, Hector Mendoza."

In grave silence she shook hands all around, the flesh on her frail fingers so thin it was almost transparent. Now that they were closer, Jonathan realized that she was so stooped with age that her chin barely came up to his belt buckle. Somehow he had pictured a grand virago, larger than life. Still, about her clung an imperious air that commanded respect and made her appear much taller.

When the company parted so that Hector could step through, her unfathomable obsidian eyes suddenly gleamed with pleasure. She held onto his hand and pulled him toward the screen door, speaking to him in clipped, staccato phrases to which he answered by animated bobbing and, "*¡Sí! ¡Sí!*"

At the doorway she waited, holding open the screen until Arpad caught it. Her tone was cordial but dictatorial. "You may wait here on the porch or come inside. The boy will be first."

From behind Jonathan, Kelvin hissed, "Push on. I didn't come all this way out to this roach trap to wait outside in the dark and get dive-bombed by friggin' June bugs and eaten alive by mosquitoes big as warthogs."

They filed past Arpad into the gloom of a small front room, heady with incense and furnished with two red upholstered chairs and a sofa, all with dark carved wooden backs and arms, probably brought in from Mexico. They didn't look terribly comfortable. Jonathan took one of the chairs, Kelvin the other. Elise and Arpad sat on the sofa. The room was lit by an overhead fixture designed for three bulbs. It held one.

La curandera led Hector through the opening into what had once been a dining room. The space was barely more than an alcove, and the only light came from several candles set about the room. The table was strewn with bottles, incense burners, candles, and a crystal ball. High on the wall facing the living room hung a crucifix, and below it, on a carved shelf, stood a small statue of the Virgin Mary. The corners of the shelf were fitted with glass votive holders, where candles flickered unsteadily until the group had settled down. At the end of the room, only partially visible from where Jonathan sat, loomed a massive dark buffet, littered with feathers and an unending assortment of bottles. The room seemed crammed with furniture and imbedded with ritual unyielding as a hinge into a tomb.

La curandera pointed to a chair at the side of the table, indicating that Hector should turn it sideways. With considerable effort, she dragged the large arm chair from the end and placed it directly in front of him so that when she sat, their knees almost met. With one hand on the back of his neck, she drew his head forward until his bandaged forehead touched hers. Hector's eyes were wide with fright until she began singing a slow droning incantation as old as *Chichén Itzá* itself. They all watched his lids suddenly drop shut as if he had fallen into a coma. Somewhere in another room a clock made small, steady notches in the quiet as Jonathan held his breath.

When she had finished, released her hold on his neck and moved back, he slumped forward. Gently she guided his body, turning it so that his head rested against the tabletop. She resumed humming softly as she lit a candle under a tiny porcelain-clad pot, into which she put pinches of herbs from several of the bottles. As the dried leaves began to heat, their combined odor turned the air acrid. She monitored the small pot closely, shaking it like a popcorn pan, then flipping its contents like a flapjack. Finally, satisfied, she blew out the candle and poured the warmed herbs into what appeared to be a rehabilitated Bull Durham sack taken from the folds of her dress.

As if on signal, Hector raised his head. *La curandera* took his hand and curled his fingers around the bag, speaking earnestly, imparting, Jonathan guessed, instructions. Elise confirmed this, whispering, "Medicine for his mom."

When they had finished, Hector, still dazed, came through and stumbled out the screen door, mumbling something to Elise as he passed. She said, "He wants to be alone for a while."

At the sound of Elise's voice, the old woman's attention shifted to her. Without rising, she lifted one finger. "The young lady will be next."

Jonathan disguised his disappointment and sent Elise a high sign as she walked uncertainly into the alcove and toward the place vacated by Hector. But *la curandera* indicated the chair on the opposite side of the table, facing Jonathan. Good. He could watch her reaction.

Without speaking, the healer placed both palms on Elsie's forehead for several minutes. Then she moved them to envelop the crystal ball as she began to sing in some language that certainly was not Spanish, Jonathan could tell from the puzzled expression on Elise's face. Kelvin shot him a look that plainly said, What a crock of shit. Jonathan cut his glance to Arpad long enough to see his pilot staring into the darkened room, spellbound.

At length *la curandera* lifted her gaze from the globe, which Jonathan fancied seemed to glow for a moment. But that was surely his imagination. When she spoke, he had to strain to hear.

"You are taking a great step. It is a right thing to know one's ancestors—and you have many, still living. Do not neglect a single one—grandparent, aunt, uncle, cousin, your own offspring. Someday many will cross over ahead of you and will be your protection and guidance. So your fear should be forgotten. You will be made whole by knowing them."

Elise's lips parted in a dry smile. "So you're saying my dad'll welcome me into the family."

Tía Carlota inclined her head to one side. "Do not forget your mother also has family. You are on the verge of finding great love. Do not delay accepting it. Tomorrow you must go."

Again Jonathan felt disappointment. He harbored a secret hope that Elise would stay with him until Arpad returned from Belize.

As Elise returned to the front room, Jonathan rose, expecting to be summoned. But the old woman said sharply, "No! The dark young man will be next."

Stunned, Arpad looked up questioningly. "Me?"

"But he's not—" Jonathan began.

"He will be next." The firm tone left no room for argument.

Arpad shrugged in apology to Jonathan, got up and went into the alcove, dragging his club foot, approaching the table as if it were the gallows.

31

Jonathan took Arpad's place on the couch beside Elise. She squeezed his arm, whispering, "Did you hear? I've been worrying for nothing." He tried to hide his dejection but she squeezed harder. "Anyway, you don't need me to interpret after all. Who'd ever dream she'd speak perfect English?"

There was no time to say more. They strained forward to hear what the healer would tell Arpad as she took his palms in hers. But the sharpness of her tone took them by surprise.

"Pah! You are a fraud! You lie even to yourself! Don't you know that will make you sick?"

The pilot pulled back as if slapped, but she held on, speaking more gently but no less forcefully. "There is within you a core that must be honored. You cannot ignore it. If you try, it will kill you. So you have no choice."

Arpad answered with reverence, his voice low and earnest. "I do not understand, Little Mother. How do I lie to myself?"

"You know the answer perfectly well. You pretend that roots do not matter and yet you think of little else. Am I right?"

There was a long silence, while Arpad squirmed. Finally he mumbled, "One doesn't like to admit a painful truth. I was born in America. At birth I was abandoned in a Boston dumpster."

A sharp gasp escaped Elise's lips, but Jonathan pressed her knee hard, a signal to keep quiet.

"Then you are the most fortunate of men," *la curandera* said.

Arpad stared at her dumbly, so she went on. "Your blessed mother, although very poor and probably very young, carried you to term, possibly at a threat to her own life."

"Then threw me away like the garbage." The bitter words cut the air like a knife.

"Have you considered that in her culture she might have believed that she was sending you to a better world? One that did not include poverty, starvation, and possibly physical abuse?"

Arpad said nothing. *La curandera* clapped the elfin hands in delight. "So! We celebrate, eh? The gods smiled on you and gave you a fine life on this earth in spite of everything. So you have much to honor your mother for."

"Better that I honor the one who has given me all that I have," he said, turning to indicate Jonathan.

La curandera refused to be diverted. "What have you done with this life you have been granted? What has been your aim?"

Arpad's handsome face creased in thought, as if giving the wrong answer might again incur the healer's wrath. He seemed to be casting about for the truth. Then he straightened as if a light had come on. "To make a name for myself."

"Ah. So you have made a name for yourself." She raised her arms as if indicating a multitude. "Everyone knows who you are."

"It's not like that," he said lamely. "It was also to make enough money to support—something...." He waited, but she didn't reply, as if expecting more. If he thought she would permit less than a full disclosure, it was obvious that he was mistaken.

After a long awkward pause, he blurted, "Ever since I was a boy, I've researched in the library and online, inventing my likely heritage. A significant number of Boston East Indians originated in the same poor section of India. In my mind, at least, I'm convinced that is where my forebears came from."

She gave a knowing nod. "And if you are correct, you may have many relatives there."

His enthusiasm was growing. "Although many have been forced to leave India, a surprising number remain."

"Why is this surprising? It is their home."

"It's a very poor desert area, you see." He cleared his throat as if to hide embarrassment. "I've often thought of supporting some of the poorest."

He glanced sheepishly at Jonathan as he admitted, "In fact, I already do, to a modest extent. I...answered an ad. I help support a family in India."

Elise leaned over and whispered in Jonathan's ear, "Better give that man a raise."

La curandera seemed to understand. "And by supporting them, you have made them your family. They know your name, they revere you, they're beholden to you as their benefactor."

When he didn't deny it, she went on. "They belong to you, so to speak. Tell me: how long has this family lived on the desert?"

"They have always lived there, I'm sure."

"And before you came along, who supported them?"

He couldn't answer.

"Would it be likely that in the desert country of your mother's birth, or her mother's, she could walk a hundred miles in any direction and find a bed to sleep in? Why? Because they were all of one family, all kin?"

"I suppose...."

"And if you die tomorrow, will life change for your adopted family? Will they leave that place? Will they remember you?"

He hunched his shoulders in a show of defeat. "You've made your point, Little Mother."

"Not quite. We are always blessed when we give, but we must examine our motives. You do not give out of compassion for their great need, but out of your own need to 'make a name for yourself'. The greatest happiness comes from giving with no expectation of return, but simply for the joy of sharing."

"You make my motives sound petty," he said. "I am chastised. But I was deceiving myself."

She got up and shuffled to the moldering buffet, wrenching open the top drawer which stuck as if unwilling to yield up its contents. From where Jonathan sat, it appeared that she took out a large Irish potato, but when she placed it before Arpad, it hit the table with a thud. "Keep this," she said.

Arpad stared at it. "A river rock?"

La curandera resumed her seat. "Here is a forgotten fact: you may lie to others, you may even lie to yourself, but you cannot lie to a stone. Speak to it and see for yourself that a stone demands the truth, the simple truth. Whenever you are in doubt about a course of action, look at the stone and you will know your true motives. If you are a praying man, remember that God works only in truth."

Arpad cupped his hands around his treasure. "Thank you. I am humbled by this great gift."

"Ah! So now we can begin." After a moment's meditation, she clamped her palms to his forehead as she had done with Elise. Soon she again stared into the crystal, singing a high nasal evocation. But with an abrupt motion of her head upward, she broke off. "There is something more, something you are planning? Would you like to tell me about it?"

He shifted in obvious discomfort. "It's—a—surprise."

"One that will not interfere with your destiny, I hope?"

At the mention of the word "destiny," Jonathan leaned forward to hear Arpad's answer: "My destiny?"

"To know your family, *señor.*"

"But I can't *really* ever find my true family."

"Did I say 'find'? Listen carefully. You must allow nothing to interfere with your destiny, do you hear me? Nothing."

Arpad appeared deeply disturbed, but she went on with a smile. "Your salvation is close at hand…within the year. It lies in surrounding yourself with relatives."

Jonathan had visions of a stream of sari- and loincloth-clad peasants descending on his pilot's simple apartment, straight out of steerage from India.

Apparently Arpad had a similar image. His features clouded with alarm. "No! I couldn't—"

"If you are wise, you will not fight it, else the core of you eats away at you and you die. But not the kind of death you would choose." With that, she rose, a signal that he was dismissed.

Arpad returned, cradling his rock, a troubled moue darkening the perfect Aryan features. He sank into a chair, head bowed.

This time Jonathan did not rise but waited to be invited. Instead, the old woman turned to Kelvin and said, "You wanted to see a miracle?"

Kelvin bolted to his feet but recovered his composure and sauntered into the alcove, a swagger announcing his intention to control the interview. "I wouldn't mind seeing a real miracle, lady. But so far—"

"Sit," she commanded, then folded her bird-like hands on the table and continued in a more convivial tone. "So you drove the big automobile, eh? Are the windows all tinted?"

"All but the windshield. By law we're not allowed to have—"

"You watched the road and the landscape carefully?"

When he didn't answer, she said, "Most beautiful sunset today, eh? Pink and purple and orange covering the whole sky...."

He shrugged. "I guess. I was busy driving."

Jonathan could see what was coming. He sent Kelvin a silent message: Man, when you're in a hole, stop digging.

Before Kelvin could finish, she leaped to her feet and slapped him hard across the cheek. *"¡Idiota!* A once-in-a-lifetime miracle happens before your eyes and you do not even notice! Pah! Enough of you! I don't waste time on imbeciles."

She pointed an imperious finger at the door and Kelvin, like a castigated schoolboy, slunk across the room without looking up.

Jonathan's pulse quickened as she fixed her gaze upon him, at long last. "And now for the gentleman who claims to be dying—the one I first mistook for Ramón."

This was news to him; perhaps a resemblance to the cave-in victim would be in his favor. As he rose, she raised a warding hand. "Your case is very special, *señor*, requiring that I burn the fires of evocation all night. At dawn I will read the embers, then go into a trance to communicate with my sacred ancestors. Then I will be ready to speak to you. Come back at noon tomorrow."

***

Hector, Guayo Cutzel, wandered far from the lights of the house so that he could see the stars in the wide black sky, the same stars that shone upon his village in Belize. It had been a mystical experience and yet it had been real: he *had* traveled to his village, tethered to his body by a silvery cord; *had* comforted his squat little mother and his wife Chacach with the promise that he would soon be there in person.

La curandera had her reasons for not transporting him home immediately. We are all connected, she'd said. Your destiny is entwined with those who will deliver you to your homeland. If I intervene, the fate of the others will not unfold as it is meant.

Patience, she told him. And faith. I will prepare a mixture that can be brewed for tea to banish your mother's *susto*.

Only a powerful *curandera* could do such a thing.

The sight of his womenfolk struck with the force of a lightning jolt. When he left Belize, he soon learned to thrust them from his thoughts so as to bear the pain of separation. Proof that his recent visit to them was real and not merely a clever trick of *la curandera*'s lay in the thudding of his heart when he saw the face of his dear *mamacita*. And in the pull of his groin when he gazed on the rump of his beloved Cacach, bent over her kettle as she was when the sight first stirred his juices.

Chacach was an old-fashioned girl, taught by long tradition to kneel and present her backside when he wished to satisfy his needs. She was still a child when he first detected the woman-odor about her. It seemed a crime to violate one so young, so he had claimed her in marriage. How could he have left her so soon?

During his long sojourn north, he had seldom succumbed to his manly urges, for warring in his belly were the customs of his ancestors and the admonishments against them by the Catholic priests. Finally, when he could bear the torment no longer, he had knelt in the confessional in a vast Juarez cathedral and revealed his few indiscretions.

The priest had been broad-minded. Far better that you relieve your blood's heat while you are alone in your room than that you commit adultery, he said. Such a suggestion shocked Guayo Cutzel, whose tribe taught that a man's seed must never be wasted. Even so, he had spilled much outside the womb. Sometimes demons came, dancing through his dreams with their throbbing, insistent passion, and when he woke, the sticky evidence of his fantasies dampened his bed. Why, oh why had he ever left home?

The creak of a screen door returned him to the present. The driver Kelvin was briefly illuminated by the porch bulb before he disappeared into the darkness. Hector saw an instant's light within the limo, then the beam of a flashlight, which soon vanished underneath the vehicle. Kelvin must be trying to disconnect the tow chain, meaning they would soon be leaving.

With soaring spirits, Hector went in search of Miguel, to tell him goodbye and—no, he could not share his recent soul-journey home with anyone; it was too sacred. But there was more that he must say. Although he was not an eloquent man, he must pour from his full heart his gratitude to Miguel for sponsoring him, for persuading the a*nglo* to bring him here to see the great *curandera* and afterward to fly him home to Belize.

Voices approached from the road; he recognized one as Miguel's. Concealed in the shadows of mesquite, he waited by the roadside until three men passed. Then he whispered, "Miguel!"

The old man turned aside, motioning for the others to go on to the house. Hector waited until they were out of earshot to emerge. He did not feel like making small talk with strangers.

Miguel hadn't said a word, but Hector knew what he was waiting to hear. "Your aunt is the greatest *curandera* in all of the north," he said, and he heard Miguel's breath expel.

"So," Miguel said. "So."

Hector shifted, then motioned toward the car. "The driver is taking off the tow chain. We must be getting ready to go."

Miguel grunted, then he too pointed to the vehicles. "My relatives are going to unload the *gallos*. One is a cousin; the other is his son."

"Ah." Hector did not know what to say next.

"A strong boy," Miguel added, then they both fell silent.

Finally Hector blurted, "I could have killed the *anglo* when I first got on the bus."

"I know." Miguel sounded grave.

"But you hit me over the head with the *gallo* crate." Hector said it with a chuckle, which set Miguel chuckling, too. Soon they were laughing out loud.

The tension broken, they grasped each other like two old comrades and started for the chicken yard.

32

Jonathan stood in the motel shower and willed the water jets to wash away his crippling despond, while in his bedroom, Arpad and Kelvin waited for his decision as to whether they should go on to San Antonio the following morning or stay in Crystal City.

Thirty-six hours ago, Jonathan was a happy man, or so he now imagined. But since that on-board phone call from Dr. Allman, he had suffered more hardship than he had endured in all of the rest of his life. It was as if the Fates had belatedly noticed he hadn't experienced enough bleakness, had missed the natural pulse between light and dark, and were determined to even the score before he died. He had spent a miserable, hungry day waiting in a dilapidated trailer at the gravel pit, endured a punishing ride with a whole flock of smelly, squawking cocks in an un-air conditioned bus with no shocks. He had been threatened with a knife, fed chicken water, treated by a vet like a wounded prairie rat, had shared a desk-top bed—but not the chair pad—with a hi-jacker. He had been starved, dehydrated, heat-stroked, nauseated. He had been ignored by his family and abandoned by his lover. Most significant: he had been condemned to extinction by the most capable and expensive medical team money could buy. No amount of water, not even baptism, could dispel all that. Apparently it was his due, but it still wasn't enough.

He turned off the shower and took a cautious step onto the tile floor. Arpad, who had taken the adjoining motel room, hadn't wanted to leave him to bathe unattended, but Jonathan insisted, saying the day he couldn't take care of himself was the day they could shoot him in the crotch.

Arpad stood by the open door leading to his room while Kelvin lounged on the end of the bed. The room smelled of ancient dust-weighted carpet. Jonathan, wearing the terry robe Arpad had bought for him at Wal-Mart, looked from one to the other and said, "I've made up my mind. I want you to go on tomorrow as planned." He didn't expect them to understand, but he added, "This is my last shot. I *have* to take this seriously. I don't want an audience watching from that old woman's front room while I make a fool of myself."

Arpad walked over and touched his arm lightly with a fist. "I could take you out there, then come back for you later. We could wait here at the motel. I'd feel much better about it."

"No. Hector's mother is ill. He needs to get back to Belize in a hurry with the medicine *la curandera* gave him—"

Kelvin broke in with a whine. "I need to get back home. Don't forget that." But Arpad fixed him a glare that would fry a rasher of bacon and he shrugged. "Then again a few more hours wouldn't matter, I guess."

Arpad said, "I'd feel better if Elise was staying with you."

So would I, Jonathan thought. But he got into bed and said, "Quit trying to mother-hen me. It doesn't become you. Go pet your rock. And close the door on your way out."

Arpad sighed his resignation. "I'll arrange some sort of transportation for you in the morning. And I'll get you a new cell phone before we leave."

Kelvin said his goodnights and left, promising to have the limo gassed and ready to roll by nine o'clock the following morning. Arpad headed for his room and had almost closed the door when Jonathan thought of something else.

"What *la curandera* said about you going back to India—think you'll take her advice? I mean, I could really die and you'd be left without a job."

"She didn't tell me to go back. She said to surround myself with relatives. I could bring them all over here, if I could locate them. I took her to mean that I should try to find them. But even then, they might not want to come."

Jonathan was puzzled. "Why wouldn't they want to leave such a desolate place?"

Arpad smiled and shook his head. "You still don't understand roots and tradition, do you? There are things more important, more real than creature comforts...Anyway, I wouldn't do anything unless you..."

Say it, Jonathan thought. *...Unless you die.*

"...didn't need me anymore."

A discrete tap on Jonathan's door brought Arpad back into the room. "I'll get it."

He opened the door to Elise, who glanced from one to the other and said, "Hope I'm not busting up a twosome here."

Arpad said, "Come in. I was just leaving."

Jonathan didn't even attempt to sit up. He wasn't dressed for receiving company and besides, he was dying. Surely that carried some perquisites. He pulled the covers higher and said, "What's up?"

She waited until Arpad had left the room then plopped down beside him. Her face was freshly scrubbed and her hair hung in damp strings that smelled of lilac soap. "So what's the verdict? We leaving or staying?"

"Leaving. I'm a big boy."

"Oh sure. Now's the time to go stoic. Well, for what it's worth, I'm feeling guilty about going."

"Don't. I'll be fine," he lied.

"I mean, you rescued me from the highway, you're delivering me to my dad's door...well, you're *causing* me to be delivered. Here you had this whole carload of people that needed to belong to somebody, and you're responsible for every single one of them getting connected with somebody who loves them—I mean, it's ironic, isn't it? You can't seem to connect with anybody."

Jonathan eyes suddenly stung and he looked away. He couldn't have put it better himself. He swallowed a couple of times but still was unable to answer. She crawled up beside him and lay on his pillow, flinging an arm across him.

"You know, you really don't have to be brave. What good does it do?"

He choked, determined to maintain composure. Good lord, the final degradation: breaking down in front of a mere girl. Finally he was able to say, "At least I'd like to die with dignity."

"Oh there you go! Do you get extra points for that?"

"Did you inherit that smart mouth from your mother?"

"Okay. So you want to die with dignity. A dying man ought to get at least *one* thing he wants. But hell, I don't want to die with dignity! I plan to go out kicking and screaming. I don't want to go, and there'd be no use pretending it's okay by me."

She squeezed him across the chest and whispered into his ear, giving rise to unbidden but welcomed libidinous urges. "Tell the truth: don't you just want to tear off a huge tantrum?"

He couldn't resist saying, "Blow in my ear again and that's not the only thing I'll think about tearing off."

She pinched his side, but not hard. "Behave, or I won't stay with you tonight."

At once he was alive. "You'd *sleep* with me?"

"Well...I figure I owe you that much. I can't let you stay here all alone."

He couldn't believe his own voice. "No...Thanks anyway. I don't need a pity lay."

She was quick to acquiesce—too quick, he thought. "Okay then. Emphasize 'sleep.' On top of the covers."

He sighed. She could at least have put up a token argument. "It's better than nothing. It's probably better than I deserve."

"Don't sell yourself short. If this were to turn out to be the last day of your life, you could be proud of how you've spent it."

He supposed he had done a few honorable things in the past twenty-four hours, probably more than he would have accomplished at home. It was amazing what a miserable job he had made of his life. Now he regretted not being a better husband, a better father, a better son: three things it had not occurred to him to be until today.

He should have been more unselfish; he should be more altruistic at this very moment. Instead, he recognized a welling dissatisfaction that he had experienced before, one that he felt safe vocalizing to Elise. "But I didn't have any fun."

It came out whiney.

"True." She rolled onto her back, put her hands behind her head and stared up at the ceiling. She had allowed the soft fuzz to grow in her armpits; he found it unspeakably sexy. It bespoke vulnerability, naiveté, nubility. A person should be shot for such tantalization.

"Okay, say tomorrow's the last day. How would you want to spend it? Forget all the crap about making amends to people for all the horrible stuff you've said and done over your lifetime. Pretend you've done that already. Pretend you've said your goodbyes to your family. There's no obligation hanging. Say the day is yours, as if you were in prison on death row and could order anything to eat—only in your case, you can do anything you want, too."

He tried to recall what on earth gave him pleasure, tried to think when was the last time he had any fun. Maybe he hadn't enjoyed himself since college.

But his mind slipped easily beyond college back to age ten, when having fun came naturally. Also at age ten he seemed to have made most of the decisions about the rest of his life, when he had figured out that he was special and that there were strategies to getting what he wanted.

It wasn't time spent playing with friends that came back to him now; it was the periods of solitude. Although he recalled with pleasure the summer he and his buddy Lidge Rutledge built a tree house down by the creek that ran behind his family's property, he cherished most the hours he spent there alone, staring off at the meandering ribbon of water, dreaming.

"When I was a kid," he began unsteadily, "I thought I was destined to have an extraordinary life. I was fated to do something outstanding, to become famous."

"I know, babe. Me too."

That stunned him. "You too?"

"Is that so hard to imagine? I figure I had better prospects than you did. After all, I've got the genes of a movie star."

Movie star: conjuring in his boyhood mind, instead, television star. As a ten-year-old, he intended to become, if not another Gregory Hines or Savion Glover or Gene Kelly, another Clint Eastwood: strong, tough, fair, with a wry sense of humor. He would live in the open— yes, out west, on a ranch. Later he would incorporate Sondra Locke into his fantasy: he once believed Sarah bore a striking resemblance to Sondra Locke. So maybe he had honored one promise to himself. But there were many broken ones, about what he would do and be.

Maybe every child felt full of potential at age ten. He could feel it now: exactly as he did thirty-seven years ago. "This is weird. Inside right now, I'm still a ten-year-old kid."

"Right. In psychology—which is mostly a crock of shit—they talk *incessantly* about honoring the inner child. That part they got right. Even an old blind sow finds an acorn occasionally, Mom used to say."

"But all the cells in my body have changed out at least five times since then. There's not a molecule left that I started out with. So how can I still be me, that ten-year-old boy?"

"There you go, sneakily trying to make a case for a soul and immortality again," she said.

He almost denied it, but it was too late for subterfuge. "I want to be more than this body that's betraying me."

"Or maybe it's the other way around," she said. She let it hang there for him to chew on for a while.

"Be nice to that body," she said finally, throwing one leg around him in a bear hug. "It's the only one you're likely to get, and it's still habitable."

He reached for the light switch and plunged the room in soothing shadows, then settled into his own departing flesh with profound gratitude for its stubbornness. Her breathing all too quickly became deep and regular, but he still needed to talk.

"I used to make all kinds of outrageous vows about what I would do and be someday. Some of them I might have gotten around to, if I had lived long enough."

"Like what?"

He couldn't tell her. She was too young to remember, too female to understand. "It doesn't matter now."

"Apparently it matters a great deal to that ten-year-old."

"What do you mean?"

"You can't renege on a promise to a kid. Don't you know how vicious a ten-year-old can be? He'll kill you if you ignore him. He'll beat the holy shit out of you. He'll throw his *rock* at you."

In the pit of his stomach, Jonathan could feel the truth of it. He said, "If life were fair at all, there would be second chances."

"True." She kissed his ear, then turned her back to him, a signal that she meant to go to sleep. In a drowsy voice she added, "Who knows? Maybe *la curandera* deals in second chances."

Jonathan closed his eyes and spoke silently into the ether, *If only...if only there were magic....*

33

Despite the droning air conditioner that ran continuously, Elise found the air in Jonathan's room stifling, heavy with death. When it became apparent that if she stayed, she would lie clenching her teeth until daybreak, she slipped out silently and returned to her own room. Jonathan, in a deep brow-furrowed sleep, did not stir when she left. He would never miss her, and besides, it would serve no good purpose for Arpad to find her with Jonathan, leading him to erroneous conclusions she had no wish to foster.

The air was oppressive everywhere. Too still. She sat by her window staring out at the night, watching the occasional flash of light to the west, not realizing at first what it was. At last the distant rumble of thunder announced an approaching storm, one of those quick and volatile summer disturbances that wrack the southwestern landscape with unpredictable devastation. Almost immediately needles of lightning pierced the blackness very close-by, illuminating convoys of ominous clouds converged overhead.

Apropos, she thought, picturing herself drenched and shivering as her father opened his door to her for the first time.

In her fantasies, it was her father who opened the door, never his wife—and surely he must have one—or one of his children. The concept had only recently taken root that there must be other Harwoods: a step-mother, half-brothers and sisters younger than she, an entire clan of blood relatives. And grandparents. *La curandera* had been specific about that. She had been specific about grandparents on both sides of the family.

Strange that her mother had never mentioned her own parents. There must be another mystery there as to why, during all these years, there had been no contact—why Salome had so firmly closed the door on her past. In doing so, she had closed it for her daughter as well.

When the storm hit, Elise went into the bathroom and took another long shower, then climbed up in the middle of her bed into lotus position and tried to meditate. But she couldn't turn off her thoughts, or the sounds of the storm's bluster. For the rest of the night rushing water gargled in the drainpipe outside her window.

At dawn, she dressed and went down to the coffee shop. It was still raining hard, and every few minutes the whole structure seemed rocked by sudden gusts of wind. To her surprise, Arpad was already there, sitting in a back booth looking glumly out at the lightning-bright landscape.

She slid in beside him and said, "Boss still asleep?"

"Yes. Good sleeping weather, I suppose."

"Then why are you up so early?"

"I have to arrange transportation for him. I've already discovered you can't get a digital phone in this town, at least, not at this hour, not activated. So I'll have to leave him mine, if I can find another battery. Mine went out the window with his phone."

"So you mentioned. Four times."

He studied her eyes, which she figured had circles and bags. "Big day for you. Guess you were too excited to sleep, huh?"

"Something like that." She felt queasy in the gut, but hoped it was only hunger. She picked up the menu and decided on dry toast and juice.

They ate in silence, watching the rain through smudged plate glass still wreathed with Christmas tinsel. Maybe he felt ill-at-ease because he presumed she had just risen from Jonathan's bed. She could think of no way to assure him that she had not.

When they finished, Arpad paid the bill and said, "Get your gear and be ready to leave as soon as I'm back. I want to be in San Antonio as early as possible."

"What about Kelvin and Hector?"

He pointed behind her; she turned to see Kelvin and Hector coming in for breakfast. Kelvin's black shantung mortician's suit hadn't been helped by the weather. She spoke to Hector in Spanish, then asked Kelvin, "Want me to stay and translate?"

He cleared his sinuses and grinned. "Hell, darlin', I'd be a piss-poor West Texan if I couldn't communicate with Mexicans."

"He isn't Mexican," she said.

"Whatever. Not that we wouldn't enjoy your company, if you'd like to stick around." He addressed her, ignoring Arpad.

"Thanks. Guess I'll go check on Jonathan."

"He's up," Kelvin said. "We're supposed to take him some breakfast."

"I can do that," she said, glad for the opportunity to perform at least one small service for Jonathan, and relieved that there would be no more awkward minutes with Arpad.

She waited in the restaurant for a take-out meal, then delivered it to Jonathan's room. She found him dressed and shaved and looking rested. "I brought your road kill," she said, marching past him without invitation. A grunt was his only answer.

She laid out his breakfast on the table by the window then sat opposite him as he ate. The egg was hard-fried, edged in brown lace. She thought of offering to order him another, but he seemed not to notice. He picked at his food in morose silence.

She said, "I gather you're not a morning person, so I'll keep quiet."

"No, you're wrong. I'm just worried."

"Something new?"

"Yes. *La curandera* was going to light an all-night fire of evocation and read the embers at dawn. Unless she planned to build it in the house—and I didn't see any fireplace—the rain obviously will have put the fire out." He took a sip of coffee from the foam cup and made a face.

She didn't try to conceal her astonishment. "You're really into the program, huh?"

He pointed his plastic fork at her for emphasis. "You see why I don't need you people around? I can do without any nay-saying."

"Sorry." She tried a new diversion to cheer him. "So what're you going to do until time to go out to *la curandera*'s?"

A glimmer of life lit his eyes, grey irises narrowing as the pupils dilated. "I've been thinking about you said. You were right: I've neglected that ten-year-old kid. Maybe I won't plan anything. Be spontaneous."

"Good for you. Fill up your reservoir. Did you ever notice golfers, how deadly serious they are? That's not play, for God's sake. Kids play to have fun, and they never ask if what they're doing is worthwhile. And they have no ulterior motive."

"And when it's not fun, they quit," he said.

She reached over and pinched off a bite of his bacon and held it aloft. "I hereby declare this a vegetable," she said, popping it into her mouth. It tasted heavenly, and she felt dreadfully wicked. "I shouldn't have done that. Children understand the sacredness of the world. I've desecrated a poor little pig."

"Is that your child talking?"

She shrugged. "Kids love the world."

"True. They're beset by wonder. Life lies ahead full of magic and mysteries. That's got to be healthy."

She inventoried him in amazement. "You know what? I wish I'd had a dad like you."

He laughed, but she could see he wasn't entirely pleased, so she hurried on, "For one thing, you're a damn fine cuddler."

He appeared mollified. He pushed his plate aside. "Maybe what I've been missing is a daughter: a cuddleable person."

Best to go while he was in an up-mood. She rose, leaned over and kissed the top of his head. It smelled of institutional shampoo. "Promise me this: that when

Arpad comes back for you, you'll stop in Uvalde and meet my dad and see me in my new surroundings."

"Deal." He half rose and gave her a one-arm hug. "And thanks for the peaceful night's sleep. Just the offer you made took ten years off my life, or I should say, off my age."

She left, feeling guilty for keeping up the pretense that everything would be all right for him. She picked up her backpack from her room and went to wait in an alcove of the motel lobby. There, lulled by the rain beating on the aluminum shingles, she dozed, jerking awake from time to time to think, Dear God, why does it have to rain today?

It was more than an hour before Arpad returned. They were ready to leave before they woke her; no time to run back to Jonathan's for one more goodbye.

Arpad rode in the front of the limo beside Kelvin, while Elise and Hector had the back to themselves. As before, Hector took a jump seat.

She wanted to put him at ease, so she said in Spanish, "Makes you feel like royalty, huh?"

Hector, black eyes gleaming, lifted his chin and drew back his shoulders. "I *am* royalty. Descended from Mayan kings."

"Gosh. I didn't know."

"In our forest, the days flow easily like the meandering waters. We live with our ancestors, who never leave us. My royal fathers wait for me to come home. I should never have left." He touched the shirt pocket containing the bag of herbs; his nails were still rimed with weeks-old motor oil. "But this potion makes it worthwhile."

"Right. If you hadn't come, you wouldn't have met *la curandera*."

"I came north to have a better life, to find a fortune. It would be nice to take one home."

"But you learned money isn't everything," she said, regretting at once sounding self-righteous. "Look at Jonathan."

He smirked and turned to watch the grey-drenched countryside slip by. "Only someone who has always had money would say a thing like that."

The trip to Uvalde took forty minutes, the expectant quiet punctuated only by the rhythmic thwack of the windshield wipers. On the outskirts, Kelvin got directions to the Harwood ranch, which was some twenty miles south on the Batesville road. Elise was glad of the delay; somehow she must drain off the mounting apprehension before they reached their destination.

The name "Harwood" on the mailbox at the ranch entrance sent a surge of pride through her, putting her momentarily at ease. She was home. Home. At long last. Where she belonged? Hector got out to open and close the metal gate, then galumphed through puddles and threw himself on the jump seat, dripping puddles onto the floor.

"Southfork it ain't," Kelvin said. "But then, it never is."

The low-slung house ahead showed no sign of life through the pelting storm. Again dread rose up to swamp her. "I should've phoned first," she muttered. She wished they could go back to town at least for a bathroom break but Kelvin would have a hissy fit if she suggested it.

Arpad turned and shot her a look of encouragement. "At least he won't be out tending cows in this weather."

Kelvin said, "I've never known a summer rain to last so long. It ought to be over soon."

As they pulled up in front, she glanced around reluctantly. "I'll leave my backpack here, so I'll have an excuse to come out and say goodbye."

"Don't worry," Arpad said. "We're weren't planning to leave until we're sure someone's there."

As she sprang from the limo and sprinted through the downpour to the long porch, she saw a curtain part in the front room. The motion brought both relief and a sense of impending disaster. She slaked the water from her face and pushed uselessly at her sodden hair. This rain was an omen. Why had she come?

Almost immediately the door opened and as she had always imagined, she faced the man she supposed to be her father: he was tall and broad, but disappointingly overweight and balding. Three horizontal creases etched his leathery forehead. He appeared much older than Jonathan.

His gaze swept beyond her toward the limo. "Yes ma'am. Looking for someplace?"

Her hammering heart echoed in her ears above the sound of the rain. "Are you Chuck Harwood?"

"Yes ma'am I am....Do I know you?"

"Not yet. I'm Cherilita Hobbs' daughter."

He appeared to have trouble placing the name. Then he glanced over his shoulder toward the interior of the house and stepped out onto the porch, holding onto the screen door behind him. "Well I swan!" The weathered features tightened as he squinted down into hers. "You don't look much like her."

"No. I always figured I must look like my dad. Only now that I've seen you, I don't think—"

"Hold on. Are you trying to say that *I*—She told you *I*—"

"Had to be. I was born September 20, 1974. Figure it out."

Still holding onto the screen, he backed up as far as he was able and gazed out over head. Maybe he was doing the arithmetic. With obvious effort, he smiled, showing a gold filling on his left canine. "Well by dog. If that ain't somethin'!" But he couldn't maintain even the semblance of pleasure for more than a flash. He craned toward the limo. "Your—mother's not…"

"Oh no. She's not with me. I hitched a ride here with friends."

Obvious relief. "You all just passing through, then."

She swallowed; her heart thudded. "Right. Just thought I'd stop by and…meet you, since I was in the neighborhood."

He shifted his hold on the screen door to the other hand so that he could stick out his right one. The smile resembling a grimace was now etched in concrete. "Well it's a pleasure to meet you…uh, what's your name?"

"Elise." Her eyelids batted wildly. She let him shake her hand while she tried to think of something else to say. "I just graduated from the University of Colorado."

"Great." He pumped her hand harder, then released it and stuck his own in his hip pocket. The pasted grin was withering. "Well it's mighty nice of you to drop by. Too bad we couldn't have better weather for you."

"Oh." She looked around at the water sheeting off the roof as if she hadn't noticed it before. "That's okay." She swiped a hand across her eyes and shifted her weight one more time. "Well ...I don't want to keep the others waiting."

"No, guess not. Not in this downpour." He nodded out toward the mesquite-dotted pasture. "We need it, though....Cattle need it. Grass was getting spotty."

"Oh yeah. Sure. Well..." She stuck out her hand again. "Nice meeting you...Dad."

He winced noticeably but took her hand briefly, rolling his fingers against his thumb when he let go. Then he waved at the limo, never releasing his hold on the open screen. He called, "You all drive careful, hear? Watch that slough between here and town. It fills up a right smart."

It was her signal to bolt off the porch and splash to the car. As she reached it, she saw Arpad and Hector make a quick seat exchange. So no need to try to save face; they must've watched her whole humiliation. She dove into the back beside Arpad and dissolved against his chest, wracked by sobs.

Despite that she was soaked, Arpad held her firmly and patted her back. Finally he said, "This is for the best. I was wondering how Hector and I would make that flight to Belize without an interpreter."

34

The morning dragged by; the wild rain spumed against the motel windows without let-up. Jonathan paced the lobby an hour ahead of time on the off-chance that his hired car would appear early. He noticed a few newspapers arranged on the counter.

The Wall Street Journal was too much to hope for. He picked up the *Uvalde Leader-News* but found no business news, other than an article about the nearby Falcon Lake area that was apparently a winter tourist resort. He did note with some gratification that the town at least had a hospital.

Then a small item caught his eye:

***

FORMER RESIDENT BELIEVED DEAD IN CAVE-IN
Roswell, NM. June 7, 2000: Ramón Fuentes, former resident of Crystal City, was the apparent recent victim of a cave-in at the Llano Sand and Gravel facility east of Roswell, although no body has been recovered....

***

He scanned the rest of the article and smiled. Doss was a good PR man as well as an efficient manager. Maybe they wouldn't try too hard to locate the body. Without a corpse, who was to say that Ramón hadn't simply taken this opportunity to disappear? It was possible that the outstanding warrant for cock fighting had caught the attention of the Border Patrol, and he had decided just to vanish before he was deported.

Or maybe the whole thing was an elaborate plot of Fuentes, uncle and nephew, to extort money from Llano. It could happen. He must talk this over with Hal, see if they had a case for avoiding payment to Miguel altogether.

He was on the verge of returning to his room to phone Hal when his driver appeared in an old yellow Ford Pinto with a magnetic sign stuck on the passenger door that read "Ramirez Taxi". It was apparent, as it clacked under the covered portico and shuddered to a stop, that the narrow token back seat was a joke; besides it was crammed with plastic bags that appeared to be full of cans. The young driver did not get out, but leaned over and gave the door a kick with his right foot.

As Jonathan slid into the passenger seat, the driver examined him with indifference. "You Tyler?"

"That's me. You're Ramirez, I take it." He tried to shut the door but discovered that it was sprung. The driver stretched across and slammed it hard enough that it caught, but not enough to prevent the rain from blowing in. Jonathan edged as close to the middle as he could.

"Wrong. I'm Mellinger, my dad's name. My mom's Ramirez."

"So this is her cab?"

"Nope. It's mine. But how much business would I get in this town, with this car, with Mellinger on the door? Tell me that."

"Right." He glanced into the cluttered back seat. "I gather most of your fares are single."

"Only today. That Indian guy who hired me said you'd be alone, so I thought I'd take my cans to the recycling center. On your nickel."

The taxi slued across the road into the sparse traffic. They rode in silence. Jonathan tried to think of something to say besides the obvious but could not. "Some rain."

"Yeah, a real frog-strangler... For this place." Mellinger switched on the radio but the crackle of static made them both jump. He turned it off, but Jonathan got the message and kept quiet.

In silence they jounced along the slippery road leading south. Frequently the driver grabbed a greasy rag from the dash and wiped the fog from the windshield. Jonathan began to understand the necessity of not adding to the moisture-laden air by talking.

When they arrived at *la curandera*'s, Mellinger bent over and wiggled the door handle, then hefted a foot past Jonathan's middle and kicked the door open. "When do you want me back?"

"In about half an hour. Can't you just wait?"

Mellinger snorted. "Hell, mister, ain't nobody going to get cured that fast on a day like this."

So Arpad must've told him, the rat. But then, why else would someone seek out a healer, particularly on a day such as this? He said, "Okay, what do you suggest? Can't I just call you?"

Mellinger pointed toward the dashboard. "You see a two-way radio in this crate? I just roam, man, and that's how I pick up fares. Tell you what: I'll check back in an hour or so. No extra charge if you're not ready."

Jonathan got out and made a dash up the muddy path, leaving the driver to contend with the car door. As he stepped onto *la curandera*'s front porch, she appeared at the screen. He tried the handle, but the screen was locked. Behind him, the yellow Pinto sputtered off toward town.

The old woman glowered up at him through the wire mesh. She did not appear glad to see him. He felt like a tardy schoolboy.

"You told me to come at noon," he said.

"That was before the rain. There is no need to come now."

Blood rushed to his ears, pounding. "What does that mean?"

"The elements have spoken. The fire would not burn. There is no future to read about."

Jonathan's heart thumped wildly. His voice cracked, letting in a shrill note of hysteria. "Are you just going to let me stand out here and die then? Is that it?"

The healer's black eyes seemed to bore into him, and her voice was surprisingly strong and unrelenting. "The rains tell the story. Of course you are reluctant. Reluctance is man's perpetual state. He is reluctant to be born. He is reluctant to give up his mother's breast, reluctant to use the potty. He is reluctant to marry, reluctant to become a father. He can avoid facing many of those things, but all the reluctance in the world will not save him from death."

With that she closed the door.

It was unthinkable that she meant to refuse to help him. No one could be that cruel. With frantic insistence he beat on the screen frame, sending shudders through the whole porch wall. When there was no response, he kicked at it, flung himself at it, tearing the screening from its moorings. Still no one came.

"Dammit, you old crone, open this door! Open this door!" His cries were torn from his throat by a blast of wind that sent a blanket of rain against him from the west. He kept banging and screaming until his hysteria turned to sobs and his knuckles were raw and bleeding.

Arpad. Where was Arpad?

Where was everyone?

Mother? No. Dead. Dad? Never. Who? Was there anyone?

He could think of no one to call out to, couldn't even remember their names. He was going to die, here in this God-forgotten place. Alone. Abandoned. Like Arpad.

He stumbled down the steps, staggering against the storm, blinded by his own tears as he howled out in rage and despair. His chest heaved, convulsed with a welling misery too pervasive to bear. His body was deteriorating, his spirit was dissolving, and there was no one to care.

Midway down the dirt path, he slipped and fell face-down into the mud. Reflex alone caused him to snort, clearing his nostrils of the thick slime, but he did not lift his head from it. He made no effort to get up, but let the rain hammer mercilessly against his back as he wailed out his desolation, sucking in gritty gobs of mud like mucus with each breath, coughing them out with each exhalation.

At times during the past two days when he had pictured his death, turning the scene over in his mind like a quaint foreign coin that he never expected to encounter, he had imagined lying in a hospital bed, surrounded by grieving and repentant loved ones. Their identities remained blurred, so that he could never name the mourners. Because the vision lacked reality, he had injected it with humor, imagining that, as they waited expectantly for his last words, all they would hear as his soul departed his body was one long, contemplative fart.

Now there was not one to hear. Fate was denying him even that.

35

Enroute to Belize City

Twice during the flight from San Antonio to Belize City, Arpad came back to check on Elise, bending over her chair and speaking in a solicitous tone. Hector could only guess at what his words meant. He felt sorry for the girl, who kept her sunglass-shielded eyes closed most of the time. But nothing could dampen his own elation. He was going home. Regardless of what he found when he got there, even if his mother were dead, it would be good to be home. Regardless of what the other men said about his failure to return wealthy, he would hold his head high and ignore them. He would never leave again. Never again would he subject himself to the indignity of being an outcast, to that bereft, intense solitude of being alone in an alien and hostile land. At least at home there would be family to welcome him, who called him by his right name.

Not so for the *muchacha* Elise, who had no family or name. Hector suspected that she was not sleeping, for occasionally a shadow of intense grief crossed her face. However, she kept her head averted toward the window so that he couldn't be sure. Hector sat in a comfortable swivel chair opposite hers and watched in reverence as the plane seemed to drift ever so slowly past towering pillars of white. Never had he imagined that he would see Father Sky at such close range, at least, not while he was alive.

Arpad's voice on the loud speaker roused Elise, who turned to Hector and translated. "We're beginning our descent into Belize City Intercontinental. Fasten your seatbelt and lock your chair stabilizer."

Hector watched the changing air patterns with rapt anticipation. For a few long moments the white seemed to press in on him, blocking the view, rendering him stifled and helpless. But just as abruptly the plane broke through the fog, and he could see a ceiling of flat-bottomed clouds growing more distant. Ahead an airport beacon swiped a yellow finger through the thinning mists.

The plane must be approaching from a westerly direction. Below, the peculiar brownish green marked the great swamp of the north. To the south, visible ahead to the right, the mountains rose. He pointed and said to Elise, "There is my home. Where I left my *nahual*. The only part of this country free of the *caxlan*."

She frowned. "I don't know *caxlan*. It must be a *Quiché* word."

"*Sí*. It means *ladino*."

"Which is...?"

"Someone who rejects the Maya heritage and the Indian ways. Someone whose blood is not pure. There is very little pure blood left in Belize."

"Okay...I think I know what *nahual* is. Isn't it what we call a 'familiar'—an alter-ego, or double?"

Hector supposed she understood, as well as a white woman could. It didn't seem worth explaining that the *nahual* is like a shadow, a protective spirit; still, he felt compelled to say more, because his *nahual* was so proud. He explained, "We are prohibited by our community from talking about our culture and customs to outsiders. This is because your Anglican priests and teachers have condemned our ways. They have tried to take them away from us. In Belize, everyone is required to go to school and learn English and Englishman's customs. We have to hide in the mountains, sometimes crossing into Guatemala to keep away from the schools that steal our heritage."

"I understand," she said in a grave voice. "We're a bunch of jerks."

"I will tell you this much about the *nahual*: we are not told what our *nahual* is until we are ten or twelve, so that we will not take advantage of it while our personalities are being formed. There is a different *nahual* for every day of the week, and our day of birth determines our *nahual*."

"So what's yours?"

Hector was momentarily offended that she would ask. Then he remembered that she was only an ignorant white girl. "I can not tell you, because that is one of our secrets."

He wanted to shout to the world that he was a Tuesday child whose *nahual* was a bull. When he left home his mother had comforted his sobbing wife, "There is no reasoning with a bull. He must butt his head against the world."

Some said the bull made a man bad-tempered. But it also made him invincible. Hector was proud to have been born on a Tuesday. He had grown to manhood confident that the bull's strength would be with him always. But on his trek northward, by the time he reached the Texas border, he knew for certain that his *nahual* had abandoned him and returned home. He wasn't sure how long it had been gone—possibly as far back as Mexico City, whore of a city, with her bright lights and smoking automobiles, her women with elaborate hair fashions, painted faces, sooty eyes—and high heels that caused their hips to sway, tantalize.

Elise interrupted his thoughts. "I've noticed that, ever since we took off for Belize, I've had trouble deciphering your Spanish."

He smiled. "I learned to speak Spanish in order to make the trip across Mexico. *Quiché* is my language, but it is a very complex tongue. Each tribe has its own version, and we often cannot communicate with each other if we wander too far from home. That is why the British and the Spanish so easily conquered us."

He peered out at the green landscape, puzzled. "I thought we were going to land. I still do not see the city."

"We were probably fifty miles away when we began our descent. But remember, the airport is ten miles from Belize City. You won't actually go into town."

"So you told me." He was not sorry. Once he had been eager to see Belize City for himself, but no more. He had had enough of cities to last a lifetime. He did not even care to see the capital, Belmopan, although it was smaller than Crystal City, back in Texas. But regardless, if he walked overland instead of following the coastline, he would inevitably pass through Belmopan, which was on the only road west at that point.

Before they left San Antonio, Arpad, through Elise, had explained that he had obtained permission to fly Hector to Belize, but that he and Elise, and the other pilot whose name Hector did not know, would have to remain at the airport while officials examined their papers. Arpad had phoned ahead to the American attaché, who would provide what Hector would need. The plane would then be made ready for an immediate turn-around flight. Thus they would be unable to help him get the rest of the way home.

Hector had scoffed at the idea of needing help. Hadn't he traversed the whole of Mexico and part of Texas and New Mexico unaided? But he didn't object when Elise said, "Jonathan instructed Arpad to arrange for a bus ticket for you, at least as far as Monkey River."

Hector was hardly aware when the plane touched down until he saw that outside his window was only hot, forbidding concrete. Two men in coveralls wheeled up in a small vehicle as the plane taxied into a berth next to the terminal. He stared at the bustling crowd inside the terminal's plate glass windows. It was a miracle! He was home!

He said, "I cannot wait to have a *temascal*—a steam bath. And a large drink of *atol*. No one can make it like my mother."

"What's that, some kind of wine?"

"Oh no! It is made with maize dough and sugar and milk. I don't know what else. When I get home, I am going to learn how to make it myself. Often I wished for it while I was away, but I had never paid attention to how to do it."

After a long wait on the ground, Arpad and a strange official came back to escort them off the plane, while the co-pilot stayed behind. At the gate, Arpad handed Hector a great wad of bills—Hector called them *quetzals*, but the government called them Belizean dollars.

Elise said, "This is as far as we can go. Jonathan said to buy you a bus ticket and give you enough money so that you can take your family a nice nest-egg."

It was more money than Hector had seen in his lifetime. Great waves of gratitude welled up in his chest, but he kept his features motionless. Solemnly he shook Arpad's hand, then the custom official's, then Elise's. She surprised him by leaning down to kiss his cheek. It burned as if he had been stung.

He followed the customs man through the gates and out to a waiting bus. Arpad had arranged everything. He climbed aboard and, head low, settled beside a black man in the first available seat. When his courage began to return, he looked around. Most of the passengers were black or mestizo; Hector was the only Maya. But then, he was used to that. He touched his pocket uneasily. Surely bandits would take his money if they knew how much he had. But no one would suspect a Maya of having money.

As the bus pulled out and headed south on the highway, it passed what seemed to be a large *finca*, or plantation, and Hector had a fine idea. He would take his mother a gift. In Monkey River he would buy a burro for her, and he would ride it home in style. The whole village would turn out to welcome home Hector, the bull. Home with a burro and medicine from *la curandera*—and a fortune!

His chest swelled with pride, and he realized that his *nahual*, the bull, had returned; he felt its surge of power rising from his groin to his throat. Silently he addressed it, "I thought you were gone, but perhaps not. Perhaps in the United States you took a human form to guide me home. Perhaps your name was Jonathan."

And maybe that was why, now that the bull no longer needed a human form, Jonathan must die.

Therefore, since the *nahual* was here, Jonathan must already be dead.

36

On the flight from Belize to San Antonio, Elise allowed Arpad to persuade her to accompany him to Crystal City. After collecting Jonathan, the three of them would return to San Antonio. She could see them off for Boston and then—what? Crawl back to her mother, she supposed, apologize for leaving her hosed in that Boulder hotel. Arpad had already informed her that a ticket for either Los Angeles or Boulder would be her remuneration for acting as interpreter on the Belize trip, whenever she made up her mind which place she wanted to go.

She considered the disparity between her odyssey and Hector's. Probably by now Hector's family was celebrating the return of its prodigal. Her appearance at Salome's door would be marked, if at all, by a sort of wake.

They took the same rooms they'd had before at the Potosi on San Antonio's Riverwalk. Elise slept soundly, as if she knew exactly what lay ahead. Her sleep was not restful so much as drugging, anesthetizing her against future pain.

The next morning, while Arpad reported in to Boston, Elise put in a call to her mother, steeling herself to grovel for running out in Boulder, before asking permission to come home. She phoned their Brentwood house, realizing belatedly that of course her mother would still be asleep. Even the staff would be stumbling around at this hour: in California it was only six-thirty. Eventually the cook answered, and Elise left a message that she would be flying home the following day and would explain everything then.

Thus she had twenty-four hours to invent a story about what happened to her new Mercedes. Maybe she had been kidnapped and the car confiscated by bandits who let her go after she pleaded for her life. Yes, that was as good as anything, unless with luck her mother had been so drunk after the graduation exercises that she didn't remember giving her the car.

A few minutes before nine-thirty she stopped in the hotel gift shop for a vial of perfume, dabbing her wrists and temples before meeting Arpad in the portico where he was to pick up a rental car. She had hoped for something sportier than the four-door Camry the co-pilot Whitlock had been using, but Arpad had ordered the biggest Lincoln available, explaining, "The chief will have to lie down in the back. We'll need shocks that squish like grapefruit."

As she slipped into the passenger side, she sensed that her extra grooming effort had earned his appraisal of appreciation. She wore sandals and a yellow mini shift, the only dress in her backpack. Why she put it on, she wasn't certain, except that she had nice legs and so far he hadn't noticed. All her life men's heads had turned when her mother walked into a room; just once she would like it to happen to her.

To cover her discomfiture as he slid in beside her, she asked, "Did you call Jonathan?"

"I tried, but he must've been in the shower. I left a message at the desk that we're on our way. He'll probably be waiting for us in the lobby."

"Did you get through to his doctor in Boston?"

"Of course not," he said. "Who ever heard of being able to talk to a doctor? But I reached the chief's office and told them he'd be back this evening, if possible."

"No word from the wife, I suppose."

He hesitated before answering. "Theirs is not a particularly close relationship. Not the sort of marriage I would have if…well, if I were to marry."

"So why haven't you, ever?" She figured he must be maybe thirty. Definitely past the Game Boy stage, but not Viagra bait.

He shrugged, concentrating on entering the freeway's flow of traffic. "Too busy. Too broke."

"Oh come now. Surely Jonathan isn't on the go *that* much."

"You'd be surprised. And I'm left twiddling my thumbs in strange airports waiting for him to finish… whatever. Can't wander too far. Can't party. Certainly can't drink."

"I can see that." She crossed her smooth brown legs and watched his gaze flicker toward them for an instant. "But surely he must pay you well. What's this 'too broke' business about? Do you really send that much money to support an Indian family?"

He let out a dry laugh and shook his head. "Brash Americans! Is nothing sacred?"

She felt wounded, dismayed. How often, during her Swiss boarding school days, had she scrambled to live down the crude American image. How carefully had she groomed herself not to fall into that pattern when she returned to the States, and yet, how quickly had she lapsed. "Sorry. Forget I asked."

Anyway, what was this "you Americans" crap? He had told *la curandera* he was born here; he was as American as she. She decided it was Arpad's way of distancing himself from her.

The ensuing silence dragged on until their mere muteness became awkward. Well, let him sulk. Elise turned her attention to the sweep of plowed fields, their immaculate furrows separating lush rows of green, probably spinach. There was something so substantial about a growing crop, something compelling about that expanse of land that drew her, but she seemed destined never to experience the rootedness it implied.

Finally he cleared his throat and said, "Actually, I don't mind telling you all that much. As a cast-off, abandoned at birth, I had nothing until Jonathan took me in, gave me a chance to prove myself. I…owe him my life." His eyes left the road to look at her full in the face with frightening intensity, as if he were trying to convey something more. Something almost sinister.

She could think of no way to draw the portent of his words into light. Braiding the mundane into the apocalyptic, she said, "So that includes your leisure time as well. I gotcha."

A chill ran up her back as a possibility too terrible to contemplate inserted itself as sharply as the blade of a dagger. She picked her words carefully, like steps through a minefield. "If you owe Jonathan your life, then you must plan to live the life he won't have a chance to live."

He didn't answer. The land whizzed by, a blur of greens and browns. She saw it only from the corner of her eye; she dared not turn to face that grim profile for fear of what she might read.

Her question didn't seem to require an answer. Instead, after two light years of no sound but the roar of tread against concrete, he changed the subject. "Did you get through to your mother?"

"No...two-hour time difference on the coast. But I'm positive she'll let me come home. If I want to."

"You sound ambiguous about wanting to."

She wasn't positive about anything—hadn't been, even before she learned about her dad. Her degree fitted her for nothing more than clerical work. If she was serious about finding a job in her field, she would need to go to grad school. But all those months before graduation, she'd never even considered applying, or even taking her GRE. And now there was the question of money for tuition.

"I've sure made mess of my life." She spoke more to herself than to him.

He snorted. "You're too young to have made a very big mess yet."

"I don't know what to do with my life. I ought to be out there in the trenches, making my mark. Instead, I feel sort of...lethargic."

"Translation depressed. Is that it?"

She heaved wearily, knowing it was true. The dull blah was a long-standing condition. She said, "I can't remember when I didn't feel like I have a slow leak."

This time his silence was curiously comforting. Eventually he said, "It isn't pathological to be distressed over a lack of family. That's both of our dilemmas, I imagine."

"Maybe we both ought to talk to your rock," she said.

"Curious you should mention that. I think *la curandera* had it backward. Instead of talking to the rock, maybe we need to listen to it. From my parochial school days, I remember something from the book of Job: 'Let the stones of the field teach thee.'"

"I see. So did you listen to your rock last night?"

"No, but I can hear it now. It's calling me from my flight bag in the trunk."

She giggled; at least he had a spark of humor. Up till now, he'd been slightly less amusing than a proctoscopic exam. But she had the good sense not to point that out. "What's your rock saying?"

"You're right. I owe Jonathan my life. I ought to do something with it. Live the life he won't get a chance to have." Again his gaze captured her full-face, his expression one of surprise. "Maybe that's what *la curandera* was trying to tell me."

"Oh? What's that? Go to India? Trace your roots?"

"No, put down new roots. Start a family of my own."

The news hit her like a lead ball in the gut, and she couldn't fathom why. She managed to murmur, "Oh yeah. Sure. So, congratulations."

His startled glance left the highway once more, darting to hers. He had lovely black lashes. "Congratulations for what?"

She felt a blush and despised herself for it, but she went doggedly on. "For your upcoming marriage or whatever. I mean, starting a family implies…"

"…that I should begin looking." A warm glint lit the depths of his eyes, a light that was the same in any culture and easily interpreted by women and even small girls around the world.

A corresponding ember sparked to life somewhere deep inside her, dispelling in an instant that long overhanging oppressive shadow that had lingered relatively unnoticed for years. For much of the time she was trapped in a fettered state of inaction, but not at the moment. The spinning tires continued their monotonous whine but the sound no longer depressed her.

Maybe she could hear the stone, as well. Of course there was something she could do: she could put down roots of her own, too. The ember glowed with hope, and the certainty, or possibility, of what she was meant to do. And Arpad had ignited it.

When she noticed the landscape once more, they had passed beyond the green truck crops to unbroken land dotted with mesquite. The rest of the drive sped by too quickly in a companionable lull which Elise had no wish to break. It was much too soon for dreaming, particularly in view of the seriousness of their mission.

Still, it would do no harm to put a small sign in the window.

She took up the thread of conversation as if no time had elapsed. "Yes, I should do the same...I mean, look around for—uh—companionship."

He said, "You didn't leave a cadre of hopefuls back in Boulder?"

"Hardly. Men aren't drawn to smart women." Might as well get that part out in the open from the beginning. No more shame about a high I.Q. If he minded, it was best to find out early.

She went on. "There was one, though. We met at a show tunes party. I wore a brown leotard and borrowed my roommate's dog's reindeer antlers and went as 'Doe, a deer, a female deer'. Almost as soon as I got there, I met this guy dressed all in yellow. Right away I knew he was 'Ray, a drop of golden sun' and I thought, Wow! It's Kismet! Only it turned out he wasn't in costume at all—he just liked to wear yellow. That can get *so* old after a few days, you can't believe."

"I imagine," he said.

"Especially when he has only one yellow outfit and he wears it *every day* and *never* takes it off, even to wash it. *So* gross!"

He didn't answer.

"I think he was mental." She petered off. No need to look to know she had lost him. "I'm rambling," she said lamely.

He came to. "Sorry. Guess my attention wandered. I...have a lot on my mind."

They had spoken relatively little of Jonathan in the past two days, but now the burden of his plight settled upon them, unspoken, but dry and palpably brittle, like the countryside itself. Drenched only forty-eight hours earlier, it already appeared parched by the sun again, wilting, starving for relief.

As they neared Crystal City, she said, "How long do you think he has?"

"There'll be no drawn-out piecemeal farewell for Jonathan. When all hope is gone, I think he'll die rather quickly."

"With little suffering?"

"No. Anyone who dies prematurely suffers greatly. The suffering, being condensed into a smaller time period, may be even more intense." Again his countenance clouded, becoming troubled, burdened, sliding backward into that old mind-set.

Her panic returned. "Whatever you've been thinking...about your obligation to him, it isn't so. Not that kind of obligation, Arpad. Remember what your rock told you."

He didn't answer.

When they reached the motel in Crystal City, Arpad drove under the portico and honked. When Jonathan didn't appear, they both got out and went directly to his room. But there was no answer to their knock, and Elise felt uneasy. Lord, had it happened already?

In case Jonathan was only in the bathroom, Arpad instructed Elise to wait outside the door while he went down to check the coffee shop. But soon he returned, concern hardening the set of his mouth, agitation glittering his eyes, telegraphing that the worst of their fears might be realized.

"He hasn't picked up his message from the desk, so he must still be in there, sleeping or showering. The clerk tried to ring but got no answer."

Elise responded by knocking once more, louder this time. But she had doubts that it would do any good. "I can't imagine that he'd be sleeping this late." The specter of Jonathan lying dead in his bed loomed unremittingly. Heart thudding, she added, "Maybe we'd better get the maid to let us in."

Arpad sprinted off in search of the housekeeping staff while Elise continued pounding, calling at full volume, "Jonathan! Open up!" with increasing urgency. But obviously he couldn't hear.

After an interminable wait, Arpad returned at a run, followed by a reluctant squat little maid, scurrying to keep up. His sleek hair stood in wild ridges, raked by frantic fingers. His stunned expression shot a shudder of dread through her.

"The maid's already been in Jonathan's room this morning. She says his bed hasn't been slept in. There's been no sign of him for two nights."

37

Crystal City, Texas

Jonathan, clinging to consciousness in *la curandera*'s front yard, was aware of being rolled over and hoisted, with great effort, onto a metal contraption by two or three Spanish-speaking men. Rain still hammered down hard, drenching his head so that mud streamed his face and threatened to invade his nostrils and tightly clamped eyes. He forced his mouth shut, which had a tendency to loll open. A wide strap held him in place, cinched around his middle and tightened behind the contraption with a ratchet that made a clicking noise. It was when the men tilted the mechanism upright that he realized he was strapped to a dolly.

One of the men held his upper body firmly against the dolly's handles to keep him from sagging forward, while the other two attempted to maneuver their cargo—not up the walk toward the house, but across the bumpy yard toward the bus, now parked near the chicken pen. Above the rain's hiss and the occasional clap of thunder, Jonathan could hear *la curandera* shouting orders in clipped Spanish from the direction of the front porch

At the door of the bus, he was unstrapped and half-carried, half-dragged up the steps and placed on one of the bench seats. Rough hands stripped away his wet clothing and wrapped him in a scratchy blanket, which he imagined to be a shroud. The rattle of rain against the bus roof blotted out all other sound. In emotional exhaustion and shock, Jonathan lapsed into sleep.

The noise that woke him was not the rain, but neither was it a welcome sound: chickens! He raised his head enough to see the cages arranged in the back, just as they had been—when? He wondered if he had been dreaming this labyrinthine time, if the bus was still parked on the highway outside Fort Stockton, if the whole episode at the vet's—and everything else since he fell into a dehydrated coma out on that hot, surreal prairie—had been a delirium fantasy.

An ancient voice at his side made him jump; it rang with the timbre of one who had lived deeply. "The *gallos* had to be moved back inside. The shed has too many leaks."

La curandera was sitting on a campstool in the aisle. Her weathered face, bright with a kind of second innocence, was only inches from his as he jerked around. The trace of a smile twitched among the creases, but she spoke sternly. "So you have feelings after all. At least now we can see what to do."

She mopped his forehead with a cool washcloth, and he realized he had been vaguely aware of this activity for some time before he actually woke. He could think of nothing to say; he still felt betrayed.

She continued. "So long as you insisted on being strong as a stone, I could not work. There is no way to get through stone except by dripping water. Perhaps the rain did the trick. The human inside the stone finally broke down and cried tears, and the man appeared. The man might possibly be helped." She raised a boney arthritic finger in warning. "I did not say 'cured'."

He worked his tongue against his parched mouth. As it clacked, the old woman bent and picked up something from the floor: a small earthen jug with a little crooked spout.

"Drink this," she said. "It is water mixed with aloe and cactus juice."

He would have drunk goat piss at that point. She held the jug a few inches above his head and allowed a stream of greenish liquid to arc into his open mouth. It was delicious.

"*Lo siento*, I am sorry, even if it were my Ramón who lay on my path, I have no bed in my house for you. You were covered with mud. Besides, Miguel is using my only spare cot. He is very old, and it will be his cot so long as he lives. This bus belongs to you, and so you will stay in it until you are ready to leave. After you have repaired the roof of the shed, you can move the chickens out, and you will have more room."

"*Me?*" He struggled to rear up on his elbows, flooded with outrage. She was manipulating a dying man, using his guilt about the cave-in, cleverly comparing him to Ramón, in order to get a roof patched. If need be, she would wring the formaldehyde out of a cadaver without a second thought.

She made a small shrug, the thin shoulders rising only slightly beneath her black silky shawl. "How else will you repay me for the meals you eat? But Miguel will do what he can to help, and perhaps his cousins will lend a hand when they all come back from the meeting."

"But I am dying," he protested. "You said so yourself."

"As are we all," she answered. "In the meantime, we are all living. It is well to do meaningful work while we can."

He sank back with a snort of disgust. "And your idea of meaningful work is roofing a chicken shack?"

"All work is meaningful. There is redemption in all work, regardless of the outcome. Our charge is to do whatever work is set before us. As to the degree of its importance, that is for God alone to decide, no? Who knows?" She gestured back toward the cages of chickens. "In God's eyes, Miguel's *gallos* may be more important than all of mankind put together, or at least more important than you."

For the first time, he looked across the aisle and noticed his clothes: they had been washed and now hung dripping on a hanger from the overhead rail behind her. Her gaze followed his and she said, "We can take your clothes outside now to hang in the sun. In this heat, they will dry very quickly. Then you can get up and eat. I have fixed Ramón's favorite soup and *frijoles*. Miguel will bring you some when he gets back. He, too, has gone to the meeting."

"What meeting?" Jonathan, remembering the unsigned release form, pictured a contingent from *la raza unida* marching onto the bus, dragging him out, stringing him up to a tree.

"There is a poor artist from San Antonio named Joe Luis Lopez whom God favored with only one hand. His father named him for the champion boxer, knowing that, being born with such a handicap, he would have to be a fighter all his life. But Joe has worked hard to make something of himself without fighting. He is an artist.

"Now he is in the fight of his life against a great California wine company. They are suing him because he is selling Tee-shirts that say, *'Puro Gallo'*."

With effort, he dipped back into high school Spanish. "*'Gallo'*—that's cock, I know. And *'puro'* must be—"

"'Pure rooster.' It is a saying we have in our culture about a brave and strong man. We had it long before there was any wine company. It does not belong to a wine company. It belongs to our *raza*."

Jonathan recalled another run-in years earlier which the same winery had had with California farm workers led by Cesar Chavez. He didn't remember how that was resolved, but he doubted that the Hispanics had won. "How can a one-armed artist fight a giant?"

"He will not fight alone. All our people will help. Miguel and his cousins have gone to the meeting to see what we can do to right this injustice."

He marveled at her naiveté, realizing, as *la curandera* could not, the muscle a large corporation could muster. Tyler Technologies either won its battles or continued litigation ad infinitum, banking on its staying power. For a while he listened to the drip, drip from his newly washed clothes until he was overcome by the need to enlighten this woman. "What chance does a one-armed artist have against an industry giant? Does anyone honestly believe he has a chance?"

She waited a long thoughtful while before answering, so long that he began wondering if she had heard him. At length she put the jug carefully on the floor, placed her hands on her knees, and rose stiffly from the campstool, gathering the black shawl about her with one tremulous hand. She turned her deep wistful gaze down upon him and answered in a voice wearied by the accumulated burdens of her ancestors. "*Señor*, do you believe you can be healed?"

An ominous cloud of despond enveloped him. The answer, he had to admit, was no. He struggled to sit up, then looked at his watch. A whole day of his precious life had evaporated. By now Elise had been united with her father and Arpad and Hector must be on the way to Belize. Sarah was still neck-deep in exotic Scottsdale mud, while Chip and Whit were dissipating their futures with some foolhardy activity, under the mistaken impression that they were immortal. His father had reached Hawaii by now and was resting under a beach umbrella with his bride before embarking on the final leg of the flight back to Philadelphia. None of them, even his seventy-two-year-old father, was worried about death. They all still had an open-ended contract, or so they believed.

"And anyway," she said, "a man must follow his calling, whether he wins or not. All of life is not about winning."

It sounded vaguely familiar. Arpad could almost have said it. Joe Luis Lopez didn't need two arms to fulfill his destiny. He was living out his dream, and at the same time, doing good: instilling pride in his people with his Tee-shirts.

She went on, "Do not waste your pity on Joe Luis Lopez. Feel sorry for the great wine company. Anyone who interferes with the destiny of another is doomed never to discover his own."

He wanted her to leave so that he could try to absorb her words. He closed his eyes, hoping she would take the hint, but suddenly he remembered Mellinger of Ramirez Taxi. "Has the cab driver come back for me?"

She nodded. "It was late yesterday, after the rain stopped. But you were sleeping and I sent him away. He will be back, I am sure, because he said he had not been paid."

At the bus door she turned, a wispy gnome silhouetted against the windshield, and pointed toward a ramshackle outhouse beyond the chicken shed. "There is your toilet. The water in the well by the back door is good enough to drink. Just prime the pump a while. Miguel will bring you a cup and also a wash basin."

The prospect of using an outdoor privy was disgusting, but, wrapping the blanket around his waist, he got up, found his shoes, and headed out. Anything was better than listening to the squawks and smelling those damn chickens. Since any breath might be his last, he opted for the odor of human excrement.

38

The mesquite, whiskered in an improbable dew when Jonathan made his way to the outhouse, had lost its moisture by the time he finished breakfast. In that hang-fire heat, his clothes dried and stiffened quickly. By mid-morning, just as he retrieved them and returned to the bus to put them on, an old green Impala sputtered into the yard and disgorged Miguel before clanking away. *La curandera* stepped out onto her porch and intercepted Miguel's progress to the house with a few terse words. He turned and hobbled toward the bus, carrying a well-rumpled grocery sack. With obvious effort, the old man pulled himself up the bus steps. As the two men faced each other, Jonathan gasped.

He had not looked at Miguel so closely, not even when they first met. Or perhaps he had not been ready to recognize what was now so apparent: Miguel did not have an open-ended contract, either. Jonathan was studying the face of a dying man, who knew with certainty that his time was growing short.

To cover his discomfort, Jonathan, in the process of buttoning his shirt, paused and stammered, "*Buenos días.*"

In answer Miguel reached into the bag and pulled out a Tee- shirt, thrusting it at him. "That's maybe not so good shirt for building. This is more better."

Jonathan's mouth fell open in surprise. "You speak English!" So he hadn't been hallucinating, back in Fort Stockton, when he heard what he thought was Miguel's voice speaking words he could understand.

The old man gave a one-shoulder shrug. "Everybody talks a little English. Me? Remember I said I got a present when I came back from the dead? That was it." He unfurled the Tee-shirt to reveal the poorly executed portrait of a red rooster and the words "*Viva Puro Gallo.*"

Jonathan brightened. "Ah, you got it at the meeting. Your aunt *Tía* Carlota told me about Joe Louis Lopez." He did not add that, if this were an example of the man's artistic ability, he was in trouble.

The old man's countenance lit up in response. "*Sí.* We got to raise money." He held up the bulging grocery bag. "Sell all them Tee-shirts." As Jonathan examined the shoddily printed shirt, Miguel added sheepishly, "Not Joe Lopez shirts. Joe Lopez shirts are *mucho mejor*— much better. *Muy hermosa.* More colorful, you know. Better *gallo.* But hard to get. *Muy popular.* My cousin's youngest girl drew this one and her boy friend had it copied onto the shirts. Everybody will buy one anyway, to help out."

Jonathan took off his shirt and pulled on the Tee, considering the irony that he might well die wearing this wretched chicken image. He said, "What does the artist think about this?"

"Don't know. Never met him."

"You mean…you're doing all this—risking bringing a lawsuit down on yourselves—to support someone you don't even know?"

A veil dropped before the old man's eyes and Jonathan could feel his retreat. As if he didn't expect to be understood, Miguel said quietly, "We do it for ourselves, for *la raza*." With that, he backed carefully down the steps and made his measured way toward the house.

When he reached the porch he turned and called, "¡*Gringo*! Hammer and nails in the shed. Ladder out behind."

So. Hoof-in-mouth. He'd be shown no mercy. They planned to go through with it. They would exploit him even if he dropped in his tracks. If they knew how unskilled he was, they would find someone else to do the job….Although he had built that fort as a kid….

He ought to refuse, ought to get back to town somehow—hitch a ride, or maybe the elusive Mellinger of Ramirez Taxi would show up. He could lie in his motel room with its godawful clacking air conditioner and its smoke-permeated drapes and wait for Arpad to come and take him away.

But *la curandera* had offered the only hope through work: it was redemptive, whatever that meant. He had worked all of his adult life and this is where it had got him. Obviously, the healer meant something else: physical work. Doubtless she had little appreciation for what it took to build a multi-national corporation from scratch, and to become a multi-billionaire in the process.

Well, why should that impress her? None of it was doing a thing to save his life. He knew something of physical work—on the racketball court, in the gym—even sensed its salubrious effect. But exercise, he must admit, was not the same as work. A quiet knowing informed him: *It is physical labor that heals. It is an organic connection to primary sources.*

He found the tools and ladder and spent the hottest part of the morning trying to reattach the metal roofing strips to their underlying wooden beams. At first inspection, the task had seemed simple enough, but the metal had been bent, warped by the wind, and was not easily straightened. To make the task more difficult, some of the pine beams had rotted and had to be reinforced from underneath with whatever material he could find lying around the yard.

After only a half-hour's labor, he was transported to his fabled boyhood fort project. In that mythical summer, he had risen uncharacteristically early every day, eager to return to the site down by the creek, where he would saw and hammer unto exhaustion with an exhilaration he had seldom felt since. He recalled the sense of melancholy when the fort was completed, remembered how he and Lidge constantly looked for other small things to do to it, as if work itself were its own reward. Even on this current project, in which he had no vested interest, it was enormously satisfying— palliative even—to secure metal to wood, to watch the cracks close due to his own effort. Maybe he was meant to be a carpenter. Maybe this was the destiny for which the ten-year-old pined. Such a simple prescription for health. If only he had grasped the lesson of his boyhood and applied it all these years, he might be a well man today.

Or so he thought until the sun was well overhead and streaming perspiration blinded him, forcing him several times to feel his way down to solid ground until he could see again.

At noontime Miguel appeared on the porch carrying a cup and a flat square pan. He called, "You want to eat on the bus? Or up here?"

Despite his hunger, the mere thought of choking down food in the presence of those stinking chickens made him nauseous. Apparently *la curandera* had no intention of extending him the hospitality of her house. The shade of the small stoop seemed his only option. He climbed down from his perch and stopped off at the pump to gulp a few mouthfuls and wash the grime from his hands, noticing with a certain awe the drop of water that clung to the spout like a pearl. How lovely was water, giver of life. He would never again take it for granted.

He trudged toward the house, feeling a physical exhaustion near collapse that he had been completely unaware of until now. He dropped onto the top step and swiped his forehead with the tail of his Tee. Miguel handed him the cup and pan, then, surprisingly, sat on the step beside him to watch him eat.

The cup contained a delicious watery tortilla soup which served to wash down the contents of the pan: several rolled tortillas filled with pinto beans. Jonathan ate ravenously without speaking.

As soon as he had finished, *la curandera* appeared at the screen door and motioned for Miguel to give her the cup and pan.

"*Gracias*," Jonathan told her. *Muy delicioso*." He hoped, by extravagant compliment, to be offered seconds, but she only scowled, her eyes like black beans.

"Where is your water jar, *señor*?"

He pointed toward the shed. "I left it there."

"Always carry your water jar with you. That way you can always fill up your stomach."

Miguel added, "You need to drink more water, anyway."

As Jonathan hesitated, dreading to leave the relative cool of the shady steps, Miguel pulled himself up and said, "I'll get it."

"No!" Jonathan rose quickly and started across the yard, the grey-dusted stones hot underfoot through his soles. He retrieved the jar, drained its contents, and returned to the pump for a refill.

Miguel called from the porch. "Maybe it's a mistake to wear that shirt in so much sunshine. Looks like you gonna go up like gunpowder." Before Jonathan could intercept the old man, he had stumped out to the bus, returning to the porch with Jonathan's own shirt. Obviously he meant for Jonathan to follow. So he was to be given a reprieve after all.

As Jonathan approached the stoop, he examined his arms, now a rosy pink. Miguel handed him the long-sleeved shirt and said, "It is better to sleep when the sun is high. You can use the Tee-shirt for a pillow and stay up here in the shade. When the shadows get over the chicken shed, you can finish up."

Touched by this extraordinary kindness, Jonathan switched shirts and sank onto the small porch floor, from which his feet dangled. He positioned himself so that the screen door could still be opened. "What about you?" he said gently. "You look as if you could use a *siesta* yourself."

The old man gave a brusque nod. "*Sí*. I will go into the house, to make *Tía* happy. But not for long. There will be plenty of time for sleeping in the grave."

As Miguel opened the screen, Jonathan thought of something else. "Why did you pretend you couldn't speak English?"

Miguel shrugged and grinned. "Do you know of a better way to find out what is going on, and which *anglos* to trust?"

It was mid-afternoon when Miguel tapped him on the arm with the toe of his shoe and, as soon as Jonathan was roused, said, "*Señor*. I have told *Tía* about your burned skin. She is going to treat you before you go back to work…in the bus."

"I see. The bus. Not the house."

Miguel lowered his voice. "You would not want to take off your shirt in *la curandera*'s house, surely."

"Guess not," Jonathan muttered under his breath as he scuffed to the stinking bus and climbed aboard. He stripped off his shirt and waited on the front bench until *Tía* Carlota appeared, draped in her black shawl and carrying a jar of ointment. He jumped up and assisted her to climb the steep steps.

Without looking at him, she motioned for him to sit, then opened the jar, humming that low-throated mantra that had first entered his consciousness when she had sat beside him earlier. He sensed that he should not interrupt as she applied the pungent salve to his skin, as if somehow to her the physical act was only part of a greater ritual. The dressing did seem to draw some of the burning sensation.

When she had finished and rose to go, Jonathan hastily pulled his shirt over the sticky ointment and said, "Please. One question. You and Miguel are very old. I envy you your long lives. Could you tell me your secret?"

She shook her head. "Ah, ah. You tempt me to take credit for the Grace of God. You tempt me to boast of being good, or obedient. But many good and obedient people are taken very young."

His spirits sank. Had he come all this way for nothing? Obviously she couldn't heal him. The least he could hope for was to learn this one thing. He persisted, "Isn't there anything you can tell me? Anything at all?"

"Oh, there is much I could tell you, but we do not learn from talk. We only learn what we experience." She fell silent for a very long while, apparently studying the chicken cages in the rear. But when she spoke, he knew that her thoughts had been a long way off.

"Perhaps I could tell you this much: The soul is very shy. It is nourished by silence and by darkness. Your soul may be craving its solitude. And I could add one thing more, since there is a blind spot in your being that will never be known: Do not attempt to separate your soul from the rest of you. It is all one, and all very mysterious."

That said, she clapped her hands upon her knees, picked up her salve, and left without another word.

He was not sorry to see her go; the stench of the coops drove him out immediately behind her. The sooner he finished repairing the chicken shed, the sooner those verminy fowl could be moved.

Halfway across the yard, she turned and called, "There is one thing more to watch out for: Too much mulling over your history wounds your being. Reliving the past hampers the soul's work."

The sun had shifted so that the chicken yard was partially protected by the cottonwood's shade. The afternoon light marbled the side of the shed with a treasonous promise of respite. Sweat had already begun to trickle down his temples as he climbed the ladder.

His thoughts returned to *la curandera*'s compelling words about darkness. Perhaps, in his headlong rush—to what end?—he had failed to heed his own rhythms, failed to nurture his own dark wisdom, failed to comprehend the presence of mystery until it was too late.

Then he caught himself. Was he not doing exactly what *la curandera* warned against?

He concentrated with all his might on the job at hand, refusing to allow his mind to wander again.

Miguel waited until he had finished, to give him a grudging compliment. He walked out onto the porch, as Jonathan was sousing his head under the pump. He motioned toward the shed and said, "Good work."

The praise pleased Jonathan more than he could have possibly explained but at the same time left him feeling embarrassed. Miguel couldn't possibly have meant the compliment, he knew. He said, "It's a good shed, well made. Did you build it?"

"I helped. Mostly my nephew did it. Ramón: the one who perished at your gravel pit."

The gratification was swept away by guilt from which he wished to escape as quickly as possible. He changed the subject. "I noticed some tears in the fence. If I had some wire, I could mend them."

"Maybe my cousins have some. I could go see." The old man strained to his feet. "You could wait in the bus, take another nap."

Jonathan could hear the cocks from here. A fat lot of sleep he would get on the bus. Despite his long day of labor, he didn't feel tired in the least; in fact, he felt exhilarated. He said, "Any objections if I go along? The walk might do me good."

Miguel covered his astonishment poorly, shrugging as if it didn't matter. "It's pretty hot," was all he said.

Jonathan elected to ignore his discomfort and walk with him anyway. It occurred to him that work might not be the whole answer to health. He had the impression that Miguel had worked as little as possible in his ninety-seven years. There must be something else. If this turned out to be his last day on earth, he nonetheless wanted to know the secret of life. Perhaps, at this point, he cared less about deciphering the meaning than capturing the rapture of it.

The old man went back into the house without a word. In a few minutes he returned with an even larger fruit jar full of water and two battered straw hats, the better of which he thrust toward Jonathan with obvious magnanimity. The band was frayed and dirty, but what was worse, the leather inner band, from which emanated a perceptibly organic odor, was deeply stained by greasy sweat. Jonathan managed to hide his distaste and reluctance and accepted the hat in the spirit it was offered.

But at the sight of the water jar, he began to have second thoughts about the excursion. "Is it that far?"

"Just up the road." Miguel held up the jar and explained. "This is for you, in case of another spell."

Touched by this thoughtfulness, Jonathan followed him down the steps and out of the yard. Despite the scorching mid-afternoon heat, the old man set off at a brisk pace that Jonathan was able to match only with effort that soon left him panting. In minutes he could feel fresh perspiration trickling down inside his shirt, and salty rivulets seeped from under the hat band and stung his eyes.

The ancient man's vitality was amazing. Despite that earlier Jonathan had glimpsed hints that Miguel's life was coming to a close, most of the time the nonagenarian appeared to possess all of the physiological attributes of a man half his age. Jonathan recalled Miguel's lifting the heavy cage and crashing it down on the knife-wielding Hector's head without even getting winded. Surely there was more to explain his stamina than just good genes.

He said, "What's your secret, Miguel? How have you lived so long and remained so spry? Surely it's not clean living."

Miguel laughed, not taking his eyes from the shimmering dirt road ahead, but Jonathan could tell that the question pleased him. "No clean living....But *much* living."

"That's the secret? Much living?"

"*Sí*, part of it." He fell silent for a while, but as if to prove his point, he swung his free arm briskly, the one not cradling the jar of water. Finally he went on more thoughtfully. "Inside of me is a voice that tells me when I am tired. Then I rest. When it says eat, I eat. Play, I play. When it says women—" He broke off laughing again. "Only it don't say women so much no more."

Jonathan recalled what Elise had told him about Socrates' *daemon* described by Plato, but he still did not understand its nature. He said, "This voice—could it be called intuition?"

Miguel shrugged and didn't answer. Jonathan sensed he had missed the mark. Elise said the *daemon* was an inner force that, from childhood on, led him toward his calling—or should, if it were not resisted. Her mention of childhood had brought a momentary recollection. What was the "other" in himself that he had communicated with back then? Was it *daemon*, or genius? Or guardian angel? Divine Knower? A pattern of energy? Or, as he now hoped, soul, the Beloved? But Elise had told him the *daemon*, or genius, was something else, a "nonhuman escort," she had called it. A sort of innate calling, a factor of destiny not explained by genes and beyond the realm of environment. "It is something within you that remembers what you are supposed to do with your life even when you forget," she had said. Was this the voice that spoke to Miguel?

He dared a sidelong glance at the old man, whose face was partially obscured by the battered hat. The slight stoop, the set of resignation on his wizened features, the shuffling gait were those of an unschooled peasant in whom the notion of guardian genius seemed preposterous. Nevertheless, Jonathan said, "When you were a boy, did the voice tell you what to be when you grew up?"

Miguel turned abruptly and shot him a peculiar hostile glare. Then he softened and spoke with some patience, as if addressing an idiot. "In the early days of the last century, in this place, my people had no choices. When we were needed by the ranchers or the farmers, we were *vaqueros*, or we picked vegetables. Otherwise...." He seemed to lose heart with trying to explain to one such as Jonathan.

In the uncomfortable silence, broken only by the rasping buzz of thousands of cicadae hidden in the squat mesquite and cenizo on either side of the road, Jonathan tried to think how to bridge the rift. Finally he made a new, cautious attempt. "Did—did you always like to keep fighting cocks? Is that something the voice told you to do?"

The old man did not answer immediately, but considered the question as if he never had before. "*Quizá*...perhaps. It is something we always know from boyhood. The *gallo* is a symbol of our manhood. There are not always bulls to fight, but *gallo* can always fight *gallo* for a man's honor."

Jonathan wondered how far he should go without risking offending his host. He said cautiously, "Does it worry you that cock-fighting is illegal?"

"Not illegal to *la raza*."

He pressed on, moistening his dry tongue by swallowing several times. "I mean, some people think it's inhumane treatment of the birds."

Miguel laughed. "*Gallos* are not human, last time I looked." The rationale apparently satisfied him. Despite the heat, he picked up his pace as if to leave the subject behind.

"But birds get killed or maimed, don't they?" Jonathan huffed to keep up.

Miguel stopped abruptly and handed Jonathan the water jar. "You better drink some," he said gruffly. "You don't sound so good."

As Jonathan mopped off the perspiration and gulped down several tepid mouthfuls, Miguel said, "I treat my *gallos* like my children. They are *better* than children. *Niños* are ungrateful for what parents do, but my *gallos* pay me back by fighting bravely to honor me. They would die for me. None of my children would do that."

He took the jar and tightened the cap before continuing up the road, leaving Jonathan to catch up so as to hear him add, perhaps to himself, "Them birds, they love me. More than anyone but my mother, and I love them more than anybody, besides my mother."

Jonathan sensed a tinge of melancholy in Miguel but did not comprehend its source.

As if by prearrangement, the cicada song increased in volume, then died down. They walked mutely the rest of the way, no more than a half-mile in all. Jonathan was not sure he could have made it much farther in that punishing heat. Miguel, appearing unbothered by the swelter, led them around the side of a grey frame house that was almost the twin of *la curandera*'s. In the back, under the shade of an ancient gnarled mesquite, two men sat hunched over a chipped porcelain-topped table, intent upon a domino game. They waved casually at Miguel's greeting, but on catching sight of Jonathan, both rose. One, about Jonathan's age, came forward and gave him a nutcracker handshake, speaking in broken English and pulling Jonathan into the shade of the tree. The welcomed drop in temperature was dramatic, restorative. Jonathan felt relief almost immediately.

"So you are better now, eh? Miguel told us how you brought him home," the man said, as Miguel flushed and turned away.

The other man, possibly the first man's father, stepped forward but did not offer his hand. "Him and his *gallos*," he said.

"You didn't look so good the last time we saw you," the first man added. "All that mud."

They all chuckled, and the conversation lapsed into Spanish as Miguel explained the nature of their errand. While the younger man disappeared into the leaning garage in search of wire, the older man addressed Jonathan. "Can't let them *gallos* get away, eh? Not before the big auction."

Jonathan turned questioning eyes toward Miguel, who again appeared flustered and said with some reluctance, "I'm having a big auction on Sunday, selling off my cocks."

"Selling your birds?" It didn't compute. Jonathan couldn't believe it. "Why?"

Before Miguel could answer, the other man jumped in. "We got to raise a lot of money to help a brother who is being sued by a big wine company."

"I know about that!" Jonathan said. "But what can you do, against an industry giant?"

"We will do what we can. We are going to get some signs painted and have a big rally, maybe get on television or something. Then we will send all the money we collect to help the poor one-armed artist pay for a lawyer." He turned and cast a worshipful gaze toward Miguel. "Miguel, he is the richest of us, and he is giving all he owns. If you didn't bring him and his *gallos* home, we couldn't have our rally, couldn't do nothing."

The younger man reappeared with a small roll of wire which he gave to Jonathan. Miguel refilled the water jar from an outside tap and said rapid goodbyes as he nudged Jonathan out of the shade and toward the front of the house.

When they were back on the blistering road, hot even through his shoes, Jonathan said, "So why didn't you tell me you were selling the chickens? Afraid I wouldn't repair the coop so well if I knew?"

Miguel did not appear resentful. "I only decided after I went to the meeting today. Besides, the work *Tía* gave you was more for your good than for the *gallos*. You're supposed to learn something, maybe."

They scuffed along the dusty road toward *la curandera*'s without wasting breath on words, as Jonathan attempted to fathom Miguel's mysterious motives. He was stunned by the extent of the old man's sacrifice. Now he understood his melancholia: He was giving up something that he loved above everything else. Obviously he was far more complex than Jonathan had reckoned.

Again at midway Miguel stopped and exchanged the wire Jonathan carried for the jar. "This is not so good water as ours," he said. "Ours is well water. This is city water. Full of chlorine. But you better drink it."

Gratefully, Jonathan consumed most of the contents, leaving only a little, which he knew Miguel would not touch, anyway. As they resumed their labored trek, the old man suddenly began to speak, as if he had been rehearsing what to say for some time. "Part of living is something to spark your life. It's like the pilot light on your water heater. It fires you up when you need it. For me, it's *la raza*. Helping a brother keeps the spark burning."

It was difficult even to imagine having a cause to believe in to that extent, something larger than himself. Not since Tyler Technologies went public and bumped him up to multi-billionaire status in the span of an hour had he even felt inclined to give. At that moment, he recalled having the thought, *Now I can do some good, without ever feeling a pinch.* The occasional political or charitable donation could be counted as no more than a tax write-off, or the buying of a little influence. Or a lot. Never could he imagine an act as magnanimous as Miguel's, giving up his entire claim to wealth, and the thing he loved with all of his heart.

Actually, at this moment, Jonathan loved nothing with all his heart—not even his spoiled unlovable sons— except his life.

As they neared the house, he suddenly knew what he must do. He said, "Wait here a minute," and trotted off to the bus. He climbed aboard, opened his briefcase, and wrote a check for one hundred thousand dollars. Then he bounded off the bus, feeling ten years younger as he returned to Miguel, who still stood by the path, black eyes narrowed quizzically.

"What's this?" Miguel said, as Jonathan handed him the check.

"I want to buy the cocks. All of them."

Miguel snorted and tried to hand the check back. "This is no good."

"Yes it is. Just deposit it and see," Jonathan insisted.

Still Miguel thrust the check forward. "I can't take this. First place, who would cash it for me? Second place, I can't cheat all my friends who are coming to bid on the birds. The auction is a 'cash only' sale. You want to buy my birds, you come and bid like everybody else. But only if you have cash."

He thrust the check into Jonathan's pocket and turned toward the house. Jonathan started to protest; suddenly owning those chickens had become an all-consuming goal. He always achieved his goals, one way or another, and this time must be no exception. In frustration, he recalculated when Arpad would return. Tomorrow was Saturday. If he got back before the banks closed, he might be able to come up with that much cash; Jonathan had no misconceptions about being able to get that amount from the ATM machines around Crystal City. In the meantime...

A second epiphany dawned, and he called, "Wait one more minute" and trotted back to the bus.

Again he opened his briefcase, this time retrieving the signed release form, which he brought back to Miguel, now standing on the first step of *la curandera*'s porch.

"I want you to have this back," he said, handing Miguel the form. "You should never have signed away your right to fairer compensation for Ramón's death. You should sue, or threaten to sue, big time." He laughed, light-headed, just imagining the chaos to come back at his office. "Make those corporate lawyers squirm. Make them earn those fancy fees for once."

Miguel puzzled over the paper while Jonathan, buoyed by a giddy sense of purpose, said gleefully, "And if you settle, don't settle for a penny less than a hundred million."

The figure, if not covered by insurance—which would apparently be the case—would wipe out his personal capital not tied up in stocks. But Sarah had her own legacy, and both boys had trust funds. Nobody, certainly not Jonathan, needed that money. Anyway, the sacrifice was no sacrifice. He was not giving up something he loved with his whole being, like Miguel. It seemed impossible for Jonathan to match Miguel's sacrifice. He would have to think of something more. Because he wanted this feeling again. Never had he realized what wild joy could come from simply giving something away.

But for now, his small gesture was a start. And it left Jonathan with something he recognized immediately: a deep smoldering spark that must have been banked for a very long time.

What's more, lifted at least momentarily was the overwhelming sense of guilt he'd pushed aside ever since he determined to deprive Miguel of ample recompense for Ramón's death. He should have known he could never escape it; from infancy Episcopalian guilt had been spooned in with his Cream of Wheat.

But his elation was short-lived. Miguel thrust the paper back at him, sticking it in his shirt pocket. "No, *señor*. I signed that paper. If you knew Ramón, you would know he wasn't worth no more than you already offered. Ramón, he was even mean to his own *gallos*. Maybe when the mine caved in, God was punishing him for not taking care of them."

"But that's not the point—"

Miguel interrupted. "Anyway, you are making a big show, *señor*, because you hope the gods are watching. You still think there is a way to buy your life. But it will not work. Nobody can bargain with God, *señor*, not even Satan. Besides, do you think you are the only one who is dying? Does the world have to stop for your big scene? What about me, *amigo*? You are trying to steal my one great gesture before I die—Pah!" He spat at Jonathan's feet.

Jonathan's head throbbed from the effort of trying to avoid the truth of Miguel's words, and he suddenly felt dizzy. He wanted to believe that he was acting from pure altruism. But he recognized the presence of the secret hope that somehow he could gain a positive balance, could give more than he got, and by the law of osmosis, good would come to him. He cupped his forehead in one hand and pressed hard, willing that fleeting feeling of euphoria to return.

Before he could protest further, behind Miguel, the screen door opened a sliver as *la curandera*'s bony fingers appeared along its edge. From the dark interior of the house came her surprisingly commanding voice.

"*Señor* Tyler. It is time to return to your work if the chickens are to be in their pen by sundown. And Miguel. Gather some wood quickly. I will make another evocative fire. Time grows short. It appears that if *Señor* Tyler is to have a reading, it will have to be soon, very soon."

39

Jonathan completed the fence repairs by the light of a lantern which Miguel hung over a post during his foray of the chicken yard for kindling for *la curandera*'s fire. Barely able to stand at that point, Jonathan insisted on helping Miguel transfer the fighting cocks into the pens, but in his exhaustion he became careless and allowed himself to be spurred on the shin by an irate *gallo*. The wound bled so profusely that he had to tie his handkerchief around his leg. The fabric quickly became soaked, but with time, perhaps it would stanch the flow. He did not mention the wound to the others, for Miguel had returned to help his aunt light the fire, set in an open area between the house and the pen. The flames made the cocks nervous, and they continued to chatter far into the night.

The bench on the bus was too short, and he slept with one leg propped up against the window and the other, the one with the spur wound, on the floor, to steady himself to keep from rolling off. Light from the blaze invaded his sleep, but he mistook it for the old lamps that lit Boston's cobbled walks, its charming winding "cow paths" that he thought he had forgotten. In the middle of the night he became vaguely aware of liquid running down his leg, but he was too physically depleted to get up and look for an alternate bandage. Before he fell asleep again, he could swear he heard singing accompanied by a guitar.

By morning a narrow, slow-moving ooze of blood had reached the bus steps, and Jonathan scarcely had strength to sit up when Miguel came to check on him. The old man hurried back to the house and returned with a clean bandage and a mug of orange juice which he forced between Jonathan's lips. The first swallow lit a fire in his esophagus and sent him into a spasm of coughing.

"What is in that?" he said.

"*Tequila.* It will build your strength."

"Or kill me....I heard singing last night. And a guitar. Was that you?"

The old man ducked his head. "I thought you were asleep."

"It was very beautiful. You never told us you're a musician."

"No more than anybody. We are all born to play and sing, but after we are grown, we have to remember how all over, to ease that tight wire, you know, between what goes on out here and what we are inside. There is always something down there that wants to be heard."

Miguel appeared anxious to escape and bounded off the bus with rubber-band energy, promising to return with breakfast. Jonathan harked back to that first meeting, when the old man made such a show of decrepitude. Was it a show, or had returning home restored the plasticity of his youth?

Miguel brought him a mug of coffee laced with Mexican chocolate and a hearty plate of *migas* which he boasted that he had cooked himself. He even fed Jonathan a few awkward spoonfuls until he gained the stamina to take over the job.

Between mouthfuls, Jonathan said, "So your aunt has delegated my care to you. She's apparently having nothing to do with me again." Somehow he wasn't surprised.

Miguel wiped greasy fingers on his shirt and regarded him with pity, as if he were incapable of comprehending the obvious. "Since before dawn she has been studying the embers and ashes, getting ready for her trance. When the sun came over the trees, she went inside."

Jonathan swallowed the temptation to ask why *la curandera* did not first heal his wound. The profusion of blood both perplexed and troubled him. But perhaps Miguel did not even mention it to her. Maybe it was important not to interrupt the ritual preceding his healing session.

As if reading his thoughts, Miguel said, "When you are ready, we will go in the house. She will be in a trance and you will sit very quiet until she speaks from the deep place that she goes. But take your time. *Tía* says it is important to be ready, to clean out your mind before you come."

Even though his heart pounded in anticipation, Jonathan forced himself to follow instructions. While Miguel sat across from him, implacable as a stone, he sipped the chocolate coffee and attempted to delete the negatives from his thoughts. But his Boston dream inserted itself, and he ground his teeth. The city, even that city, had become for him a dysfunctional arena of unnecessary complexity and competitiveness; he could find no vestige of the sylvan serenity that radiated from the bleak landscape outside his bus window.

Without thinking, he blurted, "Small is very nice, isn't it? Small and simple, human-scale things, are very satisfying."

Miguel smiled and rose from the bench. "I think you are ready, *señor*, unless you would like to remove your whiskers first."

Jonathan went to the well and pumped water, baptizing himself for a shave, using the same emergency razor he'd used for two days. The painfully arrived-at results were patchy at best. Sarah would be scandalized; he smiled, cheered by the thought.

Finally he felt strong enough and presentable enough to accompany Miguel into the house, although the new makeshift bandage was already damp and sticking to his trousers. When the larger issues were behind him, he would ask *la curandera* for some herbs to stop the bleeding.

When they reached the front door, Miguel stepped aside, putting a finger to his lips. The old man eased the creaking screen open a little at a time, until Jonathan could slip inside. As before, a heavy pall of incense hung in the close air. As his eyes became accustomed to the darkened interior, he saw *la curandera* sitting stiffly erect in the dining alcove, head thrown back, eyes closed. He turned to check on Miguel, but the old man had disappeared.

He approached the dining table and sat to her left, taking care not to scrape the chair legs against the bare floor. She gave no indication that she was aware of his presence. Should he clear his throat? Say something? He dared not break the spell, so he settled back to wait.

After what seemed a long time, she spoke. "What is it that you most want?"

The question surprised him. The opportunity was too important to waste. Instinct warned him that it was probably too late to expect a healing. Two days ago he would have unquestioningly asked to be given a long life. But that was before the epiphany of last night, following his "gift" to Miguel: that its accompanying surge of euphoria was addicting. He had no doubt that the phenomenon could be explained by brain chemistry, but he didn't care. He only wanted more of it. It had somehow to do with the spark, the ember, as well. He was even more intent on preserving that than his life. From the depths of his memory came a Gaelic term a visiting Scottish lecturer had used once in a college ethics class: *Anam Çara*, or "soul friend." The ember seemed to be a friend of his soul, and he wished with great urgency to explore this legacy further.

Thus he surprised himself by using his one request in asking, "Why am I here on this earth?"

Without pause, she said, "You are here to make the world receptive to that spirit that is the real you."

This was stunning news: the inner spark existed not to serve him, but to be served. He was supposed to make this spark happy. The truth of the concept washed over him with a certainty and a palliative flash whose source could only be that ember itself.

Of course. The professor had spoken of moral obligation which he called *eudaemonism*. It had to do with achieving personal well-being through a life governed by reason. Which, supposedly, made the *daemon* happy.

He dared to speak again. "Is this spirit my soul? My psyche? What is it?"

"The name is unimportant. It is an attendant something, your personal genius. It is that compelling force which calls you to your destiny. You knew it well as a child. As a man, you have to become reacquainted."

"Attendant? But if I must serve *it*...."

"If you serve it, it serves you. It is the believer who never gives up on you. It is charged with hope." Her voice dropped to a whisper. "It believes in the magic of wishes and the miracle of dreams."

The inevitability of it washed over him, bathing him in peace, sweeping away the fever to know. He preferred to leave the rest a mystery. His life, past and present, stretched around him as a thing of great beauty. He had not realized how much his heart yearned for beauty. This compelling force might be nothing more than a thirst, even a demand, for beauty.

He was through analyzing his life. His incessant thinking had kept him from relishing the natural world here and now. With a new resolve, he would trust his instinctual gift for self-guidance. In a sense, he inhabited the infinite, didn't he? So what if he was dangerously ill, close to death? The danger was the source of salvation. Perhaps it was not salvation in the religious sense, but the *notion* of divinity had brushed against his sleeve more often than he cared to admit. He had a momentary sense of the omnipotence and omnipresence of everyday mystery, whatever it was.

The danger is the source of salvation.

He presumed the interview was at an end, and he pushed his chair back and started to rise. But the old woman's hand closed over his arm. He looked up, surprised to see her glittering black gaze fixed on him with the hint of a smile.

She said, "There is much that I saw in the embers. Do you want to know?"

He hesitated, heart thudding. Here was temptation again. Only a moment ago he wanted to be through with trying to know everything. Or so he now wrestled to convince himself. Finally he said, "I'm not sure."

She nodded, obviously pleased. "You are wise. I will impart only the wisdom of the embers that complements your own."

As he settled back, she released her hold on his arm and pressed her palms atop the ever-present crystal ball, but her eyes never left his face. "Erase concern for your family, *señor*. When you do not suffer who you are, others must suffer for you. Now that you know, they are set free. They will make their own mistakes. But you do not want to hear about that.

"You are leaving the time of striving, entering the un-time of being. You will value idleness, which can be present even while you are working hard with your hands. It is during idleness that listening occurs. You will stop trying to cure your symptoms in favor of letting the symptoms heal you. Your fantasies point to new directions. They are your spirit's secret desires. But never forget that action must accompany your convictions."

He fidgeted. The desire to know overwhelmed his best intentions. "I can't stand it. Does this mean I'm going to live?"

She regarded him sadly. "Your affliction will not kill the essential man, but perhaps the former life is dying."

"That's it, then? I finally get a teaspoon of insight and I have—what?—twenty-four hours left to mull it over?"

She shrugged as if it were a matter of no consequence. "Who promised you hours? Look instead to how you will spend your moment. You will no longer allow amassing to absorb you. Instead you will become absorbed in the world. You are learning that failure is a gift, that loneliness is a gift, that listening to what your body tells you and thanking the pain, is a gift."

With a stubborn surge of hope, he recalled Arpad's definition of *syntrophy*: the body's drive to heal itself.

Elise had said that the heart produces the same chemicals as the brain. She called it a "thinking organ." He settled deeper into his own body, craving its comfort, ready to bat away the healer's words, if they should be condemning.

La curandera continued. "Sometimes you will forget about all this, about the knower inside you. The world wants you to forget, just as the presence tugs at you from the opposite direction. If you lose it, you can find it by going into the wilderness and waiting for the ghosts of your ancestors to guide you.

"Or you can find it in menial work, getting things in order. Nature appears to be in chaos." She waved her hand toward the drawn curtains behind the sideboard that shut out every vestige of light. "But that is because we don't know how to see. All of nature is in order. Therefore, you should own only what you can keep in order all by yourself."

He studied the unending clutter on the sideboard, and she read his thoughts. "You are right, *señor*. I have accumulated more than I can care for. It is time to give it away. I had hoped to pass it to Ramón, but now...."

A pang of guilt assaulted him, before he reminded himself that he had, after all, not caused the cave-in.

She changed the subject. "Central to all is solitude. You can reach solitude even in a crowd by returning to childhood, which is always with you. Breathe in and say, 'I have arrived.' See how simple it is. But do not be beguiled by the past. Puling over misfortune will drive away all hope of living."

Jonathan closed his eyes, took a deep breath and murmured, "I have arrived." The scene spread before him was the creek bed behind his boyhood home, and the person who inhabited his body was the Jonathan he had always been.

She said, "Breathe out and say, 'I am home.'"

He let out his breath and repeated, "I am home. Home." He felt great peace.

He wasn't sure whether it was *la curandera*'s voice or his own—or some inner other's: "*Whatever your circumstances, I am here. You need never go through anything alone. Stop and listen, for I am where I have always been.*

"*I am strength to overcome obstacles, courage to face challenges. I am your very life, your core, and you are mine.*

"*In all things, you can rely on me, because I want what is best for you. I am your rememberer, to whom you once made a promise, and I am here—now and now and now.*"

After an interlude of overwhelming joy at remembering his destiny, an unmistakable sound filtered in, galvanizing him into instant alert. It was Elise's voice.

"My God, what have you done to him? Is he dead?"

His eyes fluttered open to see her bending over him. He was lying splay-armed on *la curandera*'s dining room floor.

40

Elise bent to touch the death-white face, but Arpad gripped her arm, pulling her away. "Let him alone. You've brought him out of a trance too abruptly. That could be dangerous."

La curandera tossed the fringed shawl over her shoulder, sending off fusty waves of antiquity. It was plain that their intrusion irked her. "There is no trance. *La curandera* is the only one who goes into a trance. Your concern should be about his leg. He has a wound that keeps oozing. It may be infected."

So why don't you heal it, you old fake, Elise wanted to say. Instead, she knelt and put a hand on Jonathan's forehead, noting again its high patrician contour, like the Italian nobleman who at one time had almost become her step-father. One part of her mind wondered if all rich men have this noble bone-structure, to go along with an air of self-possession. No, some were baby-cheeked and fat-lipped, like The Donald. Jonathan's natural regality was due to centuries of breeding—overbreeding, most likely—that now had done him in.

His head was hot; given his spectral pallor, she had expected him to be cold. Her touch brought his wandering eyes to focus upon her face. They were avenging-angel bright, lit with a strange ironic glint. She could almost classify it as a twinkle.

He looked from one to the other of them, not questioning Elise's reappearance, so she swallowed back a carefully rehearsed explanation. She had dreaded telling him about her father's rejection. Now he was too far gone to care.

His gaze drifted to Arpad and settled, and words began fluttering from the parched lips like bats leaving a dry cave. "Finally! Arpad...I need cash." The timbre of his speech was thready but determined, punctuated by gravelly rumbles that sounded almost like chuckles.

As Arpad reached for his wallet, Jonathan lifted a blue-nailed hand. "No! A hundred thousand. Cash....Get to the bank before it closes....Take my bank cards, checkbooks."

A dubious cloud stole across Arpad's face. Elise fantasized the Hindu god Krishna looking down sadly, entreated to grant a senseless boon. He said, "Even on a weekday, I'd be pulling rabbits out of a hat to get it so soon."

Elise glanced sharply at the old woman and wondered: Was there an extortion attempt going on? Was the healer promising some cure for an exorbitant fee?

But as if reading her mind, *la curandera* inclined her head in the faintest show of diffidence. "There is an auction tonight. Miguel is selling his *gallos*."

Elise got to her feet and cast around the poorly-lit room. "Now I *know* he's delirious! Where's a phone? We've got to have an ambulance—"

"No!" It came from Jonathan again. Clutching at her ankle, he lifted his head from the floor, belligerence blazing from feral red eyes, like a rabid Tasmanian devil. Great honks, what had they done to him?

"Got to stay for the auction," he said, calming with obvious effort. "Miguel says it's the only way I can buy his chickens. And I have to bring *cash*."

Arpad hesitated. His Adam's apple bobbed as he took an uncharacteristic stand against his employer. "I tend to agree with Elise this time, chief...."

"Dammit!" Jonathan's eyes flashed like a crossing signal. "*Go!*" He flailed around like a madman, writhing from side to side in an effort to sit. Elise almost popped off about clearing the area and calling in the diffusing squad. But he immediately fell back—and chuckled again.

Elise knelt once more and put a supporting arm under his shoulder. "At least Arpad can help me move you to the sofa."

Jonathan flung her aside. "No! Go, Arpad. Get my bank cards ...and hurry!"

Without further argument, Arpad spun and dashed for the door, tossing a look of promise toward Elise. "I'll be back as soon as possible. Take care of him."

La curandera followed him to the screen and called out to Miguel, who soon appeared, trailed by two men. In rapid Spanish she instructed them to carry Jonathan out to the bus.

Elise's outrage erupted. Forgotten was any deference for the woman's age, or any vague fear of her supernatural powers. "*Surely* you can allow him to stay in here, where it's cool! He's burning with fever!"

Jonathan reached for her hand. His own was icy cold, a peculiar contrast to his febrile head. "No. The bus is home. I've lived long enough in swinish luxury. One place is... as good as another."

The two Latinos hoisted him between them and dragged him, arms trailing, out the door. As Elise and Miguel followed, she noticed droplets of blood seeping from Jonathan's pants leg.

She turned to Miguel. "What happened to him?"

"*Gallo.* They got lethal spurs. You got to be careful around fighting cocks," he said.

"I didn't know that," she said. Neither had poor Jonathan, obviously. Miguel should have warned him. "When did it happen?"

As they reached the bus, the old man stepped aside to allow her to climb aboard. "Last night. I guess it don't want to stop bleeding." He indicated the bloody trail on the floor.

The men placed Jonathan on the bench and stood over him. The older man glanced at the bus windows, clouded by the accumulation of decades. "You goin' to be all right? It's awful hot in here."

Elise said, "If we could just get him back to the motel..."

Again Jonathan spat out, "No!" Stubborn old toot. Gorked out of his head. He thanked the men, dismissing them with a weak wave. They shrugged and climbed off the bus, and Jonathan motioned for Elise to come closer.

She sat on the floor beside him, stunned afresh by his translucent appearance. Here was a man in free-fall. A spot on each cheek had now taken on an unpleasant tinge. His sunken glass-button eyes swam independent of one another in their black shadowed pools. The grayish lips were cracked, almost scabrous. He already looked like a cadaver, but his voice, considering, was surprisingly strong and light-hearted.

"I've found something here, that pearl of great price. Nothing else matters....Never did, if I'd only realized."

She supposed it was the fever talking, but she humored him. "What did you find, Jonathan, dear?"

"What I'd planned to *be*. I *can* be—what's his name? Clint? Sondra Locke's boyfriend? You know...Every Which Way But...."

Whoa. Reality check needed here, she thought.

"Fight for the underdog. That's what he does. We are, after all, all one....I am in communion with—" He broke off. The barest flicker of humor played around his features. "Can't describe it!" He seemed astounded by the fact. "Now I see what Zen sages mean about those who speak about it not knowing, and those who know, can't speak. Maybe that means I'm beginning to know."

He plucked her shirt-front, pulling her closer; his eyes nailed her for an answer. "It's too tenuous. What if I go to sleep and forget—even if I scrub the recesses of my brain, what if I can scour out no trace of it? What if I lose it completely?"

"Lose what?" What had he seen? Some sort of *ker*— the angel of death, maybe. She doubted she would get a straight answer from someone who'd obviously come untethered from the mother ship.

He fell back, remote, turning inward, but staring at some chimeric vision beyond the bus ceiling. Finally he said, "I'd lost my sense of play. I'd begun taking myself too seriously." He faced her with a silly grin. "*Everything's* funny! When I discovered this...voice, I had to laugh!"

So. Dementia had definitely set in. His head had been spaced-warped away by that old broad. She ached to bring him back to earth, but now he was revved up to explain what it was that made him so giddy, as if it were his last chance to make sense.

"You know, Elise, we set out to live the best lives we can. *I* did. But I fell short. I didn't intend to make mistakes, didn't deliberately set out to hurt people."

Thinking of her father and her mother, she grudgingly conceded it was probably true.

He lapsed into a purposive fatherly mode, delivering a breathless lecture, while she took a surreptitious peek at her watch, wondering how long Arpad would be gone. This was obviously important to Jonathan, so she settled in to listen.

"The...dichotomy...is between wanting to behave to please others, and in the end having to obey that inner voice."

She shrugged, not sure how to respond. He lifted a warning finger. "You're too young to take this seriously, but don't ignore it for long. If you do, it'll demand to be heard. It'll lash out and kill you if necessary to make you listen....or did you tell *me* that once?"

While she tried to decide if he expected an answer, he changed the subject. "I didn't intend to hurt anyone by running away. It's just that a magnet draws me to anyone who recognizes what I can't even see myself: this core in me, which is like the yeast in the bread, everywhere present but usually unacknowledged."

He shrugged as the hope drained from his face. "Rantings. Pay no attention. They're from a desperate man who can't imagine not always being here. Or somewhere." He closed his eyes and his mouth quivered. His voice was bitter. "I've got to get past that delusion."

Miguel appeared at the door with a water jar and a clean cloth. The multiple creases in his face were beaded with sweat. "*Tía* thinks he needs to drink. And here is a new bandage."

He put the items on the other bench seat and backed out quickly, as if he were—what? Guilty? As if he didn't want to be present at the moment of Jonathan's death? She poured some water onto the bandage and handed the rest of the jar to Jonathan, who took only a sip. After she had cleaned and dressed the dark ugly gash, she rummaged through her backpack for a tank top, which she dampened and placed on his forehead. He lay very still, eyes closed, his breathing shallow. Only a sphinx smile indicated that he was conscious. Poor dork; he'd exhausted himself with talk.

"How precious," he whispered. "The human touch."

A half-hour later Arpad's cell phone, shut in her backpack under the bench, began to ring. It had to be Arpad; no one else knew the number. She hurried to answer it.

Arpad's voice had assumed the power to turn her to mush, despite the businesslike tone. "Two items: The chief's office called. What they believe to be Ramón's hard hat has been found in the cave-in rubble. They could locate the body in a matter of hours, if there is a body. Maybe Ramón faked his own death to avoid deportation. But we can't count on that. If they find a body, we need to get the chief out of town before that happens, in case there are repercussions."

She sucked in her breath. Maybe she wouldn't mention it to Jonathan. "Where are you?"

"I'm at the First National Bank. The banks in Boston are already closed, but fortunately, the chief's reputation is well-known and revered in money circles. So the banker has kindly arranged a conference call with the elder Mr. Tyler in Philadelphia and the chief's wife Sarah in Scottsdale, to verify the chief's identity and mine. Can you put him on?"

Elise tapped Jonathan on the shoulder, handed him the phone, and moved off a discrete distance while he answered several personal questions. At last he placed a hand over the mouthpiece and turned to her. "I'm going to have a couple of private conversations with my family now. Would you…"

"Oh. Sure." She climbed off the bus into the bleak death rays of midday, glad at least to be out of the stifling, breathless interior. She ambled over to the shade near the chicken yard, where Miguel and the two men were maneuvering an old wooden table and several chairs near the outer fence.

In answer to her unasked question, Miguel glanced up and grinned. "Getting ready for the auction." He waved an arm toward the other two. "Cousins, from up the road."

Since neither man looked her way, Elise saw no reason to acknowledge the off-hand introduction. She said, "Why're you selling your birds? I thought you were so wild about them."

"Long story," Miguel said. "Little girl like you wouldn't be interested."

As if she weren't there, the older of the two men, his dusky closed face sodden with senility, said, "I still think you should have it today, before everybody's paycheck is drunk up."

"They want my *gallos* bad enough, they'll save back some," Miguel said, dragging the last chair across the rough yard.

The younger man, who, from the appraising way his gaze raked her, probably considered himself God's Gift, mopped his face with his sleeve. "Anyways, if we had it tonight, nobody would come. Everybody'll be at the rally."

The older man slapped his forehead. "*¡Madre de Dios!* What's the matter with me?"

Miguel chuckled and struck the man's head with his own palm. "Yeah. What's the matter, Ernesto? You gettin' too old to remember?" He turned to explain to Elise. "The man we are raising money for might be at Lalo's Icehouse tonight. Everybody wants to go meet him, in case he comes."

"He would come, I bet," Ernesto said, "if he could get a ride."

The younger man hitched up his jeans and spat across the yard, a spectacular distance, then checked to see if she noticed. "I would go to San Antonio and get him myself if my transmission was fixed."

"Maybe he'll come," Miguel said, as Elise, no longer interested, wandered off. But she heard him insist, "Lalo invited him to come, I know that."

Sticky with sweat, she waited by the bus door until she heard Jonathan finish his call, then she climbed aboard. He appeared so surprisingly refreshed that she cackled with pleasure. "You have amazing recuperative powers!"

"I had a great conversation with my wife and father, like I could never have had before....Also, Arpad's bringing the cash. Will you...be staying for the auction tonight?"

"Sorry to be the bearer of a disappointing news flash, but apparently the auction's been put off until tomorrow," she said. "Seems everyone's going to Lalo's Icehouse tonight to meet the guy from San Antonio that they're raising money for."

Jonathan shot up like a coil spring. "Joe Luis Lopez is coming here? What a break!"

Before she could protest, he swung past her and flung himself off the bus, almost crumpling when his feet met the ground. But he recovered and stagger-trotted over to Miguel and his kin, propelled by glee. The transformation was astounding.

"Oh Lord," she muttered. "Surely he's not thinking about going with them."

Apparently that was exactly what Jonathan had in mind, and apparently Miguel was going to let him. Jonathan spoke with the men for a long animated period while Elise plopped into the driver's seat, drumming her nails on the steering wheel. By some trick of the sun, the image of her hands was caught in the slanted windshield: a ghost of herself trapped forever on this bus. So that when she went back to Boston with Arpad, a part of her would remain imprisoned in the glass forever. Even after she was dead, her hands would be there still, drumming, waiting. Maybe everywhere she went, she left a part of herself.

What had come over him? Had the fever fried his brain? He had yet to question her presence there, to ask about her reunion with her father. It was as if his life had begun when he rose from *la curandera*'s floor, and all else had been forgotten.

At last Arpad's dusty rental car rumbled into view. She recognized it from a long way off and marveled that the mere sight should zap her innards such an erotic charge. When had this shift taken place? When her father rejected her, her first thought had been of coming back to beg Jonathan to take her in. Maybe she would have married him. But sometime during the trip to Belize, Arpad's hovering kindness had stepped over the line—in her mind, at least—and become affection. So much so that, by the time of their second stay at San Antonio's Potosi, there was no need for separate rooms.

She watched, entranced by the starkness of the landscape which allowed her to observe his almost mythical approach in a shimmering cloud of haze. As he neared, she got off the bus to meet him. Jonathan came to wait beside her as Arpad pulled in next to a beat-up boat-sized Impala parked behind the bus.

Before Arpad could get out and shut the door, she was upon him, twining her arms around him, grinding her mouth to his, having almost forgotten the musky taste of him. Behind them, Jonathan howled. "Jesus! I must've slept through the best part."

Arpad's dark reserved face flushed by her open display. He disentangled himself and handed Jonathan a large manila envelope. "I'll fill you in sometime, when I figure it out myself. Here's your money. Put it in a safe place."

Again Jonathan guffawed: a full-throated revived blast. Before this afternoon, she could not remember hearing him laugh. "Safe from who?" he asked. "The money's for them, anyway." Nevertheless, he stumbled off toward the bus, calling back, "Got to stash this and get ready. Miguel says we're leaving in about ten minutes. We want to be sure to get a seat."

At the doorway, he turned to call, "We can win! Arouse the public! The only thing that prevails against mindless corporate greed is public outrage. I oughta know."

In answer to Arpad's nonplussed gape, Elise said, "He's gone batshit. He wants to split to a place called Lalo's Icehouse to meet the guy they're raising money for. It's hero worship."

Arpad nodded. "I heard about it in town. Miguel's selling his birds to contribute to the defense of some one-armed artist who's being sued by Gallo Wineries."

"Oh brother," she said. "Talk about your hopeless cases. This sounds more like something *I'd* do."

Arpad pointed to Jonathan, who had again sailed off the bus like a kid, faltering only momentarily before he wobbled gamely on and joined the others, heading for the Impala. As he passed them, he managed a robust thumbs-up. "Don't wait up."

But the unnatural brilliance of his eyes perturbed her. She had heard of deathbed rallies and suspected this was what one looked like. At best, it was a fever-induced dissociation from reality. But in Jonathan's case, maybe that wasn't all bad. Her heart constricted and tears sprang to her eyes, hot as the desert air. She blinked them back and pressed Arpad's arm.

"He's lost a lot of blood from the chicken wound. And it's still bleeding. Why won't it stop?"

"Maybe the bleeding will keep it from getting infected." Arpad's reassurance sounded too morose to be comforting. "God knows there's a lack of sanitation on that bus."

She swallowed hard and waved as the Impala sputtered onto the road. Tejano music blared from the car's open windows, and someone inside—was it Jonathan?—let out a war whoop. "Oh Arpad, this is going to kill him."

"Possibly," he said. "But at the moment, he's really living."

41

Uvalde Leader-News, July 11, 2055
EL CURANDERO GRANDE, FAMED HEALER, MYSTERY
MAN, DEAD AT 102
Special to the Leader-News
By Juanita Espinoza

Crystal City, July 10, 2055. Juan De Los Milagros (John
of the Miracles), better known in South Texas as *el
curandero grande, hombre de misterio,* was found dead in his
home today by devotees who swore by his powers. He
had been ill for several days, suffering from a rickettsial
disease. He was reputed to be 102.

Mystery shrouded the identity of the healer for more
than half a century, and speculation continues even
after his death.

Hispanic citizens of Crystal City remain convinced
that *el curandero grande* was Ramón Fuentes, a former
resident who fled the state to escape several arrest
warrants and later was alleged to have faked his own
death so that he could return home in disguise to take
on his great-aunt's mantle as the local healer.

The circumstances surrounding Fuentes' supposed
death in a cave-in at a New Mexico gravel mine were
little noted by authorities at the time, even though it

was rumored that excavators never located a body. A recent search of death certificates issued during that time yielded no positive corroborating evidence.

However, the mine's owner, Tyler Technologies, Inc., made a sizeable settlement, reported to be in the millions, to his next-of-kin, leading to the assumption that sufficient evidence existed that Fuentes had indeed died in the disaster.

Still, those close to Fuentes' great-aunt, Josefina Carlota Rulfo, a legendary *curandera* in her own right, claimed to have heard her prophetic statement: "Now that I have someone to pass my mantle to, I can leave this earth in peace."

La curandera, as she was known, lived to the reputed age of 117. She and her nonagenarian nephew perished in a fire in 2000, apparently the result of candles on an altar they erected for *día de los muertos*, the traditional Day of the Dead observance.

Legend maintains that nothing remained of Rulfo's house except the dining room containing her potions. The room, located in the center of the house, was miraculously untouched by the flames, a fact her followers saw as a sign that Milagros, who also lived on the property, was to continue her work.

The healer Milagros is said to have come into his legendary powers shortly before the death of his mentor. Thereafter many healings were attributed to Juan De Los Milagros, whose name is possibly a nickname meaning John of the Miracles. His followers describe a typical curative prescription as a combination of herbs, homilies, and hard labor.

Tyler Technologies' multi-million dollar settlement apparently did not improve the family's lot. Rulfo and her aged nephew Miguel Fuentes continued to live in the same modest home as before their windfall. After the fire, Milagros, sole heir of both Rulfo and Miguel Fuentes, continued to reside in an abandoned bus in the back yard, having used the inherited settlement to set up the Carlota Rulfo-Miguel Fuentes Human Rights Foundation, appointing as administrator, in a strange quirk of coincidence, Arpad Patel, a former pilot for Tyler Technologies.

This association with Patel was to have lasting consequences for Milagros.

His most celebrated client was the former movie actress known as Salome, who early in the century was brought to the healer by her daughter, Elise Harwood Patel, Patel's wife.

The fading film star consulted *el curandero grande* for relief from painful and crippling arthritis, which disappeared after several sessions with him. The arthritic condition was thought to be the result of free-roaming silicone that had leaked some thirty years before from surgical breast implants.

So complete was her recovery that she went on to star in the one-woman show bearing her name which ran on Broadway for an unprecedented six years, a record for a single-cast production and a tribute to the aging star's physical stamina.

Following her retirement, the actress, once famous for her jet-set lifestyle, returned to Texas and became the healer's wife. But his refusal to abandon his converted school bus for a more conventional dwelling led to their early separation.

"Why should I move from this place?" the eccentric healer was quoted as saying in an interview following the break-up. "I learned most of what I know about living, right here. And over the years my friends have made it most commodious. I have a bed, a camp stove, a TV tray, a can, a tub, and books out the gazoo. All this and great sex, too: What else could any wife want?"

No petition was ever filed for divorce.

The former actress, who claims to be 82 (making her nine years old in her steamy film debut, "Salome"), still maintains a residence in nearby Utopia, coincidentally her original home. Despite her distaste for roosters, she made regular conjugal visits to her husband whenever she was in town, even as recently as last month.

Patel's appointment as administrator of the Rulfo-Fuentes Foundation gave rise to an early rumor that the healer Milagros, the chicken baron Ramón Fuentes and the billionaire Jonathan Whitley Tyler IV were one and the same person.

Tyler, founder of the multi-billion-dollar techno-giant Tyler Technologies, reportedly died in 2000 while on a business trip to South Texas, succumbing to a lingering auto-immune condition. His pilot Patel claimed that without fanfare he had personally flown the body to Philadelphia for interment in the family mausoleum.

At the time, a spokesperson for Tyler Technologies and Tyler's personal attorney, Hal Lieberman, stoutly denied the rumor that someone other than Tyler could be entombed in the family crypt, although shortly before the billionaire's death, he transferred the bulk of his fortune to the Rulfo-Fuentes Foundation.

"There is no doubt in my mind that Jonathan Tyler is dead," Lieberman said. "If I thought that urn was not Jonathan's, I'd insist that it be exhumed immediately. The man is dead. Just ask his doctor about this."

Tyler's attending physician at Sloan-Kettering Hospital, who declined to be quoted by name, verified that his former patient suffered from a terminal illness. "Medical science is never mistaken about the course of these autoimmune conditions," he said. "They are always fatal."

Neither Patel, presently visiting friends in Belize with his wife, nor their son Harwood Patel, the Foundation's current administrator, would comment on the rumor, or on the more likely possibility that Juan de los Milagros was Ramón Fuentes, the supposed cave-in victim.

Sources say it seems improbable that Milagros was the techno-scion in disguise. At the time of his death the healer appeared to be destitute, although other sources close to him point out that he was in the habit of giving away any worldly goods bestowed on him.

"It's entirely possible for him to give away a fortune," opined a local reporter. "The man was a certifiable macadamia nut."

Asked to explain the secret of his longevity during a television interview on his 100th birthday, the cadaverous healer, who was known to be in frail health for years, said, "It appears I still have a lot of reaping to do."

Tragedy plagued the immediate family of the scion of Boston-based Tyler Technologies. At approximately the time of Jonathan Tyler's demise in Texas, his wife, Sarah Hemmings Tyler, and her masseur accidentally suffocated to death when they slipped during a sexual mud bath orgy at a tony Scottsdale, Arizona spa.

His elder son, Jonathan Whitley Tyler, V (Whit), who came into a large trust fund at that time, squandered it on so-called "show girls" and failed attempts to circumnavigate the globe over the poles in a hot air balloon.

His last journey, when he was only 21, met with disaster when the billionaire adventurer's balloon disappeared over the wilds of Borneo.

His final "May Day" call indicated that he had crash landed, and that his gondola was being invaded by a large, eager, toothless woman wearing nothing but a bone through her nose. Rescue parties located the downed craft, but local natives, described as "giggling," claimed to have no knowledge of any survivor.

Coinciding with the deaths of his parents, the Tylers' younger son, Charles Mayfield Tyler (Chip), was brutally murdered at the age of 15 by the family butler, Henry Peters, who testified at his trial that he became enraged by the boy's "insolence and intransigence" and "choked the bloody s*** out of the ugly little blighter whilst he was preoccupied making love to himself."

Peters was then himself murdered in prison by two lifers who claimed that he was "too f***ing prissy to f***ing live."

The strongest argument offering credence to the opinion that Milagros was actually Ramón Fuentes is the apocryphal account of his alleged attachment to

Guida M. Jackson

chickens. Ramón Fuentes was at one time said to be an avid cock fighting impresario.

Prior to the death of the elder (Miguel) Fuentes, Milagros purchased a number of old fighting cocks from him and shipped them to Fort Stockton to have their lethal spurs removed by a veterinarian, Dr. Sim London, whom the healer credited with once having saved his life.

Milagros presented these birds to various nearby relatives of *Señora* Rulfo, but the fowl were said to evince great loyalty to the healer and to return frequently to roost in the overhead racks of his bus, a fact that discouraged many visitors from staying past sundown.

Throughout his lifetime, with the exception of the periodic conjugal visits from his estranged wife, who "abhorred the nasty little p***ers," Milagros was never without several chickens in his home, offspring of the original cocks.

It is believed that one of these birds was the carrier of psittacosis, the rickettsial disease that brought his life to a precipitous end.

***

As Is This

***

363

Acknowledgments

The author owes gratitude to Andy Jackson for taking time from his always hectic schedule to locate the appropriate fowl in the big city of Houston and shoot the cover photograph.

After the novel's original inception, two incidents occurred that might fall under the broad category of Art Anticipating Life: Two things happened in my family that closely resembled incidents previously described in the book. Since both were integral to the story and could not be removed without altering the trajectory of the story, I elected to set the manuscript aside. However, now that many years have passed, it is unlikely that any similarities will be noted. They are mentioned here to explain why it has taken so long to give birth to this book.

Because this has been a work long in progress, numerous writers have helped me develop the story over the years—so many, in fact, that I hesitate to name any for fear of overlooking someone. Besides, their names would fill up several pages. Broadly, I thank the members of Authors Unltd of Houston, Houston Writers Consortium, the Woodlands Writers Guild, Second Friday Writers, the Wednesday Woodlands critique group, and the Eagle's Trace group for their assistance in crafting this story.

Thanks also to David Bumgardner for legal advice; to Olivia Orfield and Frances McMaster for psychological and philosophical comments; and to Jackie Pelham, Ann Anderson, and Ida Luttrell for additional last-minute critiques. Thanks to my family members, Jeff, Linda, Andy, Mary, Tucker, Patty, Annabeth and Steve, for their unfailing support and encouragement. Finally, special thanks to my mentor Jack Hume for ongoing inspiration.

About the Author

Guida Jackson has worked as a newspaper editor, magazine editor, book editor, English teacher (University of Houston), and Creative Writing teacher (Montgomery College). She has a BA in Journalism, MA in the Humanities specializing in Latin American Literature, and PhD in Comparative Literature specializing in Third World Literature, particularly West African. She is founder of *Touchstone Literary Journal* (1976) and Panther Creek Press (1999), and author of 18 fiction and non-fiction books, published by Simon & Schuster, Oxford University Press, Barnes & Noble Books, and others. She lives with Jack, Hunter, and Lili Hume in Houston, Texas.